Shut Eye

Adam Baron lives in Brighton and is a writer and comedian. As one-third of the comedy act The Baron Brothers, he has appeared on MTV, *The Paul Ross Show* and *The Lenny Beige Show*.

Shut Eye is his first novel.

Adam Baron

Shut Eye

PAN BOOKS

First published 1999 by Pan Books
an imprint of Macmillan Publishers Ltd
25 Eccleston Place, London SW1W 9NF
and Basingstoke

Associated companies throughout the world

ISBN 0 330 37063 4

3 5 7 9 8 6 4 2

A CIP catalogue record for this book is available from
the British Library.

Phototypeset by Intype London Ltd
Printed by Mackays of Chatham plc, Chatham, Kent

For my father, Charles Baron

the time of no reply
is calling me to stay
there's no hello and no goodbye
to leave, there is no way

NICK DRAKE

Acknowledgements

This book was written with the help of Jason Baron, Marcus Baron, Beverley Cousins, Naomi Delap, Dr William Drake, Lisanne Radice and Andrew Watts. General and essential encouragement came from the rest of my family, as well as from Lucy Barker, Jane Gregory, Alan Samson, Vicky Tennant and a girl I met on a beach in Portugal. Heartfelt thanks to one and all.

When I see it, this is what I see.

Teddy stretched his legs and followed the stewardesses off the plane. He joked about overtime payments with his co-pilot as he picked up his bags and headed through the blue channel. He asked Mike if he wanted to catch one before hitting the traffic, but the flight had been late and Mike begged off. Teddy wasn't surprised – Mike was a real family man. There was a time once when all Teddy had wanted to do was get out of the airport and go home too. But not tonight. He patted Mike on the back, told him goodnight, waved at the stewardesses, and headed for the bar.

Teddy could have gone and sat in the first-class lounge but for some reason he chose the espresso bar the public use, which serves a good cocktail as well as the coffee. He took off his cap, ordered a Scotch and soda, and thought of the caiporenias he had drunk three nights ago in Rio. He looked around the sterile, white airport and then he checked himself out in the bar mirror. He ran a hand through hair which was still full but turning slowly from sandy to grey. He was OK. He looked just like an airline pilot. He stretched out his face to try to lose some of the lines around his eyes, smiled to himself at the stupidity of it, and relaxed.

In the mirror Teddy noticed that a youngish man in a baseball cap, sitting three stools down, had seen him mugging

1

to himself and he was embarrassed for a second until the man gave him a broad smile as if to say it's all right, I've done that. Teddy smiled back and took a long hit from the drink that had been placed in front of him. He yawned. He took another drink. When he glanced back up at the bar mirror a minute or so later, he noticed that the man in the baseball hat was looking straight at him.

Teddy and the man in the baseball hat chatted for thirty minutes or so, mostly about Teddy's job, because the younger man seemed quite reticent. Interested but reticent. All Teddy could get out of him was that he had just got back from a week in Paris and his friend was late picking him up. Two hours late by now; he was going to have to get the train. Teddy asked him if he lived in London and when the man said he did, and it was only ten minutes from Canonbury where Teddy lived, Teddy told him he was welcome to a lift if he wanted. The man shrugged his shoulders and said, 'Sure, why not?' but didn't look too grateful. He hadn't looked too grateful when Teddy had bought him a beer either.

Teddy finished his second Scotch and soda and stood down from the stool. The younger man followed suit. The barman watched the two men walk off together at about ten-thirty, Teddy putting his cap back on, the other man swinging a medium-sized black leather grip over his shoulder. The barman knew it was around then because that was when the night barman came in. He remembered the bag because he liked it and needed one himself, although he didn't think he could afford one like it. He told the police that he had never seen either of the men before but that it wasn't all that uncommon for some of the flight staff to stop off at his bar and offer lifts home to stray passengers, if they knew what he meant.

Teddy chatted as he drove, casually mentioning that his

wife was away on business, saying how much he hated going home to an empty house after a long trip. The man just nodded now and then and said yes or it must be, and then why not? when Teddy asked him if he wanted to come in and do some damage to a case of champagne he had won in a raffle. Teddy said great and he laughed out of nervousness. It was the first time he had done this, invite a stranger into his home, and he still wasn't sure if he was doing it or not or what was going to happen. He pulled into the forecourt of his building, drove through it and round the back, and pressed a button on a remote control device which activated a door to rise slowly in front of his car. Then he scraped the wing of his Rover as he put it in the garage and, laughing it off, blamed his wife for parking her Golf convertible too far over on his side.

Teddy was talking a lot now, about anything and nothing. He thought about his brother. The man in the baseball hat followed him through the garage and the back door, into the stylish, modern, spacious, two-bedroom flat, which Teddy shared with the wife who parked in so selfish a manner, and with whom the touching of car wings was as intimate as Teddy and she had been in almost six months. He turned to face the man behind him.

'So!' he said, rubbing his hands enthusiastically. 'Champagne!'

Teddy went to the fridge to fetch a bottle.

When Teddy's wife came home next morning, four hours earlier than expected, she found it, two-thirds full, standing next to one half empty glass, and one full glass, on the side of the American-style hot tub they'd had installed in the white tiled bathroom. It had gone flat. In the master bedroom, where she had gone after calling out her husband's name, she found another bottle of champagne and she found Teddy.

Teddy was on the bed, naked. The champagne bottle, or at least the top half of it, was protruding, like the funnel of an ocean liner, from Teddy's abdomen. The rest of it was scattered in pieces across his torso. Teddy's face had been smashed in, and a long spike of glass stuck out of what had once been his upper jaw but was now a crumpled hole encompassing both his mouth and his nose. Even someone as unqualified in medical matters as Teddy's wife could see that he was dead. Very. Mrs Morgan screamed, ran into the living room, and called the police who got a couple of flatfoots round there in minutes.

The two policemen found a woman who was obviously in shock, and a day-old corpse covered in broken glass. Later, at the morgue, another police officer found more glass fragments as well as a quantity of semen, and some of Teddy's blood, a long way up Teddy's anal canal. While it is true that nothing should be taken for granted in cases such as these, it can probably be assumed that the semen had arrived there first.

PART ONE

Chapter One

I don't really know what got me into boxing. I never did it when I was a kid, or at college, or when I was still on the force. I had occasion, a year or two back, to ask some questions at a gym that was beneath a pub behind King's Cross station, and I got to know the manager. She helped me to find out the answers to my questions, and a week or so later I went back to work out and train. After a couple of visits the manager talked me in to doing some sparring and, if you can excuse the pun, I was hooked. The only reason I can think of for my attachment to it is that standing across from a man whose express purpose is to punch your lights out in the shortest possible time available to him, does tend to relegate any other problems you might have to the recesses of the head which you are trying so hard to protect. Even if it is only for an hour or so.

The gym I go to is not a professional one, or rather, it is run for profit but no professionals train there. It is more of a fitness centre and club, attracting a lot of young kids who have seen Eubank or Benn on the TV, and the kind of cars they drive, and who want to see if they've got what it takes themselves. If they do they soon leave for bigger setups and if they don't they either give up or carry on coming for the love of it. Sal doesn't mind that. She took the place over when her husband was killed and I think she keeps it as a way of feeling close to him as much as anything else. She knows she's no Frank Warren and anyway she has another source of income which makes her boxing gym something of a sideline.

I like Sal's gym as much as I like Sal. Most Wednesday nights find me down there if nothing else comes up and I generally try to slip in another night as well. I get a sweat up, punch the bag, and then I either go home or stick around for a pint with Sal and some of the guys. A few of them may feel a bit funny about what I do for a living, and about the fact that I used to be in the Filth, as they put it, but they respect Sal, and seeing as I'm OK with her, they respect me. Or at least they pretend they do. One or two of them, I swear it, genuinely like me.

A lot of affluent media types around my age go to gyms to do what they call boxercise. They train and work out, do everything a boxer does except the actual boxing. It's a very good way to get fit. My gym, however, would never permit such a thing. Not because they think that if you train like a boxer you should use what you've learnt in the ring, but because they don't want to attract the affluent media types.

I parked my car in a delivery bay opposite The George, locked it, and crossed the street. I usually walk, or ride my bike down there, but it had been raining all day and autumn was beginning to give into a Big City Winter, so I'd decided on the Mazda. It was quarter past seven, dark as the streetlamps let it get. When I got down-stairs I was late and Sal had already started the circuit training, putting fifteen or so guys through an experience close to absolute misery the first time you did it, and which never seemed to get easier any time after that. I decided to skip it. I got changed and headed straight to the weights room.

I stretched, worked out for half an hour in the slightly cramped, brightly lit room, and then I went in with Mountain Pete, a huge black guy who doesn't move around a whole lot, but who has a sizeable enough punch on the end of a long reach to make up for that. We waltzed for a round and a half and then I got under his guard a couple of times and he covered up before going to pieces a little. I backed him up in the corner, ducking and swinging round the side when he came out after me. I got a couple in under his jab. At the end of the third we broke off and stepped out. Mountain Pete could have created a sea with all the sweat running off him.

'You're getting good, Rucker,' he said to me, shaking his head, breathing hard. 'I'm fucked if I didn't used to be able to bounce your pretty white arse round this ring like a yo-yo. I'm going to have to start trying against you.' His face disappeared completely beneath a small white towel.

'Don't try too hard, Pete,' I said. 'You'll flood the place.'

'Fuck off, you cheeky cunt!' the towel said. I laughed and went to find Sal.

Sal was in the weights room herself now, teaching three new kids how to use the machines. I waited while she showed them the correct way to perform a bench press. Sal is around the forty mark, taller than most women, with a good, muscular figure and dark curly hair she only lets down outside the gym. She has a firm chin, a strong nose which she constantly reminds herself is too big, and soft, mahogany eyes which sometimes give the lie to her tough, no-nonsense exterior. Her cheeks are beginning to show the first broken capillaries of a woman who has never made friends with a bottle of whiskey because the bottle has never stayed round long enough. She is the sort of woman who never wears much make-up but who can transform herself from tough boxing coach into alluring modern woman with a silk blouse and a touch of lipstick.

When she saw me watching her, Sal left the kids, walked across to a table in the corner, and picked up the photograph I'd given her a week or so before. The photograph had a man's face on one side and my name and number on the back. I'd been showing it around for two weeks now, trying to find Edward Morgan's killer, a confusing experience which made me relish the focused simplicity to be found in Sal's gym. When Sal came over to me she was shaking her head.

'No,' she said, holding it in her hand, looking down at it. 'I thought it rang a bell when you gave it me but it's not clear enough, you can't see enough of his face.' She stared hard at the picture in her hand, trying to pull something familiar out of it. She shook her head again. 'No. I wish I could help you, Bill. I've handed out the rest you gave me but I wouldn't expect much if I were you.'

'I don't,' I said. 'It doesn't hurt though, passing out photos. It's the sort of thing that eats at you if you don't do it.'

'Yeah. People round here are not what you'd call talkative though, at the best of times.'

'I know.'

'Good luck with it though, Bill. He needs catching, he does.'

Sal walked over and put the picture back on the table. The three kids were standing by the rower, waiting for her.

'Thanks anyway, Sal.'

'Don't mention it, Masher,' she said, winking at me. I smiled at the tag and went back into the training room.

The reason Sal calls me the Masher has nothing to do with boxing, although it does sound like it might. Iron Mike, Smokin' Jo Frazier, Billy the Masher Rucker. A Masher, so Sal explains to me, is an old East End word for a man who dresses in a manner designed to attract young, impressionable women. She calls me this because two of the boys from the gym saw me going into a very swanky club one night and thought I looked just a little poncy. Telling them that I was on a case, and that you have to dress right to gain access to the places where you are trying to further your investigations, had little effect. I was a Masher.

'We'd have let you in no matter what you had on,' Tommy said. They were on the door. In my opinion, with their frilly blue dress shirts and floppy bow ties, they looked a lot more poncy than I did.

That piece of work turned out well. I had been looking for a girl who had run away from home in Sheffield and had found her working as a waitress in a place that did not require her to wear a shirt as she served the tables. I had persuaded her to call home and her family were relieved and I was five hundred pounds better off. The case I was on now was not going so well. In fact, it wasn't going at all. I had no clues, no idea where I could find any clues, and that day, after wandering aimlessly around half of north London, I had just about decided to give up on it. All I had was an unlimited supply of copies of a blown-up, grainy, indistinct photograph of a man's face, taken from the side. Not a lot. Ten detectives from Islington police station had worked their arses off for six months getting absolutely nowhere on it and it had taken me two and a half weeks of dull, solid graft to catch up with them.

The case had left me not only frustrated but deadened and exhausted. It was the biggest thing I'd had to do since leaving the force, and every day that passed meant that some poor bastard somewhere was a day closer to a very miserable death. This time of year was a killer anyway, dull slate-grey skies, ever shorter days, stained ugly buildings, and drizzle. It probably would have been a good idea to, but I didn't feel like climbing into the ring again so instead I stood watching a sixteen-year-old kid called Sanjay, who had only been coming a month or so, but who Sal thought might have something.

Sanjay was a lithe, good-looking lad, with snake-like muscles moving beneath smooth, caramel skin, and a natural cocky grace that was good to watch. His stomach was a cheese grater, the sort of thing no amount of training can give you once you've skipped past thirty. Ah, youth. He was quick too, with both his fists and his feet. Sal, however, stood shaking her head, her lips pursed and her arms folded.

'The problem,' she explained, looking straight ahead as the kid picked apart another Asian lad of about the same age, 'is The Prince. Sure, they see him, and that's what gets them into it, which is great, but then they try to fight like him. Look at this nonce.' She pointed at Sanjay and shook her head again, weary as a stallholder at Brick Lane when you're trying to save a few pounds. 'Where's the guard I taught him? What sort of a punch is that from down there? Anyone decent would beat the shit out of him.' She said this as Sanjay gave his friend a minute or two off, his gloves by his sides, dodging and smiling as his friend tried to connect. 'Christ!' Sal exclaimed. 'He'll do a fucking handstand in a minute!'

I laughed.

'The Prince is good though, Sal.'

'Good? He's a fucking genius! That's the thing. If he wasn't he'd get his teeth knocked in fighting like that.'

'And if he wasn't so cool these kids wouldn't be here.'

'I know. I've never had any Asian kids in here before the last eighteen months. Beats working in their old man's corner fucking shop, doesn't it now?'

Sal got into the ring and started swearing. Sanjay looked nonplussed, like a kid who gets yelled at for burning the kitchen down when he only wanted to help his mother. I told myself that it probably did beat working in a corner shop, but not by much, and I went to get changed.

On my way to the locker room I saw the three new kids, who were standing together watching what was going on in the ring. They were all black, fourteen or fifteen years old, equally free from concerns of weight and muscle tone. One of them was holding a bright orange object which could have been a coat or a small sleeping bag and which he obviously valued too highly to let out of his sight. He looked at me as I passed him and I thought he was going to say something but he didn't. He looked a little scared. I wondered why for a second before realizing that it's a strange thing to do, getting up on a little stage in front of twenty or so other guys, trying to hit someone and stop him hitting you. And not look stupid. I gave him a sympathetic glance but he looked away quickly. I took my things out of the locker and got under the shower.

I left the gym just as two of the black kids were

climbing through the ropes with Sal. They weren't much to watch and everyone else was milling around, starting more exercises, working on the bag. I turned at the door to wave to Mountain Pete who was skipping, trying to get some speed into those flat iron feet of his.

'Catch you next time, Mash!' he called out, getting the rope caught round his shins. I waved to Sal in the ring and she waved back as she showed the two kids how to face each other and begin. The kid who had looked scared darted his eyes over to me as Sal spoke to him. He looked even more nervous than he had before.

Outside, the temperature had taken a dive, and even though it is only half a centimetre long my hair let me know that I hadn't dried it properly. Hat time soon, I thought. The old brown Mazda started eventually but somehow it refused to drive me home, and took me to The Old Ludensian instead, a bar I frequent down on St John Street near to Smithfield. I stayed there for an hour and a half, sitting at the bar, talking to some of the regulars. I had three or four, flirted with the waitress who I always flirt with the waitress, and then went home.

Nicky, who owns The Old Ludensian, had suggested making a night of it down at The Titanic but I put him off. I didn't think I deserved a night of carousing and these days I can't enjoy it that way when I don't think I've earned it. I wouldn't have been able to stop thinking about a guy with a broad smile who was never going to smile again. Also, Nicky was probably the best-looking and most charming man I had ever met, and a night out with him often entailed drumming my fingers on the bar top while he chatted away to some impossibly gorgeous woman. Not tonight, Josephine.

'Soon though, Billy,' Nicky said. 'I don't see enough of you.' He had walked me to the door and was shaking my hand.

'You would if you let me pay for my drinks,' I told him. 'I get embarrassed.'

'After what you did for me, never.'

'OK, Nicky,' I said, shaking his hand. 'I'll see you. Probably when I've sorted this shit out, one way or another.'

'Make it soon, Billy, soon.' He slapped me on the back and I walked outside.

Nicky was referring to the time when, with the help of Mountain Pete, I had talked a certain gentleman into allowing him to remain alive. The gentleman was a mid-ranking member of an East End security association, and while Nicky had constantly refused to give the gentleman what he wanted whenever he had called at Nicky's bar, my friend had not been so ungenerous with the gentleman's wife. I did the talking while Mountain Pete showed the man how much the butt end of a twelve-gauge sawn-off shotgun can hurt somebody's head. I assured him that the butt was not the end Mountain Pete would be using next time, and the problem was solved. Mountain Pete is a member of a security association of his own, run out of Westbourne Park. Nicky was relieved and thankful, and since then neither Pete nor I had ever been allowed to part with a penny at the bar of The Old Ludensian. The incident shook Nicky up so much he didn't sleep with another married woman for at least a week.

I gunned my dream machine into life and this time it did take me back to my flat, which is above an old print shop behind Exmouth Market in Clerkenwell. No messages. I showered, poured myself a whiskey and took it to bed, drifting off into sleep with one of Nick Drake's stark mellow tunes on the stereo.

At two fifteen the phone woke me and I let the machine get it. The room seemed empty without the music, which had turned itself off. A big, angry voice said it knew I was there and told me to pick up. It was quite insistent. Why not? I did. The voice then told me that if I wanted to find the man whose face was in the photograph I had been showing around like I was a Catholic priest and it was a piece of Jesus's fucking toothbrush or some shit, I should go and stand in the entrance to the freight depot halfway down York Way as soon as I could get there. I was to wait and be sure to bring along some money – five hundred would be ample. Any less would not be. The voice said soon or don't bother, and then it became the dialling tone.

I sat up in bed and turned the lamp on.

I ran my hands over my head and yawned again, trying to bring myself to some level of decision-making consciousness. I thought about it. Standing around York Way in the middle of the night with a pocket full of money, waiting for a man who probably had, instead of information, a very big knife in his pocket, was not something I'd ever advise anyone else to do. The guy probably saw my name on the back of the photo some-where or other and thought he was on to an easy mugging. York Way is not what you would call a safe place to hang out at the best of times, but even less so when it's two fifteen in the morning and someone knows you're going to be there. But what the hell. It was the first thing approaching a lead that I'd had and I was awake now anyway as the joke goes. I wanted to *do* something, even if that something was something very stupid.

It took me two and a half minutes to climb into jeans and a sweatshirt, pull on my Red Wings, and grab a jacket. I saw my wallet lying on the kitchen table. I left it there.

Outside there was no one about and I shivered myself awake as I lowered myself on to the torn driving seat of the Mazda. I checked my watch and pulled the belt on. I inserted the key into the ignition and turned it, expecting a fight. Luckily the car started first time.

Luckily?

Chapter Two

I don't normally take cases that the police are already working flat out on. I usually spend my time looking for runaway kids, teenagers or younger, who are a low priority to my ex-colleagues on the Met but a high priority to the families they have left behind. In most other matters the Met have me beaten. They have more resources, and more powers of surveillance, entry, and arrest. They do, however, tend to stand out like sore thumbs in bars and clubs and casinos in either cheap suits or tacky undercover leather jackets, and this makes room for me. The bars and the clubs are the sorts of places where I generally find my teenagers because they are often part of the reason the teenager comes to London in the first place. The Big City, provider of action and anonymity. I don't look like a copper, I don't even look like an ex-copper, and having spent the first fourteen years of my life in Toronto I can make sure that I don't sound like one either. I can go to the places I have to go to and not have half the kitchen staff legging it out of the back door before I've even managed a sip of my Canadian Club. Also, thanks to a vicious old man I haven't seen in twelve years, I know what it feels like to be a kid and to hate your life so much that anywhere, *anywhere*, is better than home. I do OK at what I do, but I usually leave the big stuff to my previous employers.

The message I found on my machine one bright Monday morning in mid October, however, intrigued me. I had just opened up the small, sparsely furnished office that I keep in a business unit up behind Highbury Fields. A plummy middle-aged male voice informed me that it belonged to one Sir Peter Morgan, and it asked if I could please call it back as soon as I was able. The voice was nervous and far too restrained, as if the owner of the voice was afraid of what the voice might say, and held it tightly in check like a pit bull on a leash in a Montessori Centre.

The name intrigued me. It had been in the news a lot recently, although it had been sidelined in the last couple of weeks by the state of Sarah Ferguson's thighs and the health, or lack of health, of the Russian President. I have a good memory for names, though, and even if I hadn't I could hardly have forgotten it. Sir Peter Morgan was a Conservative Member of Parliament, a (now) Shadow Minister at the Treasury. He was a leading Euro-sceptic and senior member of the 1922 Committee. He was a regular guest on *Question Time*, *Any Questions*, and those political programmes you turn off immediately when carving the Sunday roast. His name was especially familiar, however, for the fact that his younger brother Edward, an airline pilot, had recently been brutally murdered in the flat he shared with his wife of six years, by person or persons unknown wielding a broken champagne bottle. I wrote down the number he gave and sat for a second, wondering why he was calling me.

There were three other messages on my machine and I dealt with those first. One was from Joe Nineteen, a regular provider of information concerning the whereabouts of errant children, and one was from a woman whose son I had located six months ago; she wanted me to locate him again. The other was from Sharon. I called Joe and told him that his tip of the day before had been spot on and that I would be round to see him soon. I called the number the woman – a Mrs Lewes – had given, and left a message on her machine stating that I would be happy to help her and that I would be in touch when I knew more. I didn't call Sharon because the message was from yesterday and I had already arranged to have dinner with her after she'd reached me at home. I sat for a second, thinking, and then dialled the number the MP had given.

A secretary put me on hold for a minute and I was just about to hang up, redial, and leave a message when Sir Peter came on the line.

'Mr Rucker?' he asked.

'Yes. Sir Peter Morgan? I'm just returning your call.'

'Thank you. I . . .' He thought for a second. 'I was wondering if you are free for lunch today. Your services were recently recommended to me and I have something I would like to discuss with you.'

The MP's voice wasn't so restrained as it had been on the machine. The pit bull wasn't on its leash any more; it was dressed up like a poodle.

'May I enquire who you spoke with?' I asked. My usual customer survey.

'I really would rather do this in person if you don't mind, Mr Rucker. Could you meet me at one today? Do you know where the Portman Club is?'

I waited a second. I don't like talking to people who give orders by asking questions, or whose tone of voice indicates that they cannot conceive of ever not getting their way.

'Sir Peter,' I said, 'I have an idea as to what you might want to talk to me about. If it is what I think it is, I really don't think that I can be of much help to you. I'm not a big organization, I don't have anyone else working for me. I usually look for missing teenagers.'

'I am aware of that,' he answered. 'My information is, however, that you are very good at your job, and that it would be worth speaking to you.'

'All the same,' I went on, 'I don't want to waste any of your time.' Or mine, I thought. 'It would be pointless to come all the way down to your club to tell you exactly what I could tell you now.'

'Nevertheless, Mr Rucker, I would like to meet you. I will of course pay for your time, whatever the outcome, and I can assure you of a most excellent lunch.'

'I . . .'

'Please, Mr Rucker. It would save me the trouble of hunting you out. If you have an idea as to why I want to speak to you then you might understand how much it means to me that I should.'

The ex-Minister stopped speaking abruptly. The leash on his voice was back and ready to snap. I thought about it for a second. Something inside me sighed wearily.

'Crème brûlé?' I asked.

'I'm sorry?'

'On the menu. At your club.'

'Oh,' he said, thinking. 'Of course. The finest west of Paris.' He managed a short laugh.

'All right,' I said, 'I'll be there.'

He laughed again, stiffly. 'Thank you.' Then he added,

'I don't want to sound patronizing but the club insists that visitors should wear a jacket.'

'I'll buy one on the way, sir.'

'And a tie, I'm afraid.'

'Right. What about trousers?' I asked. I took the address from him and then hung up.

It was perfect. Mine is as good but I don't have a blow-torch to get the top perfectly crisp while leaving the underneath firm. I make do with a grill.

I had made a few calls, looked at the file I had on the missing Dominic Lewes, and decided that I would work on him either that evening or else the next day. I had drunk some coffee in the café that serves the business units, and then gone back to my flat and donned the Paul Smith suit that I had bought for my brother's wedding but never had a chance to wear. I'd chosen an antique Ralph Lauren from the seventy or so ties in my cupboard, which I collect, but which I seldom get a chance to wear.

We were sitting across from one another in the Portman Club's dining room, a huge, high-ceilinged room, with the requisite wood panelling, oil paintings of sea battles, and huge chandeliers. Sir Peter Morgan was a tall man of forty-seven/forty-eight, elegant in a conservative way, with a greying, full head of hair, which would make him look very distinguished in a few years' time. He had a high forehead above a narrow face, with striking blue eyes and a nose that seemed just a little too small compared with his other features, making him look slightly boyish. A pair of reading glasses hung on a delicate silver chain around his neck.

Throughout the three courses we made polite conversation. I asked him how he was normally addressed and he said that Sir Peter was fine. He didn't like being called Mr Morgan but he never complained when people made the mistake because it sounded very petty to do so. He told me a little about his job, I told him a little about mine. At one point I thought he was going to get into politics but luckily he didn't. It might have been the end of a very beautiful friendship. We ate, we chatted, he nodded at the odd acquaintance, and I noted his perfect Windsor knot over a starched Hilditch and Key blue striped shirt, with matching handkerchief poking cautiously out of the pocket of an exquisitely tailored single-breasted pinstripe. He showed few signs of his recent loss beyond an unwillingness to engage any of the people who passed the table in any conversation beyond the usual pleasantries. His table manners and posture demonstrated a man who was used to being in control of himself. He was like an uncle who invites you to lunch during your final year at Cambridge in order to dissuade you from going to live on a commune in Goa, recommend a tailor, and enquire as to which City firm you would like him to get you a job at when you graduated.

When the waitress took away our dessert plates Sir Peter told her that we would take our coffee upstairs. We stood up and I followed him through the dining room and up a broad circular staircase, covered in a deep red carpet held down by bold brass rods. The walls were similarly covered in oils, but most of these were of stern old men whose faces gave the impression that, unlike me, they hadn't found the crème brûlé at all satisfactory. We walked past them and along a broad corridor, towards a heavily polished oak door which Sir Peter pushed open. It didn't make a sound. On the other side of it was a large room, filled with armchairs that were mostly vacant, next to low coffee tables liberally covered in broadsheet newspapers. I say liberally: they were either the *Telegraph*, *The Times* or the *FT*. Sir Peter led me through the speckled columns of light charging through large arch windows on the opposite wall, across to the furthest corner of the room where we sat facing each other, both of us encased in green leather.

Sir Peter shifted uncomfortably in his seat, looking for a way to begin. I waited while he sipped his coffee, listening to the faint hum of traffic on Piccadilly. I noted that he had the same colour Turk's Head cufflinks as I had found in the pockets of a second-hand Gieves and Hawkes suit I'd bought on Portabello Road a year ago.

'Mr Rucker,' he began finally. 'I find this quite difficult. I've never needed the services of a private investigator before. I . . .' He stopped speaking and gazed out of the window.

'You want me to find the person who murdered your brother,' I said. Well, I didn't have all day.

'Yes. It's as simple as that I suppose. Yes. Yes I do.' He looked at me, relieved that the ice had been broken. He seemed scared too, scared of going over what had happened, of seeing it again.

'In that case I'm afraid that this has been a waste of time,' I said. 'Except for the crème brûlée. You are aware of the amount of manpower the police are already putting in to this? Especially now.'

'I am aware that the police are doing what they can.'

'I happen to know one of the officers on the case. He's good. I don't think that there is any doubt that they'll find whoever it is who's behind these killings.' Sir Peter seemed to wince, to shy away from what I was saying. I carried on.

'The first one hardly got into the news as far as I can remember. It certainly didn't make the TV. A lorry driver found dead in the sleeping area of his cab. Stabbed with a broken beer bottle and all his cash taken. Kids probably, crackheads who needed fifty quid bad enough at certain times that they'll quite cheerfully kill a man to get it. Without breaking a sweat. No sign of sexual activity, a simple robbery that possibly went wrong.' I leant forward for my coffee cup. Sir Peter was perfectly still, his expression blank, looking straight at me.

'The second one did make the headlines. A rent boy in Brixton, only fourteen, still at school, halfway through his GCSEs. This time there was sexual activity, although it's impossible to state in this case whether or not any of the four brands of sperm found in various areas of the corpse actually belonged to the perpetrator. Again a bottle, this time Lucozade I believe, was used to pierce the victim's abdomen. Pieces of glass were discovered in the boy's anal canal, which was severely lacerated.'

Sir Peter shifted in his seat and looked at me in a way which suggested he was used to being treated with just a touch more deference.

'You seem to know what you are talking about,' he said coldly.

'I read the newspaper. I also called DI Gold after I spoke to you earlier. The officer who recommended me to you. I trained with him at Hendon, he filled me in. With the MO similar to the motorway killing a link was established and background work done on the driver. It appears that he was a homosexual, or a bi-sexual bearing in mind that he was married with three children. The pathologist still insists that there was no evidence of sexual contact the night he died, but several men were found who admitted sexual encounters with him, some of them in his lorry. It's curious. Apparently the driver's wife was more distressed when an officer was forced to relay this information to her, than she had been when she'd been informed that her husband had been killed.'

I sat back and waited for a response but Sir Peter didn't say anything. I took a big sip of my coffee before it went cold. I hate cold coffee.

'The police don't like serial killers,' I continued. 'Even if it's only arse bandits as I can assure you they refer to gay men who are the target. They put a lot of people on it. That number was doubled when your brother was killed. It would have been increased anyway, but the fact that you are a prominent politician won't have hurt things. Anything I could do would be a drop in the ocean compared to what is already happening.'

I relaxed into my armchair and threaded my fingers together. The waitress walked over with a coffee jug and refilled my cup. I should have known, in a place like that. As she refilled Sir Peter's I gave myself a little ticking off. I was not being very kind. Something about him, his reserve perhaps, or simply his position as powerful politician, reversed to bereaved supplicant, made me want to be brutal with him. It seemed to be working; his face had a deeper, more introverted quality than his previous gravity. He smiled weakly at the waitress and then waited until she was quite a way off, serving a crumpled old man who looked suspiciously like Winston Churchill.

'It isn't that I doubt the police, Mr Rucker.' There was a certain impatience in his voice. 'I have visited the operations room, I have seen what they are doing.'

'Then you must know how ineffective I would be. They have officers out asking every possible question in thousands of different places. More importantly they have forensics, DNA tests. That's how this guy, assuming it is a guy, will be caught. Unfortunately you may have to wait until he does it again, maybe two or three times, but he'll make a mistake before too long. They always do.'

'I don't doubt you, Mr Rucker.' The irritation and impatience in his voice was overlaid by an increased imperative.' 'But you see, from my point of view, it doesn't really matter what the police are doing. Edward was my brother. It matters to me what *I* am doing about it. I can't just sit back, I have to do something. I can't do nothing.' The MP's hands turned palm up and suddenly there was an appeal in his eyes, an honesty that I had not seen before.

'I can understand that, sir. But if you already know that employing me is really a way of easing your conscience, of trying to do something, then you know how pointless it is because you haven't done anything wrong and catching criminals is not your line. You're a politician, not a detective. It was not your fault, how could it have been? Also, from my point of view, I really don't want to spend my time on a fool's errand because you feel helpless. I sympathize with you but I'm sorry, there really isn't anything I can do.'

I stood up to go, but the MP let out a long sigh and pursed his lips against a swell of emotion.

'Mr Rucker,' he said. He was firm, his voice raised a little too loud. It stopped me. I sat back down again, resigned to hearing him out. I leant back in the armchair as he clasped his hands together and stared over his knuckles at me. I could see him around a table in a television studio, waiting for the jeers of a studio audience to die down.

'Mr Rucker. There is something. Something else. The police listened when I mentioned it but I could tell they were just being polite, they didn't believe me.' He hesitated. 'Mr Rucker, I heard what happened to my brother. I know the details. I was told there was evidence of sexual activity. With a man. My brother had been buggered before he was killed. I am well aware of this. But, Mr Rucker,' he looked right at me, 'one thing is wrong. I know that my brother was not a homosexual.'

His voice was lower now. He had regained control and was staring at me intently, his blue eyes not appealing to me but measured and precise, cold as an empty house. I suddenly lost all sympathy with him. So that's what he cares about, just like the lorry driver's wife.

'Sir Peter,' I said, 'it may be difficult for you—'

'I know what you are going to say, Mr Rucker; that I am an old Tory bigot who can't stand the fact that his brother was gay, who refuses to accept what the evidence so clearly displays. But you are wrong.'

'I didn't say—'

He cut me off. He leant forward towards me. 'You are not gay,' he said. He stated it flatly, like a logician beginning with a simple premise. 'You're not, are you?'

I looked at him, surprised, trying to work out where he was going.

'No,' I answered, 'I'm not, but . . .'

'And my brother was not either. He would not have slept with a man. He was not a homosexual.'

I didn't say anything. He could finish, then I could thank him for lunch, get up and leave.

'Do you know how I can tell?' he asked, his eyes fixing me now, sensing my irritation. I shrugged.

'I can tell, Mr Rucker, because I am.'

The MP sat back and smiled to himself ruefully. The room was suddenly silent except for the ticking of a grandfather clock which I hadn't noticed before. Sir Peter seemed to be lost within himself for a second, seeing things which I couldn't, things which seemed to bring him pleasure along with a dark, overshadowing wistfulness.

'Do you know, Mr Rucker, you are only the third person I have ever told that particular piece of information to. I didn't want to but somehow, ever since Edward was killed, being secretive doesn't seem to matter any more. Finding out who killed him does.' He smiled at me. 'It is amazing how simple it is to say it. Before I told my wife it was much worse. And before I told Edward I was a wreck. I was almost forty years old and I was so terrified of what he would say I couldn't eat for a week.' He laughed sadly and waited for me to say something. I didn't really know what.

'How did he take it?' I found myself asking.

'Oh, brilliantly. He said he'd been waiting for me to tell him ever since he was sixteen and I was nineteen. He was relieved that I had.'

'That must have meant a lot to you.'

'It did. My wife, quite understandably, was not so generous. We had already begun to lead separate lives within the same house but she was scared that I would "come out", as I believe they say, and it would humiliate her. She enjoys being the wife of a Minister you see, even an

Opposition Minister as she puts it.' He hesitated, and I waited for him to go on. 'Diana told me never to mention it again. To anybody. But I did decide to tell Edward. After I had told him I was then able to confide in him, to tell him of my feelings. We had long chats about it and it made the burden a lot easier to bear, knowing I could talk about how I felt, that he understood me and I would never have to worry that he would tell anybody. It was a great relief. For some reason I found that I hardly ever needed to do anything about it after that, I didn't need to take so many of the risks I was taking.'

The MP stopped for a second as the waitress came back over. She was either naturally very diligent or a member of the KGB. In the gap it afforded him the former Minister restored some of his reserve and when she was gone he said, 'The point, you see, is that I know he wasn't gay. We spoke about it and he told me he had never even thought about it for a second. He wasn't lying to me, he had no reason to. He had no problem with my sexual preference and would not have had if it were his own. Edward was a lot more open, far more relaxed about life than I am.'

'And you think it strange that he should be murdered by a serial killer specializing in homosexuals?'

'I do. Even if it was the same man I feel that the police are blinkering themselves by insisting that my brother was gay, and that this one fits a neat pattern.' I nodded my head reluctantly. The police do like things to be neat. They even go so far as making things neat when that is the last thing that they are. I'd done a fair bit of neatening myself in my time.

'You told them Edward wasn't gay?' I asked.

'I did, but I didn't tell them how I knew. They were

polite enough but I know they didn't take any notice. They think I just want to lessen the political embarrassment of what happened.'

I'd thought that myself earlier. I still wasn't sure if that wasn't the case.

'So, what you want is to employ somebody to explore the possibilities that you believe the police are overlooking.'

'Yes.'

'And you don't want a big organization because a big organization would just do what the police are doing. And they might not be, what you would call, discreet.'

'Yes. I told DI Gold that I wanted to hire someone, an individual to help me. I didn't expect to meet the resistance I am getting from you. DI Gold tried to talk me out of it, like you did, but when I told him I was determined, and would simply look in the Yellow Pages if he didn't recommend someone, he came up with your name. I am aware that it may turn out to be a waste of my money, but while there is a chance that I may be able to contribute, I will. DI Gold told me that you usually find missing children at a flat fee, but that I might be able to engage you by the day.'

'You might,' I said.

And I thought about it.

There was a chance it would be worthwhile, a chance I could dig something up, although it wasn't likely. It certainly wouldn't hurt my bank balance to try and I could probably fit in my other work around it. Also, it was a challenge, a piece of real work. I didn't know what to do, I was still shocked by what he had told me, or, rather, by the fact that he had told me it at all, here in this dusty, establishment boys' club where such a revelation was completely incongruous. I found myself saying that I would do my best for him until I'd either found something interesting or couldn't think of anything else to do. I told him he was almost definitely wasting his money and my time, but he seemed pleased. We discussed terms and then we stood up.

'Mr Rucker,' Sir Peter said, taking my hand. 'Thank you. I trust that anything I have told you will be treated in confidence.' He looked uneasy. 'My wife, you see.'

I told him that he had nothing to worry about. He nodded his thanks. Then he snapped back into Uncle mode and told me some of the history of the club, as he showed me out of the room and back down the broad staircase, which looked even more impressive on the way down. He pointed out a portrait of the club founder, and one of his own grandfather, and he told me what their motto meant: diligence and discretion.

At the bottom of the staircase we passed the waitress with another jug of fresh coffee in her hand. I could have sworn she looked disappointed to see us leaving.

Chapter Three

The drive back to my office was about half an hour longer
than the drive there and I vowed once again to leave my
car at home and use the bus more. Or walk, that would
have been just as quick. I finally made it back to Highbury
Corner and drove along Highbury Grove with the park on
my left. Through the naked trees I could see the last rash
of tennis players battling bravely on the faded red courts.
I turned right, into the forecourt of the Lindaeur Buildings, and after waving into the security booth I parked
next to the front entrance. As was often the case the huge,
stately building, put up in the thirties, reminded me of an
ocean liner. I locked up the car and, ignoring the waiting
lift, I jogged up the four flights.

When I opened up my office it was glaringly bright,
the sun having just reached round far enough to beam
straight in through the huge windows. I let the straw blind
down to about halfway, which subdued it and gave the
small room a strange, almost tropical ambience. My
machine informed me that the time was two thirty-six,
and that I had one message. It was Andy Gold, wondering
if I had agreed to help the MP, and would I like to talk to
him about it? I called him back at the station and arranged
to meet him in The Albion at four. He sounded stressed.
In the background I could hear the clatter of typewriters,

33

the other phone lines going, and what sounded like a very irate old woman telling somebody that her little boy could not possibly have done anything like that. They'd framed him the first time, I heard her say, and now they wanted to do it again. I smiled to myself grimly at the memory of day upon day upon day spent sitting in that room, feeling just as harassed as Andy did now. I told him not to work too hard and hung up before getting his reply.

I'd jotted down a few notes earlier, at The Portman, in a small hardback notebook, and I took it out on my desk and made some more. I had been engaged by a Tory MP with more money than sense (a complaint common amongst Tory MPs) to find out who had killed his brother, because the MP did not believe the police were exploring every angle open to them. The murder seemed to be the work of a serial killer with a distaste, or a very strange taste, for homosexuals. But the MP did not believe his brother would have had any contact with a homosexual so it seemed strange to him that his brother should be a target for this person. The police did not think it strange. I was to look into the possibility that his brother was murdered by someone other than the apparent serial killer, or else that the serial killer did not confine himself to homosexuals at all. Simple enough. I wrote a list of things to do, and then went through to the café for a cup of coffee.

The café is run by Ally, a very bright, attractive Italian girl, and her English boyfriend Mike. The unit is about twice the size of mine, with four small tables and more potted plants than the place really has room for. From a small, adjoining kitchen, they knock out sandwiches, hot meals and espresso to people in the other units, and they also deliver to nearby businesses. They both work a lot harder than I do but always manage to be cheerful to their customers and to each other – no mean feat considering that they share a flat as well as a business. The café is very convenient for me, being only three doors along, and I'll often leave a note on my door telling clients to wait in there for me if there's a chance that I'll be late. I have a spare coffee machine at my flat which I could bring along to my office if I wanted to, but I like Ally and Mike, so I don't. I like the fact that they are there, and it doesn't cost me much to contribute to their staying. Also, last Christmas, they had bought me my very own mug to use. It's bigger than their normal ones and it has a picture of Kojak on the side, though whether this is a reference to my profession, or to my hairline, was not made clear to me.

I had Kojak in my hand as I approached the counter. Mike was in the kitchen washing up while Ally was clearing a table from the last of the lunch rush. Mike called out hi through the open door.

'Been to see your bank manager, Bill?' he asked, looking at my suit.

'No, the Shadow Treasury Minister actually,' I replied.

'Blimey,' he said, 'your overdraft must be bigger than mine, mate!'

Ally put down the dirty plates she was carrying and smiled hello, before going round to the machine to pour me a black coffee.

Ally has the sort of smile that makes you wish sudden and calamitous death on her boyfriend, or at least that you didn't like him so much. She also has the shiniest black curly hair, and huge bottomless eyes, dark as olives. She handed Kojak back to me and made a tick in her tally book. I took the coffee gingerly by the rim, and went to sit at the table she had just cleared.

I had an hour to kill before meeting Andy Gold. I spent it sipping the coffee and staring at Kojak's ever-lasting lollipop, thinking about the seven years I had spent as a detective with the Islington Police. I had liked the job to begin with, and as I got higher up there always seemed some new aspect of the work to keep me interested. But then I got to the point where I seemed to be constantly battering my head against a mixture of a lack of resources to deal with the kind of criminals I wanted to deal with, and a lack of time to investigate anything properly. I came slowly to the conclusion that I was not employed to solve crimes and arrest their per-petrators, but as part of a political tool, a tool used to spread whitewash over the city so that the graffiti would not show through. At local election time the councillors would panic, and after a few words were whispered at the right cocktail parties there would be us, engaged in yet another useless crackdown on begging or street prosti-tution. Clean out an area, Harlesden say, by arresting a lot of very minor people, who get out after spending a night inside, to set up somewhere else. All it ever did was piss off your snitches, and make it harder to find them when you needed information about anything really important. And we never got to deal with the biggest reason the homeless or the whores inhabit any particular spot of God's green earth in any number; the pushers selling them crack pellets in Yorkie Bar foil, which they work all day and night scratching money together to buy. These guys would just disappear for a day or two and then they'd be back, leaning against shop-fronts and lampposts, keeping on chewing, giving us the smile as we walked past. And the kids kept on selling themselves and the wheels kept on turning. After seven years I found myself both cynical and bored, with a mounting feeling of frustration.

I probably would have stuck it out though. I was still only in my late twenties, and at the time the feelings which I can articulate now usually just manifested themselves in a liking for the bottle and the kind of Need for Speed which was not the sort that Tom Cruise could have related to. I would probably have gone on for years, just like Andy Gold had done, getting more and more miserable about it, tied in by a mortgage and the hope of that next step up the ladder, getting further and further away from the reasons I joined up in the first place. You could say that my brother Luke saved me from that. I owe him my new status as a happy, well-adjusted, self-employed detective, with my own office and company vehicle. And I owe him a great deal more than that, so much more that if I try to think of a way to repay him it sends me insane.

Luke risked his life for me. For various reasons too long to go into a man I'd tried to put away wanted me dead and Luke found out about it. Luke knew the man was coming for me and though he was aware it was dangerous he drove across town to warn me. Because we look alike, and because Luke was driving my car, the man thought my brother was me and he tried to kill him. Some would say he succeeded. Luke risked his life for me and because he did that I knew I could not go on living the life I had been living. That life hadn't really been much, certainly not worth doing what Luke did to save it. Not worth spending the rest of *his* life – if you can call it that – lying in a hospital bed, unable to move even his eye-lashes, kept alive by a constant stream of liquid nourishment fed through a plastic tube in his stomach, sitting helpless inside himself, a prison cell which, I was assured, he would never be released from. Not into this world, anyway.

I sipped Ally's coffee and traced my finger around the flower pattern on the vinyl tablecloth. I was sinking back into feelings of guilt, and a vein-searing impotence, shrunk by the image of Luke's inert body in the wreckage of my car, remembering the helplessness I felt, until time took me by the scruff of the neck and kept me from drowning. It was quarter to four. I shook off the thoughts I'd been having, like water from a raincoat. I got up and asked Ally for two portions of her unbelievable tiramisu to take home with me.

Ally cut one portion, placed it carefully in a cardboard carton, and then went to cut another.

'And if you could just give me the recipe as well, Ally, I'll be on my way.'

'Never!' she laughed. A long, elegant middle finger rested lightly on the top of the second piece, stopping it falling off the cake slicer. I'd been on at her for years about her tiramisu recipe.

'Why would you ever buy it from me if you could make it yourself?' she asked.

'Oh,' I said, 'I don't want to make it, I want to sell it!'

She laughed again and put the carton in a plastic bag.

'And who,' she asked, 'is the lucky girl?'

'Sorry?'

'Which privileged female will be sharing my tiramisu after you have cooked one of your famous meals for her?' Ally's eyebrows stood up into two neat arches.

'You should be a detective,' I said. 'Maybe I just think I'll be hungry later.'

'No,' she said, 'you exercise too much. There's definitely a second party involved here.'

I held up my hands.

'OK,' I admitted, 'you've got me bang to rights. But it's only Sharon.'

'Only Sharon,' she said meaningfully. 'Hmmm.'

I ignored the archness of Ally's tone, as well as that of her eyebrows, and took the bag from her.

'Actually,' I said, 'you wouldn't make a very good detective at all. Your method of interrogation is far too intimidating.'

We both laughed, and then I left, calling out bye to Mike who was still up to his elbows in soapsuds.

If you work all day looking for missing people in the squats or doorways of Camden, King's Cross, Dalston and Hackney, getting sworn at, spat at, threatened, and generally abused, then walking through the front door of The Albion, in Barnsbury, feels like St Peter has held open the door for you. It is an old, ivy-covered haven, with a wooden floor, sofas, horse brasses which somehow manage not to look kitsch, and no jukebox. It has the immediate effect of making you think that you have just been transported into the tranquil heart of the countryside and the one detective you would not be surprised to see there would be Miss Marple. I had a quick skirt around for Andy, ordered a Perrier, and sat at a small, gnarled table, with my eye on the door.

Andy Gold ducked in ten minutes after I had, at twenty past four, and he seemed to bring his day in with him. I waved off his offer of a drink, and he stood at the bar while the barmaid served him a pint of lager and a double whiskey, straight, no ice, which he drank off before coming over to sit down. He needed his other hand to hold his briefcase.

Andy is only about five-eight, qualifying for the Met a year after they lowered the height requirement. He has dark brown hair which he keeps constantly slicked back with its own natural grease, and he has the sort of face which looks like it could do with a damn good shave, immediately after it has been given a damn good shave. Like me his mother was Jewish and his father Anglo-Saxon, but his features are more Semitic than mine, his skin that Mediterranean non-brown, his nose prominent, his thick, bunched eyebrows giving a correct impression of over-anxious intensity. He's the same age as I am, give or take a couple of months, but he could easily pass for ten years older on a bad day. This, it seemed, was a bad day.

Andy sat down and took a long pull on his beer. He looked a wreck. His suit was creased to shit and his eyes were two boiled eggs in a dish of ketchup. He loosened his already loosened tie, sat forward in his chair, pushed his head forward and ran his nails hard over his scalp. Then he sat back and yawned, not bothering to cover up the fact that he had had a tonsillectomy at one point in his life, and had eaten too many sweets as a teenager. He drank his pint down to about an inch before taking any notice of me. I waited.

'So,' he said eventually, 'the MP doesn't think his bro was a homo.'

'No,' I said.

I reached into the back pocket of my trousers and pulled out two fifty-pound notes, which I let Andy see before slipping them quietly into the side pocket of his jacket. Andy nodded almost imperceptibly. Then he reached down for his briefcase which he placed on his knee and snapped the clasps on. He took out a brown folder which he laid on the table in front of me.

'You never saw this,' he said, as my hand reached out to open it.

Chapter Four

I pan-fried the sausages very quickly to brown the skins, and then I put them in the Le Creuset which Sharon had bought me last Christmas. I'd picked the sausages up from Molise's on the Farringdon Road, along with a couple of tins of Italian tomatoes, the ones that don't have acetic acid or any sugar added, and the smell of which makes you think of Tuscany, whether or not you've actually been there. I opened the tins and tipped the contents over the sausages, along with a large glug of extra virgin, six crushed cloves of garlic, a little white wine, a splash of Lea and Perrins, and two small dried Indian chilli peppers. I mashed the tomatoes up with a wooden spoon, remembered the tablespoon of honey, and then put the pot on to bubble for an hour. I made up some polenta, mixed it with two chopped, steamed leeks, and put that on to bake. Then I sat down on the sofa with some photocopies of material from the file which Andy Gold had been kind enough to show me.

It was clear that my friend and his colleagues had no doubt about Edward Morgan's murder being part of the series of gay slashings which the tabloids had taken such great delight in over the past six months. Teddy's details were in there alongside the details of the other two deaths.

John Evans was killed in the cab of his lorry. He was parked in a lay-by on the A1, just south of Stamford, and current theory believed that his assailant was probably a hitchhiker who he had propositioned, and who reacted with greater energy than the usual yes or no. Two severe contusions just above the hairline show that Evans was rendered immobile with what forensic scientists are certain was his own ten-pound hand wrench. Evans was then attacked with a broken bottle, receiving abdominal and chest injuries, which caused internal laceration severe enough to cause his heart to fail before he had time to bleed to death. The absence of any glass fragments in Evans' cab, to match those found in his body, led to the conclusion that the attack was to a large degree premeditated, because the assailant clearly had the weapon ready before he got into the lorry. Why a bottle was used in this way instead of a knife, is not known. These days, seriously effective knives are just as easy to get hold of as beer bottles. If the attackers were teenagers, then a knife would actually have been *easier* to obtain than a beer bottle.

As for motive, the report stated that a theory of simple violent robbery was hard to sustain. While it is true that John Evans was robbed of what is believed to be about a hundred pounds, Evans had no defence wounds on his arms and hands, nothing to show that he had tried, as would be natural, to stop whoever it was from stabbing him to death. He was, therefore, unconscious, or at least completely defenceless *before* he received the wounds to his stomach area which killed him. A mugger would usually have taken what he wanted after immobilizing his victim, and then left him unconscious. He would avoid

43

murder if he could help it, and in this case it seems that he definitely could have done.

But he didn't.

The police appealed for witnesses, posting pictures of the driver in service stations and truck stops up and down the A1, and they interviewed all of Evans' friends and workmates. But nobody came forward with anything useful. The murder was privately put down to a crack-head getting carried away, and while the usual amount of manpower was still spent on it, it was assumed that the perpetrator would get caught sooner or later for doing something else. At this stage of the investigation no homosexual link was established.

I turned the page.

A young lad with smooth light brown skin and a big, goofy grin stared out at me from an A4 blow-up of a studio photograph. I could just make out a blue shirt, and a red and green striped school tie. I looked at the shot for a second or two, not really wanting to turn the page again. Then I put the picture aside.

James Waldock worked as a male prostitute, probably controlled by a Brixton outfit called the 22 Crew. The 22 are an enterprising bunch of dudes who hang out in a café on the Railton Road, and are gradually maturing into an efficient whores and scores team, expanding operations as far as the Yardies will let them and as long as they give them a big enough piece of the action. For a male prostitute in the City of London and its boroughs James was a couple of years older than the estimated average. He was fourteen.

James Waldock came from what the report politely termed a deprived background. Free of any fatherly influence, his mother was a user, and it was probably she who introduced him to her own profession, anxious that at his age he should begin to pay his way. His form teacher's report, which was in the file, stated that he was a quiet, surprisingly bright kid who, when he did attend school, was always attentive and liked to ask questions. He was, however, easily led by older boys, and he often tried to hide his intelligence behind an assumed bravado which didn't seem to come naturally to him. This happens a lot to young black males, so the teacher reported. White males too, I thought. I see it all the time. The peculiarly harsh way in which some boys aged fourteen or so rebuke the child in them, as if they hate the naivety within themselves, a naivety which has conned them into some sort of hope which they begin to see can only cause them frustration and disappointment. I remembered it myself, how I'd once challenged my father to a fight, just him and me, after he'd used his belt on Luke for coming home ten minutes late. How he had kicked the shit out of me. This tacked-on manfulness can look ugly and be dangerous, but it usually passes. If the kid is left alive long enough to grow out of it.

James was conscious through most of what happened to him. His body was found in the basement of a condemned block of council flats which is being taken down slowly, floor by floor from the top. Police believe that he was being buggered in a standing position, and that during or immediately after this, his head was battered hard against the wall he was being pushed up against. His nose was broken and scrapes of dry paint were found on his skin and in his mouth. Nonoxynol, the chemical used to lubricate certain brands of condoms, was found inside his anal canal, as well as two types of semen, along with the two types found in his stomach. The presence of the semen suggests that James was not exactly Aids aware, and that the Nonoxynol came from his attacker, the wearing of the condom being his attacker's idea; a way of avoiding DNA profiling. The condom was not found.

Cuts on both the inside and outside of James' wrists, and on his hands, show that he tried to defend himself against the Lucozade bottle which was repeatedly thrust into his chest, face and neck, and eventually left embedded deep in his stomach. The amount of cuts James received suggest that it took him some time to die, although it is impossible to say how many of them he received after he was actually dead. Once again, no trace of the bottom of the bottle, or the lid, were found. Like Evans, James was also robbed. It was clear that he had had at least four other clients that night, but there was no money on his body when it was found. The police, however, couldn't say for definite that it was his assailant who took the money. There are people who will rob a corpse, even if the corpse is that of a fourteen-year-old boy lying in a dismal basement, on top of enough blood to fill a bathtub. Some of these people, I thought, as I went to turn the heat down from under my Le Creuset, are police officers.

The picture they had of Edward Morgan, or Teddy, as his brother had referred to him when we parted from each other, and he urged me to do all I could to find out who killed him, could have been lifted straight out of the BA catalogue. Teddy was tan, fortyish, squared-jawed and blue-eyed. I could see no resemblance to his older brother. Teddy looked just the man to get you down safely when they had trouble with an engine, or calm your nerves during turbulence with a joke about rollercoaster rides. Perfect white teeth. I'd always wanted teeth like that. It seemed strange to think of such a confident, strong-looking person as a victim, someone weakened, viciously humiliated. Murdered. Looking at his clear, open face, I tried to decide whether or not I thought he was gay. The picture didn't tell me anything.

I read what had happened to him, what had been done to him. Already my mind was trying to see it, to see it happening as if it were a scene from a film. I read the statements given by the co-pilots, the stewardesses, the barman at the airport and then I read the scene of crime report. I read how his wife had discovered his body and a statement from her saying that she had no idea that her husband was involved in homosexual activity. Possible images of death flitted into my head like the ghosts of pinned butterflies. I was just getting to the forensic report when the door buzzer sounded.

It was very good to see Sharon. I was surprised by how well she was looking, and how delighted I was to see her standing in my doorway with a bottle of wine in her hand. We kissed hello. I took the bottle from her and she followed me into the kitchen, towards the smell which she was already congratulating me on.

I'd done a quick tidying-up job and my place didn't look too bad. I live in a converted photo-studio with black blinds, a small open-plan kitchen and floorboards which I haven't got round to sanding yet. Sharon has often promised to come round and help me do the place up a bit, and to this end she bought me a framed Salgado print for my birthday which is the only thing breaking the purity of the whitish walls. Every time she comes over she tells me my flat looks like I've just moved into it. She uses the words shelving, cupboards, uplighting and Ikea a lot.

I poured Sharon a glass of the Rosso di Montalcino she'd brought with her and then put some broccoli on to steam. As we sat on the sofa chatting I couldn't help thinking of how I had met her, and the thing that bound us to each other. The reason we have dinner once a month or so, go to the theatre or the movies every so often. The reason why sometimes she is the only person I can, or want, to talk to, or why I spend ages looking for her Christmas present. Why, once in a while, on a particular date perhaps, she calls me in the middle of the night, her voice breaking, and asks me to drive over.

I never used to get on particularly well with Sharon but in the last few years that has changed. Sharon was my brother Luke's fiancée. As a matter of fact she still is, technically. She certainly hasn't actually broken it off with him. It has been nearly four years since Luke was injured and if I think about it I know that Sharon must have seen somebody else in that time. But on the occasions that we meet she is discreet enough not to mention anything. I still see her as Luke's girl, though I would completely understand if one day she turned up at my flat with a nervous-looking man who she would like me to meet. It might be strange, but I would understand.

Luke and I were sharing a flat at the time he met Sharon, and as soon as he started to tell me about her I could tell it was something special. Luke was working in a bar on Camden High Street at the time, having yet to establish himself as the new star of the British stage, and Sharon had come in for a coffee. Luke said that when he saw her he just knew, and he was so nervous that he spilled her cappuccino all over the table. He wasn't too nervous to make sure he had a chat with her and find out her name though. Sharon, a law student. Sharon was immediately embarrassed about her name and assured Luke that she wasn't the stiletto sort and that her parents had been into the Bible; the Rose of Sharon. In that case, Luke said, it suits you. When Sharon got up to leave he told her to make sure that she came in again soon, and Luke put himself on the rota practically every hour the place was open over the coming week to make sure that he didn't miss her. He needn't have bothered, however; she came in again next day.

When I first met Sharon I was pretty sceptical. I couldn't believe that all the hyperbolic nonsense issuing from my lovestruck little brother's mouth was actually true. I just didn't venerate women the way he did. I'd asked Luke what it was about her and he'd spent hours trying to tell me. It wasn't so much that she was drop dead beautiful, he said, but that she had a constant, radiating warmth inside her, a kind of simple, mesmerizing energy which made him feel slightly childish. She also had a steely quality that kept Luke spellbound when, over dinner in our flat, she told us about what she wanted to do with her life, how most people went into the law to make money, or because they couldn't think of anything else to do. I thought it sounded just a little prissy, but when Sharon told how she wanted to make a difference, to use the legal system to help people, it actually was quietly inspiring. She asked me if that was what I felt about being a policeman, which I still was at the time. I remember feeling uncomfortable under her earnest glare, unable to match Sharon's fervour but then telling her yes, it actually was, and being happy and surprised to know that I was actually telling her the truth. Then.

Luke and Sharon soon started seeing each other seriously and his view of her never tempered. He agreed with almost everything she said, and I could see him trying to change to match up to her. This surprised me because Luke had always been flighty and noncommittal about most things, especially women. But even though Sharon was two or three years younger than Luke, she seemed to mature him. He took himself much more seriously. He worked a lot harder at his acting, going to evening classes at the Actor's Centre, sending out CVs all the time, and I have to admit things did start to go well for him. He got a good role at the Kings Head, and then a couple of bit-parts in the West End, and some TV. Luke had always written poetry, which he never showed anyone, not even me, and Sharon persuaded him not only to show it to her, but to work on it and send it off to magazines. He did, and after a while his stuff began to appear in the *Rialto*, *Stand Magazine*, and once *Poetry Review*. In general Luke began to approach things the same way that Sharon did, with a determined, though quiet confidence which was impressive but, I thought, somewhat forced and even unnatural. He became a graver, more weighty person and I wasn't sure I really knew him any more.

When Luke and Sharon told me that they were getting married I remember having mixed feelings. Luke was twenty-six, Sharon twenty-three, and I thought they were too young. I thought that Luke was perhaps growing old too soon, that he had completely shunted aside the child in him in an effort to keep up with Sharon. Sharon seemed to monopolize my brother and the times when they were in company she could never quite relax, giving the impression of marking time until she could get him alone again. I knew, however, that this was probably jealousy. I missed Luke's infantile sense of humour, and realized that it was Sharon's distrust of any sort of frivolity which bugged me. I had begun to miss my brother (and the aspiring actresses he used to introduce me to). I was pissed off that Luke never seemed up for a big night any more, or that he suddenly started getting a ridiculously sour expression on his face when I cut up a line on the coffee table. Fuck it – I was the Fuzz, for God's sake! I thought he was taking things too seriously, something which, ever since Luke could talk, he was constantly accusing me of.

I didn't think that Luke should marry Sharon, not yet at least, but my reservations would have only caused a rift between us so I put them aside. I kissed them both and told them they were stupid and that I would happily be best man at the divorce as well. Sharon kissed me back and told me, with that unnerving certainty of hers, that it wouldn't come to that. And she was right. It didn't come to a wedding either.

After we had finished the sausages, Sharon asked me what I was working on at the moment. I told her about the usual runaways, and then I told her about the MP. I told her what the MP had told me. He wouldn't have liked it but he didn't know Sharon. She wouldn't tell anybody.

'Peter Morgan is gay?' she asked, surprised.

'*Sir* Peter Morgan.'

'He doesn't look it,' she said. 'Does he?'

'I don't know,' I answered. 'I have no way of telling. Unless it's obvious of course.'

'Like when someone is all in leather, with a Freddie Mercury moustache?'

'I suppose,' I said. 'But it doesn't have to be that obvious. I know it's a cliché, but some people just look gay.'

'Maybe that's because they choose to look gay,' Sharon said, 'in whatever they're wearing. If they chose not to then you would never be able to guess, not even if they were in the leather. Peter Morgan chooses not to. It's still surprising though. I wonder how he voted on the age of consent debate?'

'Probably against, especially as he's keen that none of his political colleagues know about his orientation.'

'Damn hypocrite.'

'I know. But in a strange way I actually feel sorry for him.'

Sharon put down her wineglass.

'For being gay? And being a Tory at the same time!'

'No,' I said. 'Because he's realized that the way he's been living his life is wrong. All the intrigues and lies, the pretence, it all seems pointless to him after what has happened to his brother. But he's too far immersed in it to break out.'

'To return is as tedious as to go over?'

'Something like that. He knows that it doesn't matter, not really, if people know he's gay. He knows that it would probably make him happier if they did know. But he won't ever let it out. His wife, his position. He's stuck.'

Sharon sat back in her chair. 'It sounds like you quite liked him,' she said, with more than a hint of disapproval.

'I did,' I admitted, 'after a while. After he told me he was gay. It took courage to do that to a complete stranger. I could tell that he cares, or cared, about his brother.'

'So does Michael Howard I should think,' Sharon said. 'If he's got one.'

'Then maybe I'd like him too,' I said. I shrugged my shoulders. 'I don't know, there was just something about Morgan that I liked. Something intangible. He has a kind of wistful, removed quality about him.'

Sharon laughed. 'He doesn't on *Question Time*.'

'No,' I answered, thinking about it. 'You're right. He definitely doesn't look wistful on *Question Time*.'

I served the tiramisu, and after we'd devoured it with the animalistic relish which it deserved, Sharon told me what she had been doing recently. Sharon finished her pupillage two years ago, and works as a barrister for the Refugee Legal Centre, defending asylum seekers against deportation orders. It's a difficult, dispiriting job, given the current attitude towards refugees, or burdens on the state as they are portrayed. Sharon's success rate is a little higher than the average at about six per cent. She spends a lot of time in miserable detention centres, talking to people who are scared and desperate. They tell her about Nigerian prisons, Turkish punishment squads, and they show her bruises and scars from cigarette burns or knife cuts, which Sharon can never prove they did not inflict upon themselves. She watches their faces when she fails to win their last appeal, and then she imagines their faces when they are sent back to their country of origin, and she never hears from them again.

Sometimes though, there are lighter moments, and Sharon is the first to admit that some people do try it on. I sat listening to her tell me about a woman whose boyfriend was applying for asylum on some invented grounds of abuse, and who wrote to his girlfriend in Albania telling her exactly what to say at the airport when she came to England to join him. Customs officials found the letter in her bag, which not only blew her claim but her boyfriend's as well. I watched Sharon as she told the story. Her lipstick had dissolved into thin lines, which exaggerated the fullness of her mouth. She systematically pushed an errant strand of her dark blond hair back behind her left ear, as it kept repeating its offence of escape. Her teeth were stained by the wine, her eyes so clear and green you could see why unimaginative people often asked her if she wore those coloured contact lenses. I thought about Luke, and remembered the time he told me about them. How he had described those eyes just like they were, and I didn't believe him, thinking he was just a love-sick fool.

I laughed at Sharon's story, and apropos of nothing I suddenly told her that I was glad she had been able to come, and that it always meant a lot to me to see her. She smiled, and we looked at each other for a second. Neither of us said anything. Neither of us were self-conscious, we just sat there looking and smiling at each other. I don't know why. Then her smile took on the faintest, most distant tinge of sadness, like caramel which has just begun to burn. I looked down at the table, at a small stain of red from a drop of wine which had missed the glass. I saw Sharon's hand, resting on the table a few inches from mine. Her engagement ring. I didn't know she still wore it. I looked at the simple ring, one small diamond set into the gold band, for several seconds. I had lent Luke the money to buy it. He still owed me seven hundred quid, the bastard. I put both my hands on the table, pushed myself up without looking at Sharon, and went to make coffee.

In fact, I had no coffee. I had stood talking to the

youngest Molise boy in the deli for a full ten minutes while I tried to remember the thing which I knew I had to get. But it never came to me. I apologized to Sharon, a little too much. She said she didn't mind though. She looked a little nervous, but then she smiled at me again, softly. I looked away from her. All of a sudden I didn't want to be in my warm, cosy flat with Sharon. I was beginning to feel claustrophobic and heavy.

I clapped my hands together, trying to make the atmosphere disappear like a magician with a fake bunch of flowers. I had an idea.

'Do you want to see the famous William H. Rucker, Private Eye, scourge of the evil and corrupt, in action?' I asked her.

'You bet,' she answered with surprise, picking up quickly on my lightening of the mood.

'Are we going to catch a killer?' she asked.

'Nothing so exciting,' I told her.

The drive down to King's Cross only took five minutes. I parked the Mazda and then took Sharon, and my second-hand Nikon, into the twenty-four-hour-café at the bottom of the Pentonville Road. As usual, the café looked shabby and the tables were all dirty. The waitress came over but she didn't bother to wipe up from the people before us. We ordered *cafés au lait*. I took the camera out of my bag and rested it on the seat beside me. Remembering a very embarrassing time earlier in my career, I made sure that the film was in it. I smiled at Sharon and kept one eye on a group of teenage lads who were standing around on the corner of the Pentonville Road and Calshot Street.

'You take me to the loveliest places, Bill Rucker,'

Sharon said, using her serviette to create a stain-free square of Formica for herself.

I was looking for Dominic Lewes, whom I had found once before. His mother didn't want me to tell her where he was, which I would not have done anyway, she just wanted to know that he was alive, and what sort of state he was in. I didn't really expect to find him. It had been eight months since I had discovered him in this very spot, and I'd learnt over the past ten years that absolutely anything can happen in eight months to a young boy from Grimsby who's run away from home. Cold, hunger, death to name but the obvious and there are plenty of things which occur that are far from predictable even to someone who has seen a lot of it before. It would send you mad to think of all the things that can happen, that *are* happening right this second, to all of those young Odysseuses who have broken free from the ties that bound them and come to the damp rooms and stinking alleys that make up their London. Any number of things could have been done to Dominic in any number of places but still, it didn't hurt looking in the place I had found him before. We had wanted coffee anyway.

The coffees arrived, and Sharon and I sipped them, chatting, while I kept an eye out on the street.

'One thing though, Billy,' Sharon said, resting her elbows on the table and leaning forward. 'You never tell the parents where their kids are. I still don't really understand.'

'It's simple,' I told her. 'Kids run away for a reason. The kids who are happy don't run away. The kids who are quite miserable don't run away. It's the kids who are very miserable that run away. They wouldn't view what they had to go through here as acceptable unless the alternative was worse. When I first started I found this girl, twelve or thirteen, and took the dad down to this squat in Streatham where she was living. I thought I had just reunited a misunderstood teenager with her worried and non-recriminating family, and saved her from all sorts of bad shit. But you should have seen the poor kid's face when her loving dad showed up. The sheer terror. I thought she was going to vomit. And the dad's face. There was no relief, no joy. His face just sort of set when he saw her, hard as granite, and I knew immediately what I had sent the girl back to. He didn't say anything, he just pulled her into his car. Of course, not all the parents would be like this, but how can I know? I never tell them. Sometimes I tell the Bill, who tell social services, if the kid is very young and into some bad shit. But I'm not sending some poor kid back to a dad who thinks he's Nigel Benn, or an uncle who can't keep his cock in his drawers.'

I took a sip of coffee. It was surprisingly good. Outside, a car drew up and one of the lads on the corner pushed himself off the wall and walked over to it. He leant into the passenger side window for a second or two and then got in. The car drove away.

'But,' Sharon continued, 'and I don't mean to be rude about your abilities as an investigator, Mr Rucker, but if you won't tell the parents where their kid is, then why do they hire you? Most other agencies don't have your scruples, I shouldn't think.'

'They don't hire me at first,' I said. 'I usually get used when some agency or other, made up of overweight failed ex-cops pushing sixty, fails to find the kid, or when they've run away so many times that the parents know there's no point bringing them back again. It's the mothers usually, who hire me. Often I'm told only to contact them, that the father doesn't know about me. Some of the mothers, I swear, are glad that their son or daughter has escaped what they haven't been able to. They don't want them to go back, they just want to know that they are OK.'

'I see,' Sharon said, putting her long glass down on the saucer. 'I bet you still lose money though, doing it the way you do.'

'Yes,' I said, 'I probably do.'

At that moment, a boy in white jeans and a black MA1 walked around the corner and started talking to the other lads. The boy had short, bleached blond hair, but I was pretty certain it was Dominic. I pushed aside my coffee.

'Bingo,' I said.

I reached for my bag and pulled out a copy of the photo I'd taken of him last time. I looked at it, then at the boy on the street and yes, in spite of the hair, which had been long and dark, it was him. I grabbed hold of the Nikon.

'Wow,' Sharon whispered, 'action!'

I focused in on Dominic Lewes, but he was in shadow. Even with the lens I had I knew I could only get him if he stepped out into the light of the lamppost. I wasn't worried about it. By the look of him, the way the other lads treated him, I could tell that he came here often. If I couldn't get him tonight I could easily come back. I was amazed once again how easy my job sometimes was. I put the camera down on the chair beside me, and smiled broadly at an old lady who was looking very nervously at my distinctly suspicious behaviour. She turned away.

I kept an eye on the street, and we sat drinking coffee until Sharon said that she had to leave. She had a case to prepare for the morning. I put three pound coins on the table before she could do anything herself, and then gave her a look which told her that I didn't want a fight about it. As we were standing up she suddenly thought of something and delved into the postman's bag she always carries. She pulled out a slim blue A4 file.

'I don't know if you've seen all these,' she said, holding the file out to me. 'I went through Luke's books again a couple of weeks ago and collected together most of his poems. I also found some that he'd hidden in his acting notes.'

I took the file and looked at the sky-blue card. I didn't open it.

'Thanks,' I said, after a second or two. I felt that I should say something more but I didn't know what. I held the file gingerly for a second and then I opened my bag and put the file inside, careful not to bend it. Luke's poems, his private thoughts about Sharon, about me. About our father. I put the Nikon in next to them. I picked up the bag and walked over to the door with Sharon.

'Aren't you going to wait and take his picture?' Sharon asked, surprised that I was leaving, nodding over towards the corner where Dominic Lewes stood with his colleagues.

'It's too dark,' I said, 'but I know where he is. And it gives me yet another excuse to visit this delightful establishment.' I waved goodbye to the waitress, and pointed to our table to indicate that we weren't doing a runner. Sharon opened the door for me and we walked out into the sharp October air, redolent with eau-de-kebab and carbon monoxide.

I offered Sharon a lift home but she refused and hailed a cab before I could begin to persuade her. I opened the door for her, kissed her goodbye, and then closed it after she had climbed inside, in the ungraceful fashion only a London cab can enforce on you. Sharon slid the window down and thanked me for the evening. She said it was good to go out and just be together without mulling over the past like we were prone to doing. I said yes, it was. I wanted to fix up a day when we could both go and see Luke together, but just as I started speaking I noticed that Dominic Lewes was walking away from his pitch. With a man.

The man was taller than Dominic and from the side looked to be a lot older. He had a travel bag in his hand – probably just got off the train. I told Sharon I would phone her, then kissed her goodbye again hurriedly, feeling her cold hand on the side of my face. The cab U-turned and just made the lights before heading along the Euston Road towards the Westway. I waved. Then I walked off after Dominic Lewes and the man to whom he was about to purvey the delights of his fifteen-year-old body.

Chapter Five

Next morning I woke up at eight, got up at quarter past, and showered. I hadn't had more than half a bottle of wine and three or four slugs of John Power's last night and Mr Hangover (unlike Mr Phone Bill) had not decided to pay me a visit. I wrapped a towel round my waist and, ignoring the washing up, made a cafetière of light Colombian and two slices of toast with Lincolnshire honey. I set the pot down on a tile on my table, next to the file with Luke's poems in it, which I'd taken out of my bag last night but hadn't read yet. I thought about going through them now. I stared at the file lying on the table next to my ever-dying orange plant. Poetry – before 9 a.m.? Later.

After I'd left Sharon I'd followed Dominic Lewes and friend to a row of Victorian houses only two minutes walk away, some of which looked ready to fall down and others which had yellow alarm boxes on the walls and which wouldn't have looked out of place in Highgate Village. Dominic showed his friend into number 23 Elm Drive which, it wasn't difficult to see, was a squat. The man seemed to look nervously at the run-down hole he was about to enter, hesitating on the doorstep and running his tongue over his lips. But his needs were obviously stronger than his fear of cockroaches and mildew because he soon went in. I wrote the house number down and then smiled to myself. The old Mazda was showing signs that my investigative prowess was rubbing off on it. It was sat directly outside.

I moved the car and parked it further down the street towards King's Cross, but facing the house. I sat in the front seat, waiting, listening to the late book on Radio 4, which at any time would have been too early. After fifteen minutes the man who had gone into number 23 emerged – but without Dominic. I saw him walking towards the car and I had the sudden urge to jump out, tell him I was vice squad and scare the shit out of him. I let the urge pass.

He walked by without noticing that I was inside the Mazda and headed back the way he had come, no doubt to a wife and kids who by the look of him could well have been about Dominic's age. He was in his fifties, tallish, well dressed but not in the Peter Morgan bracket. He looked like he'd just been away for a few days on business and had decided to make the most of his last few hours of solitary anonymity. He looked pleased with himself. I had the sudden urge to jump out of the Mazda and kick the living shit out of him. I let the urge pass.

I thought about going home. I didn't know if Dominic would come out again and even if he did I was pretty sure I wouldn't be able to get a picture of him. Hell, I knew where he lived, I could easily come back in the daylight. And I was tired. Dominic, however, came out five minutes later, while I was still deciding. He didn't walk back towards his pitch though, but turned right out of his house and then right again at the top of the street, walking quickly. I hopped out the car and followed him, just catching sight of him as he crossed the street and headed towards a medium-sized tower block which announced the beginning of the Russell Estate. Concrete forest perhaps, if not quite concrete jungle.

Two figures waited by a fire exit at the bottom of the old, stained building, wearing dark puffas and B-hats. When Dominic walked up to them they both pushed themselves off the wall and stood in front of him. It didn't take long for Dominic to reassure them, however, probably because they recognized him, or if they didn't, with a password or the name of The Man. They let him through and held the fire exit open for him as he walked in quickly. I strolled past the building with my hands in my pockets until I was out of sight of the two doormen, and then I pretended to use a payphone across the road which didn't have a receiver on it.

Dominic was out again in less than ten minutes. I let him get round the corner before going after him. I watched him cross the road, turn left, and then insert his key into the door of 23 Elm Drive once again. I walked by back to the car.

In less than thirty minutes Dominic had picked up a john, sucked him off or let him fuck him, and then scored what was almost certainly twenty or forty quids' worth of crack or horse. And in the same amount of time I had ascertained these facts and in doing so had revealed the salient points about Dominic Lewes' life at that point in time. He was a smackhead who was young enough to sell his arse rather than go housebreaking which, for all I knew, he probably did as well. He'd come a long way since I'd first seen him – here he was jiving with the guys on the corner, gaining entry to secret, exclusive places. I was pretty sure he hadn't been a user when I'd seen him eight months ago, looking bewildered and lonely, asking any man that passed if they wanted to take him home with them. Even asking me. He had come a long way all right, and I'd found him in exactly the same place he'd started from. I got back into the car, turned the key and drove home.

I finished my breakfast and made two or three calls. It was a bright, clear morning, summer making one last stand in mid-October, and I was eager to get up and out into it. Probably the caffeine. I put on a dark Aquascutum suit which had been my uncle's, a white Pinks shirt without a tie, and a pair of old brogues I could see my face in while I was tying the laces. I ran my hand over my chin and regretted that I'd been too lazy to shave that morning. Too late. I turned the machine on, left a message to un-known callers that I would be on my office number from around lunchtime, and skipped downstairs into the street.

It was still only nineish and Exmouth Market was busy with people on their way to work, or looking through the four or five stalls which give the street its name (just). Workmen were busy ripping out the old Spar minimarket which was about to become another restaurant and a group of bleached trendies who didn't seem to have gone to bed yet sat outside Fred's Café, drinking cappuccinos, probably waiting for The Face to open. I walked past them, waved at Alberto through the window and bought a paper from the shop next door to Zak's Snacks. Walking back past my flat to the Mazda I flipped over to the sports pages and saw that Arsenal had lost last night at home to

Forest. 2–0. Campbell and Thomas. It put a spring in my step. What an absolutely perfect way to start the day.

I sat outside 23 Elm Drive for ten minutes but it was far too early and I gave up. I drove through the back streets which run horizontal to the Euston Road until I reached Harley Street and then I joined the main drag. It took me twenty minutes to drive the quarter of a mile further to the Westway, and once on it I didn't move very much faster until well past Ladbroke Grove. I didn't want to use the Westway, I never wanted to use it, but there was no choice really. I listened to ten minutes of *Call Nick Ross* and then switched over to Robert Elms on GLR. He was quite funny as usual and quite interesting as usual. But there was something about him which annoyed me. As usual.

And then I came to the place. The railing had been repaired long ago and the wrenching skid marks on the tarmac were also a thing of the past. Nobody would have been able to guess what had happened there because there was no evidence left, there was nothing to see any more; it was just a normal stretch of the flyover. But there was a lot for me to see and though I tried not to I saw it all. The gaping hole in the smashed barrier, the mess the car made after it had nosedived down on to the street below. I saw the rain and the flashing lights and the crowd of firemen and medics crowding round my wrecked car as I ran up to it and pushed my way through, through to the body they were cutting out of it, covered in blood, his face blank as if he wasn't even there. The way he just hung in their arms. And then hearing the sound of someone else begging to be let through the cordon and turning round to see Sharon arguing with the officers, who wouldn't let her through. And I was glad that they wouldn't let her through.

In the short-term car park at Heathrow I looked through my case to see that I had everything. Teddy's broad face grinned at me again. He still looked cheerful and in control. Alive. I hadn't mentioned any specific time to the barman so I went through his file again to make sure there wasn't anything I'd missed, any question that I would have liked to have asked and would feel annoyed about if I thought of it later. I didn't think I was going to get anywhere on this thing but at least I'd know that I'd done what I could. I took out the pathologist's report and quickly had another run through it.

Teddy Morgan died of a massive coronary thrombosis caused by severe lacerations to the abdomen and stomach lining which induced massive stress on the heart. He had been battered unconscious by a champagne bottle which caused a lot of structural damage to his face and which broke on impact. It was then used to cause the injuries to his stomach area which proved fatal.

A quantity of semen was found in Teddy's anal canal, and the police are unsure as to when it arrived there. While it was at first assumed that Teddy had been buggered before any attack was made on him, it is possible that this may have occurred after he was bludgeoned unconscious. The lack of any significant bloodstains directly under Teddy's body ruled out the theory that he was buggered while dead: the assailant would have had to turn the body over on to its front, and this would have soaked the sheets beneath his torso.

Fragments of glass were also found a long way up Teddy's anus. The police pathologist believed this to be one of the last things that had happened to Teddy, and that he could not have known anything about it. One of the larger fragments was matched to a long sliver of glass which had broken from the main body of the bottle, probably on initial impact with Teddy's skull, and the lacerations to Teddy's anal canal indicated that they were caused by a long, slender piece of glass rather than the main body of the bottle itself. The use of the shard of glass (as well as the lack of any alien fingerprints anywhere in the flat) suggested that the killer was, at that moment at least, wearing gloves. The rest of the shard was found jammed into what was left of Teddy's face.

The last thing that happened to Teddy was that whoever used the champagne bottle on him then stuck the top half of it into his gaping abdomen, wedging it between his hip and rib bones, where it stayed until Teddy's body was discovered by his wife. This struck me as the cruellest, most cynical thing his assailant had done – an insult to someone whom he had already humiliated, a two-finger salute stuck up to whoever found him, a salute which would never leave the memory. Even I could see it and I hadn't been there, and I wondered at the mind which would take pleasure in such an act. I suddenly had the strange realization which I used to get on the force, that the person I was thinking of was out there somewhere, out and about talking to people, laughing with them, sitting at a bar with them maybe. The police psychologist reported that the perpetrator's last action with the bottle meant that he was likely to have a highly developed, ironic sense of humour. That he liked a joke. Right, I thought, as I put the file back in my case. Ha ha ha.

It was now after ten and the airport wasn't that busy. The business flights were gone and it was not the time of the week or year when us Brits can't take it any more and rush off to other parts of the Continent we are so sceptical about. I wandered through the white halls avoiding the odd bag-laden trolley and looked for the Pavilion Bar.

The bar itself was a semi-circle surrounded by aluminium stools, none of which was occupied. I took one to the left side and ordered a Perrier from the only barman, the man I had come to see. He was tall, late twenties, with long light brown hair which was receding slightly at the sides, leaving him a full, back-combed widow's peak. He was clean-shaven with smooth, even-coloured skin, a large flat mole on his left cheek, and very dark, blue eyes. He was wearing wire-rim glasses which did not undercut the loose, rather lackadaisical style he had about him. As he took my order I noticed a hint of Australian in his accent, but it was difficult to tell which way round it was, whether he was English and had been there recently, or an Australian who'd been living here for ages. Perhaps it was neither. Perhaps there's an accent which people pick up simply from working in airports too long. Whatever it was it made me think of the time when Luke and I had gone backpacking in Queensland for a month, just before Luke had met Sharon.

The barman picked up a small bottle of Perrier from a row behind him, twirled it round in his hand with a very professional absent-mindedness, and then set it down in front of me next to a glass full of ice and a wedge of lemon. His movements were cool but not showy, a natural affinity with objects he touched every day, and they seemed to strike a cord with me as if I'd seen the man before. I was sure I hadn't. I took the wedge out of the glass, put it in an ashtray and poured the water over the ice. Then I watched the barman as he served another customer. I looked at the chairs standing up against the polished wooden sides of the bar like men in a firing squad, and wondered which of them Teddy had sat on. Which the other man, the man he had met. Maybe I was sitting on it. I thought about all the people who must come every day and sit on the stool recently used by someone who was going around London mutilating homosexuals. And never knew it. I took a sip of my drink and then caught the barman's eye.

The barman got the manager to cover him, took off his apron and came round the bar to join me. He told me that his name was Alex Mitchell, which I already knew, and then he said that he'd told the police everything he could remember but was happy to help me anyway. I gave him my card.

'He came up and sat down,' the barman said. 'The other guy was already here, he had been for quite a while. The pilot had a drink on his own and then the next time I looked the other guy was sat next to him and the pilot ordered a drink for both of them. I was too busy to hear what they were talking about. They stayed about half an hour more and then left. That's it.'

The barman shrugged his shoulders and sat back on his stool. He gave me a sort of hopeless look, as if to apologize for wasting my time coming all the way out there. I opened my case, took out a pad and looked down at some notes I had made. The file with Edward's murder in it stared at me and I closed my case quickly as though something, his screams perhaps, were going to escape from it.

'The man had a bag,' I said, 'which you noticed.'

'Yeah. It was leather, slung over his shoulder. I remembered because I needed one. I told the police that.'

'I know,' I said. I thought about it.

'Did it look empty or full?' I asked.

'Oh,' said Alex, 'I dunno really. Empty. Yeah, it looked pretty empty. Is that significant?'

'I don't know,' I admitted. 'It could be. It gives an indication that he hadn't travelled anywhere, that he only had a few things in it. Things he would need in the immediate future only.'

'Like murder things?' Alex asked.

'Maybe,' I said.

Alex reached over the bar and filled a glass with water from the soda gun. He took a sip from the glass and then set it down on the bar top.

'Tell me about the man,' I said.

He thought for a second. 'Well, it's hard,' he said, frowning. 'I already sat with the police on this computer imager thing, but all we got was the baseball hat really. I suppose that's why he wore it. He was white. Well built. Young.'

'Good-looking?'

'What?' he asked. 'I don't know. He didn't seem to be. I don't know.'

'As good-looking as Teddy? As Edward Morgan?'

Alex bit his thumbnail and then looked either side of me.

'I don't know. No. I don't think so, I don't know.'

'OK. Now,' I said, changing the subject, 'if you were to guess, what do you think he did? What was his job?'

Alex seemed surprised at the question.

'How would I know?' he asked.

'Well, for instance, you said he was well-built. He had on jeans and a leather jacket, trainers. Did he look like he wore these things all the time? Or did he look the sort who had changed into them from a suit after work, say?'

'No,' the barman said, getting into it a bit more, sur-

prised that he was able to answer the question. 'No. He
didn't look like he wore a suit or nothing. I don't know
why I think that but he didn't. I can't imagine him in a
suit. He sat sort of slouched, maybe that's why.'

'So if you had to guess, what did he look like he did?
Manual work? Building work?'

'No.' Alex shook his head. 'He didn't seem like a bricky
or something like that either.'

'Well, did he look like a student then?'

'Oh no. Not that I know why. He was more . . .
weighty. In himself. In charge. He looked, I don't
know . . .' I waited.

'Go on,' I said. 'It doesn't matter if it sounds stupid or
it's just a guess. All I want to know is the impression you
had of him.'

'He looked,' Alex went on, 'like someone with important things going on in his head. Real world things, not
like a student looks. But I can't see him doing anything for
a living. Strange though, his bag looked expensive, that's
why I remembered it . . .'

'Right,' I said.

'But I can't think of him doing any sort of job.'

'Fine,' I said. 'That's fine.' I took a sip of water and then
put my glass down on the bar. I looked at the barman and
asked, 'Did Edward Morgan look gay to you?'

'Oh.' Alex hesitated for a second. 'Well, I didn't even
think about it when he came up.' He ran a hand back
through his hair. 'Not at all. Not that I'm an expert. But
when he sat with the other guy, and then they left, well, I
just assumed. Not that they touched or anything. But it
was pretty obvious.'

'And the other man,' I went on, trying to keep him
with it, 'when you served him initially, did he seem gay?'

He thought about it. He bit hard at his bottom lip.

'I don't know. Yeah, he did. Or, rather, he seemed *something*. Definitely something. Then when I saw the two of them leaving I knew what it was. Or, rather, when I found out what he did. What happened to the pilot. I can remember what he made me feel like when I served him, what he gave off. It was nasty. Like he knew stuff which wasn't nice. Not nice at all.' Alex seemed to have gone somewhere, but he came back and laughed. He shrugged his shoulders.

'It's funny,' he said. 'I can remember all that, now that you ask me. What he *seemed* like and stuff. But for the life of me I can't remember his face. I can't remember what the bastard looked like.'

I asked Alex a few more questions, without any great feats of reasoning standing in wait behind them. For some reason I didn't want to leave yet, as though there was a question that I wasn't asking but should be. When he said he'd been working at the airport for a couple of months I realized that my accent theory was wrong. He was an Australian, from the west coast, but he'd lived in Britain for the last two years.

'Thought I'd escape the crime and violence in Perth by coming to live with you genteel Poms.' I asked him if he was sure he hadn't heard anything more that the two men were saying and he replied he thought he heard Teddy asking the other guy if he wanted a lift. He remembered that Teddy had paid for all of the drinks.

After a while the bar manager began to give me significantly pissed-off looks – probably because she was actually having to do some work herself for a change. I smiled at her sweetly. I thanked the barman for his time and asked him to phone me if he remembered anything which he thought might be useful. He looked down at the card in his hand and said he would do. Then he slid the card into the pocket of his shirt as he walked back round to his usual side of the bar. I offered to pay Alex for the Perrier, but he told me to forget about it, and expertly flipped the empty bottle into the bin. This really annoyed his manager who pursed her lips into a tight O at the profligate liberty taken by one of her minions. I thanked Alex again, smiled to myself, and walked back to my car.

The drive back to Islington only took forty minutes. As I was cruising along the now deserted Westway I thought about what the barman had told me. I tried to conjure up a picture of a man, a man who seemed to have things on his mind. A man who slouched but seemed important, who knew nasty things. None came. I drove past the place again but this time very quickly and the only thing I was worried about was a traffic camera. I drove along the Euston Road and up to the Angel. I turned off Upper Street behind a 38 bus and stopped at the bottom of Cross Street in a red zone.

I made a quick visit to the library just across from the fish shop. I have a friend there who lets me take out back copies of newspapers even though this is not strictly permissible. I always take them back, often the same day. I just like sitting in my office with them, near the phone. I dumped an armful on to the back seat, got into the car again, and drove up Highbury Grove to the Studios. I parked and walked up to my office.

When I got up to the fourth floor I found Andy Gold sitting in the café, drinking coffee and quite obviously eyeing up Ally.

And looking pleased with himself.

Chapter Six

We were in my office. I couldn't put Ally through any more of Mr Gold's smoulderingly sensual glances and anyway the place had started to fill up for lunch. Andy was seated across from me and was taking a file out of his briefcase. I noticed that there were a couple of messages on my machine but I didn't think about playing them. Playing your answerphone messages with a policeman in the room is not what I'd call a good idea.

Andy placed an A5-size photograph on my desk. It was obviously taken from a security video – it was a slight downshot and the definition was poor. It wasn't a repro-duction of the whole frame, it was a blow-up of one section, but the date and time could still be seen in the bottom left corner. It showed a man's face, in profile. Alongside but obscured by him, was another man wearing what looked to be, or at least could have been, an airline pilot's hat.

'That's our man,' Andy said, turning the picture round towards me.

I looked at the picture some more. It wasn't very clear, not clear at all, but it was a person. Only one person. It was a profile which somebody might recognize. I asked Andy when he had got hold of it.

'Last night,' he replied. Andy was happy. I got the

feeling that he was about to tell me something which illustrated how clever he was.

'We'd been through all the airport security vids and we did get a shot but from directly above. No use, you couldn't even see hair colour. Then we went through the ones from the stores with open fronts but there was no sign of our Edward or if there was it was too crowded to make him out. We went through those vids frame by frame for days but didn't get anything. I even took some copies home with me and you know how I like to leave my work at the office. We gave up on the vids weeks ago but yesterday, after I'd seen you, it suddenly struck me that our Mr Ed might have stopped off for something in one of the stores that are completely contained, for some mints or some johnnies or something.'

He broke off to take a sip of the coffee he had brought through with him and also, I suspected, for me to take in the magnitude of his investigative prowess.

'Well, we checked, but naturally enough Edward and friend didn't stop for refreshments, they had other things on their minds I presume. But they did walk pretty close to the Body Shop.' Andy leant forward with a smile on his face.

'Want to know how I know?'

I sighed. I wished I had a book in the office. Andy's chirpiness depressed me; as usual it had nothing to do with catching a killer and everything to do with being the one who did it.

'Watkins and Dawson were going through the tapes, fast-forwarding to see if anyone in a baseball cap, or Ed himself, came in. I suddenly realized that whenever anybody opened the door to go in or out, which they did a lot because the place was really busy, the camera got a peek at the concourse. At the people walking by. We knew the time Edward and his new pal left the bar so we went through the tape real slow at around that time and Houpla! Edward and his chutney chum.'

'Brilliant,' I said, 'you should be a detective.'

'Lucky, I know, but we nearly missed it. We got the still made last night and then had it cut and blown up.' He put his finger down on the middle of the man's face, and pushed the picture towards me.

'That's our bastard,' Andy said.

I picked the picture up and studied it.

'Have you given this to the beat boys yet?' I asked.

'Being done now.'

'What about media? Are you going to do a *Crimewatch* or anything?'

Andy sat back in his chair and sighed.

'Now that, my dear Bill, is the prob. The Governor, in his infinite, does not believe the picture is clear enough.'

'He has a point,' I said.

'He thinks that if we put it out we'll get every old dear from Skye to Southend calling in whenever they catch a peek of a bloke in a baseball cap through the sitting-room nets. He wasn't even sure about giving it to the plods.'

I was surprised. 'Why not?'

'Well, it's not so distinct that you could clock someone with it. On the street. More like if you already knew the guy you might put his face to it. And, for some reason, the Governor doesn't think that any of our Blue Boys socialize with crazed homicidal fags.'

'No,' I said. 'And perhaps he's even right about that. So what are you going to do?'

'Use it in evidence when we catch the cunt, and until then give it to the plods but tell them not to get too carried away. And give it to the plain-clothes team who are on the thing. They'll wave it around in the right places and who knows?' Andy paused for a second and smirked. 'The Gov didn't even mind you having a go with it.'

I smiled at the memory of a fat Scotsman with a perpetual look of disgust on his face, encased in a cloud of cigar smoke, Glenfidich and Aramis.

'Still remembers me then?' I asked.

'Oh, sure he does. Said he always had suspicions about you, especially when you quit. He thinks you couldn't take being around so many beefy men all the time. Said it was a good idea giving you the picture because you probably go to all those bender bars and might even know the geezer yourself.' Andy Gold laughed.

'Charming,' I said, and I took out an A4 manila envelope from my desk drawer, and slid the picture into it.

Andy told me he was going to troll the picture round to all the people he had interviewed already and that he'd let me know if anything came of it. He said he didn't hold out much hope really, and that his team were pretty well resigned to waiting for the next one. He said we were about due bearing in mind the length of time between the other murders. He left me with two copies of the photograph and I walked him down the hall to the lift. He popped into the café to take his coffee cup back and when he came out he was smiling again, having set aside thoughts of serial killers as easily as an onboard magazine when the flight attendant comes by.

'You know,' he said, as he stepped into the waiting lift, without even the faintest trace of irony, 'I think that Italian piece fancies me.'

*

Back in my office I made a call to the courier company I use and told them that I had a pick-up. Then I called Carl at the Repro place near my flat and told him that I would be biking over a picture that I wanted doing in postcard size. Two hundred to start with. I said I'd pick the copies up later, just before he shut.

'Oh, you mean *today*, Mr Rucker?' Carl replied wearily. I told him he was beautiful, and hung up.

One of the messages was from Sharon. She said she had been given a couple of tickets for a flamenco dance show at Sadler's Wells on Friday night and would I like to go. What was today? Wednesday. Cool, why not? I called her at work and arranged it. The other message was from Mrs Charlotte Morgan. She was just returning my call. She left a work number I could reach her on if I needed to speak to her today, or I could contact her at home that evening after seven. I called the work number and Mrs Morgan agreed, somewhat reluctantly, to meet me the following morning.

After I'd given the envelope with the photo in to the biker I spent the rest of the afternoon going through the newspapers I'd picked up from the library. As I read what the press had to say about the three murders, the image of the man's face was ever present in my mind. This face was out there somewhere, and it was highly likely that its owner was thinking of ways to provide the papers with even more copy.

I started with the lorry driver and the rent boy and then I went through everything there was about Edward Morgan. What I wanted to try and see was if they *felt* the same, not the way they were reported but the events themselves. There was something about them which seemed to me to be familiar in some way, as if I had read of something like them before but didn't know where. Probably in one of those pseudo-Victorian true crime books that always used to be kicking around the station house. For some reason my brother came to mind, as if he had mentioned something like this to me.

I wondered if the man in the picture had seen to Waldock and Evans as well as Teddy Morgan. The newspapers were in no doubt as to the link between the killings. Newspapers like to serialize everything; they sell more copies that way. While they couldn't print many of the details of how the murders were committed, they were allowed to mention the use of the bottles, which they all did with varying degrees of enthusiasm. The broadsheets were quite restrained but I was shocked once again by the dramatization given by all the tabloids. Their tone was one of horrified moral outrage at the murders, but underlined with a joyous 'we've got a great story' air. The very reporters who wondered as to who could possibly perpetrate such heinous crimes were the same ones who hounded the relatives of the dead for quotes. In one rag there was even a big exclusive which purported to be by the mother of James Waldock. It was about the sordid acts which her life of poverty and drug dependency had reduced her too: theft, deceit and prostitution. And, I thought to myself, talking to tabloid news journalists. I remembered the first time I had ever encountered such bullish insensitivity, picking up some rag in a Melbourne bus station. It was a graphic report about some other vicious killings, including pictures, splashed all over the first few pages. At the time I'd thought it unbelievable, even over there. Now it's commonplace, even here.

As I went through the lurid tales in the papers it struck me that if Teddy Morgan had been killed by the same man who killed Evans and Waldock, the killer had definitely broken his pattern to a certain degree. The question was whether or not Teddy's murder was pre-planned or opportunistic. Either way there was a discrepancy between that and the other murders: even given the baseball cap, the killer had, unlike the previous two times, given people a chance to see him. If it was just a 'lucky' chance – if the killer had been at the airport anyway and just happened to meet a gay airline pilot at the bar who offered him a lift home – then it would mean he had just got a little careless. He couldn't resist his urge to do what he does, even though he knew that he had been in a public place prior to the killing. If, however, the killer had planned to go to the airport in order to find a victim then he wasn't being careless; he was being over-confident. He didn't care if he was seen because he either thought that his hat was sufficient disguise or he didn't take into account the security cameras.

Irritatingly enough, neither the chance nor planned option seemed completely credible to me. I thought about the chance idea. The other crimes were obviously pre-planned; the bottle in each case appeared to have been prepared in advance and the perp made sure that there was no one else around, or if there was then they weren't the sort to go chatting to the Bill about the activities of a recently murdered boy-prostitute. Bearing in mind his previous meticulousness it seemed difficult to believe that the killer had just happened to be in the airport and had met Edward and decided to kill him. Also, his bag looked empty. What would a person who had to be at the airport anyway be doing with an empty bag? And how did he know that he would be able to use a bottle on Teddy if he had just met him? Because Teddy told him about the champagne he had? Maybe. But even so I found it hard to believe it was chance. The barman said that the man in the hat had been at the bar for a while. Why would he sit there, in an airport, if he wasn't hoping something was going to happen?

I suddenly realized that I hadn't asked the barman if he had noticed the guy before, on other days, checking the place out. Idiot. He probably wouldn't remember, and he would have told the police if he did remember seeing the guy previously, but even so. I might have been able to get him to remember, and if I did it would prove that the whole thing was intentional – he had gone there to find a victim. I made a mental note to call the airport first thing in the morning.

I didn't think it was a chance thing but the idea that it was planned also had me doubting. Why was he so deliberately careless? There are many ways to kill people you don't know without doing so after you have been seen chatting to them in a well-lit airport bar. Agreed, a killer of gay men does have to meet his victims and this will have to be in a public place (unless of course the victim is a prostitute or a lorry driver). Maybe the guy wanted to spread more panic – make it dangerous for men to pick each other up in public as well as dangerous to give them lifts or sell them sexual favours. But then why didn't he use a bar or a gay club? Too obvious? Perhaps. Male flight staff do have a reputation for homosexuality but was he really likely to meet one in a public area? Apparently, according to the barman, he was; Alex Mitchell said that some of the gay staff came to his bar. But that still leaves him with the problem of the cameras and the fact that Teddy's uniform would make his last movements particularly memorable to potential witnesses.

I tried to think how I would select my victims if I was in the habit of murdering homosexuals. While I did think that his first two strikes made sense, I really did not think that I would go to the airport. It would take me too long to meet somebody, by which time I would have become a regular feature in the place. Unless I lucked out first or second time. Not worth it. But then again, I thought, maybe the killer isn't very bright. It isn't written anywhere that serial killers should be, that's just in the movies. Or maybe it's me that's not very bright and Teddy's murder was excellently planned.

Well, nobody's caught him yet.

I felt that the discrepancies I'd found did increase the chance that Sir Peter Morgan was right, that the murder could have been a copycat set-up. But set up by whom? There was, however, one other option to consider if the killer was the same for all three murders. Not only had the murderer planned on murdering someone he met at the airport, he had planned who it was going to be. He knew Edward Morgan and had decided that he would be next. This option presented a myriad of different possible scenarios based on who Edward knew and where he went, none of which I knew anything about. Yet. Hacking away at that option would be fruitless at the moment and anyway my head felt pretty full of different takes on the thing as it was. I decided to leave all the stuff I had put into my brain to sift itself. I packed up the newspapers, turned on the machine, and went down to my car.

As I passed the café Ally saw me through the door and called out to me.

'Hey, Billy,' she laughed, 'such nice friends you've got!'

Chapter Seven

I had half an hour before my pictures would be done so I
drove down to King's Cross and parked a few doors down
from the squat inhabited by, among others, Dominic
Lewes. It was still light but it wouldn't be for ever so I
tried to think of a way to precipitate Dominic's appearance at his front door. Bomb scare? Too drastic. Eventually
I just decided to walk right up and ring the doorbell.

'Yeah?'

It was a girl. I couldn't see much of her because the
door was only open as far as the chain would let it. What I
could see was that she wasn't one to get overly influenced
by a Timotei ad or go overboard on fake tanning cream.

'I'm looking for Dominic,' I said.

'Who?'

'Dom.' Her face didn't register that she knew anyone
of that name. 'Smallish kid,' I said. 'Bleached blond crop
and brown eyes. He lives here?'

The girl hesitated for a second. A male voice behind
her called out, 'Who is it?'

'Someone for Mikey,' the girl told him, turning round
and moving away from the door.

The owner of the voice came up and took the chain
off the door. He was a tall black guy, about the thirty

mark, dressed in a black V-necked T-shirt and camel-colour jeans.

'What you want here?'

'Mikey,' I said, 'is Mikey home?'

'He called him Dominic before,' the girl said helpfully.

'Fuck off!'

The door was slammed in my face so hard I thought the glass would jump out.

Oh well.

I picked up the pictures from Carl and sat in my flat listening to PM and attaching a small sticker with my name and number on to the back of each one. When I had done that it was nearly eight so I made a quick bowl of pasta with Molise's red pesto. I packed up a small bag and, remembering to put a bunch of the repros in the side pocket, headed out the door. I picked up my bike from the hallway and carried it down the stairs.

Down at the gym I went through the circuit training, worked out, and then sparred four rounds with a wiry old bruiser called Archie. He must have been about fifty but he was a tough old bastard and certainly didn't expect any favours. So I didn't do him any. After getting under the shower I asked Sal if she could spare a minute.

I stood next to her while she looked at the photograph under the light of her office desk lamp. She nodded her head to herself and then shook it in irritation.

'You know what, I think I've seen this guy,' she said. 'Just for the moment though, don't ask me where.' She stared at the picture so hard I thought she'd wear it out.

'What's he done, this one?'

I told her what the police wanted him for.

'Well, you know me, Bill, the further you can keep me from the Boys in Blue the happier I am but I'll tell you, if I remember where I've seen this nonce I'll get on to you straight.'

'Thanks, Sal,' I said.

'And I'll show it round the gym, see if anyone else has any idea.'

'Thanks,' I said again. I gave Sal a cheque for some subs that I owed her and reached in my bag for my bike key.

There's a gay pub called The Centre quite near Sal's gym and I stopped off there on my way home and chatted to some of the clientele. They had all heard of the murders and were interested in the photograph I had. No one could place the man, however, though one nervous-looking sixtyish teacher type did look at the picture a little longer than necessary and was just a touch too vehement in his denial. When I mentioned this to him he said that he had had a rough day, that's all, and the last thing he wanted to think about was a serial killer. I told him that if he wasn't careful that would be the last thing he ever did think about.

Back in my flat the washing-up stared at me like an angry lover. I plunged into it and felt good when it was done. I lay on my futon and looked through some more of the newspaper articles but didn't get anywhere. The beginning of an investigation is always the most frustrating; you want to make connections but you haven't got anything to make them with. I put the papers aside and then remembered that I still hadn't read Luke's poems, the ones which Sharon had given me. I got up and fetched them from the kitchen table. I sat looking at the blue folder Sharon had put them in for a long time without taking the poems out. I didn't know why. The folder was made by a company called Avery and the style was a

Guidex Bradford® BLUE 21113. I stared at it a few minutes more and was about to open it up when the phone rang.

It was Nicky, wanting me to go down to The Old Ludensian.

'I can't tonight, mate,' I told him, looking at the folder, 'I've got something I should do.'

'Should?' Nicky laughed. 'Billy! I thought you were self-employed. Didn't they tell you when you got your Schedule D number that there was no such thing as should any more?'

'I think I missed that bit of the form.'

'Come on down,' Nicky insisted. 'There's no one in the bar, it's quiet. Come and keep me company.'

'Nicky . . !'

'Come *on*!'

I let Nicky talk me into it and I drove down and joined him. The place was jumping. I thought perhaps that he'd just got a rush on, but when I finally managed to push my way through the crush to the far end of the bar where Nicky always sits I realized I'd been had. He was with two friends. New friends. Hi, hi. Hi, hi. I ended up with the blonde one and a nose full of hooter in a flat off the Fulham Road. I didn't get back to Exmouth Market until well after seven the next morning. The blonde didn't seem too upset that her friend had got Nicky, and her me, or if she was she was polite enough not to show it. Her name was Trish and she was in Advertising.

When you have a hangover and haven't slept more than a couple of hours and generally feel like a piece of sun-dried shit, the best thing to do is shave, shine your shoes, put a tie round the collar of a bright white shirt and all in all look a lot smarter than you usually do. Then, not only will you feel more together, but if you happen to run into anyone you know the first thing they'll tell you is how good you're looking these days.

I did all these things and got to my office around ten. The temperature had fallen from the day before and the cold perked me up a bit. I didn't actually feel that bad but I wasn't so foolish as to think I'd got away with it. I knew it would hit me later. I ducked into the café for a coffee and because Mike was still out making deliveries Ally was there on her own. She looked me up and down as she handed me Kojak, and smiled.

'You know, Billy,' she said, 'it's not a bad effort but you should get some of that stuff which whitens the eyes. You know, takes away the little veins?'

I looked in the mirror behind her; blood-red cobwebs.

'Any time you want to give this job up just tell me, Ally, just say the word.'

I did my accounts, paid a few bills, and wrote a couple of letters reminding people that they had actually employed me in a professional capacity and that because of such I would be very grateful if they would send me some money. I had another look at Andy Gold's file and read the notes on Charlotte Morgan. At thirty-eight Charlotte was four years younger than Edward and had been married to him for seven years. She worked for a PR firm and had met her husband when her company won the BA account and decided to boost the profile of the airline's actual staff in their corporate identity. A sort of upgrade for the pilots. They had married after a courtship of only six months and moved into the Highbury apartment in which Edward's body had been found, often spending weekends at Mrs Morgan's family home in Pevensey,

Sussex, which she had inherited on the death of her father a year earlier. Neighbours reported them to be a quiet couple who were amiable enough but kept mostly to themselves. I had to smile at this. As a DC I had been given this description many times by people anxious to keep out of the picture or protect themselves against charges that they should have reported their neighbours' activities long ago. It didn't mean anything; the Morgans could have been holding sado-masochistic sex parties which included sacrificing chickens to voodoo gods and the description would have been the same. Quiet, kept to themselves.

The police had routinely ruled out any hint that Mrs Morgan was involved in her husband's murder. The only suspicious fact was that she had been away at the time, something which could look just a little convenient if there was anything else pointing to her. But there wasn't. The two PCs who had responded to her 999 call reported that her shock and trauma were genuine on discovering her husband lying dead with a champagne bottle jutting out of him. DI Drake, who was the first to interview her, also testified to her very real grief and shock. Everything pointed to the homosexual slasher idea, and when semen was discovered inside the corpse it was generally agreed that Mrs Morgan wasn't the one who put it there.

The semen. That made me think. Had they cross-checked it with that found on James Waldock? I called Andy quickly and managed to catch him. Of course they had checked it, what sort of prat did I take him for? There was no match. Another change then – the killer had been even more careless: he'd wiped his prints but left his DNA.

So. Mrs Charlotte Morgan wasn't a suspect and had no

idea that her husband was, or even might have been, a homosexual. She hadn't seen anyone suspicious hanging around in the area before she went away on business, and when she spoke to her husband on the phone from New York she didn't notice anything different about his mood or his tone of voice. In fact, she knew nothing, nothing that was any help to the police. But maybe, like Alex Mitchell, I would be able to get her to remember things she didn't even suspect she knew.

I'd arranged to meet Charlotte Morgan at twelve, in the small coffee lounge of Agnieszka's, the Polish expat club on Exhibition Road, South Ken. I'd thought of it because it is always very quiet, especially in the mornings, and is only five minutes' walk from where Mrs Morgan told me she worked. When I suggested it I was surprised that she actually knew where it was and had even been there. Nobody else I'd ever mentioned it to had.

I parked on a meter near Imperial College and got to Agnieszka's about ten minutes early for my meeting. From the outside the club looks like a house. There is only a very small plaque on the large black door to announce its identity to the world, as well as a small sign which asks that visitors ring the bell. I did so. The doorman, a small elderly man in a dark suit and tie, opened the door and showed me into the hallway.

'Hello, hello again!' the man said, bobbing the top half of his body up and down, his mouth breaking into a huge, cracked smile. I had no idea if he remembered me or whether this was simply his standard greeting. The man looked disapproving, upset even, when he saw that I didn't have a coat to hand him. I informed him that I was here for coffee and he showed me through to the lounge.

As he sat me down on one of the broad sofas I handed him my card and I told him that I was waiting for a woman to join me, and would he show her through when she arrived. His grave nod told me that he took it on himself as a great personal responsibility to do so, and he left me to my thoughts.

The coffee lounge in Agnieszka's takes up one end of the dining room, and as I waited for Mrs Morgan I let my eyes wander to the far end of the room. The impression is one of an old faded salon. The ceilings are high and the walls are almost completely hidden behind hundreds of oil paintings, their tops jutting forward slightly from the wall as if they are all competing for attention. The paintings are passionate, dramatic, especially the portraits of beautiful, dispossessed countesses, their eyes burning, their gaze set towards distant and lost horizons. What wallpaper that can be seen beneath the pictures is a dull, yellowy-cream colour that is torn in places and hasn't been changed in years. Dinner there is reasonably cheap and can be surprisingly good, but it isn't the food that I go there for. I go because the tableclothes aren't paper, the cutlery is silver, and because, in contrast to those found at The Portman Club, the manners there demonstrate genuine warmth rather than stiff English formality.

There was no one else in the lounge so I had only Bartók to disturb me. A waiter came over and asked me if I wanted please to tea or to coffee. I said that I wanted thankyou to coffee, and to mineral water also if it was possible. He said it was. Just as he was setting the tray down on the low table in front of me the door opened and Mrs Morgan was shown in by the doorman. I stood up and greeted her.

'William Rucker,' I said, shaking her hand.

'Charlotte,' the woman replied.

After the waiter had brought her coffee and she had taken a sip of it Charlotte Morgan folded her hands in her lap and looked at me. She looked very composed as she sat there and I was reminded of Sir Peter, the control he had shown. Two people with an ever-present pain inside them which they carried through their daily lives like a tumour. I looked for a sign which might give away her current emotional state but I couldn't see one.

'Well,' she said.

I met her gaze for a second and thought how I should begin with her. Charlotte Morgan was a tall woman with black, full-bodied hair and a firm, lightly tanned face which I couldn't imagine looked any more beautiful when she was younger than it did now. Her eyes were an amber-brown like those on a toy bear and set between them was a firm, slightly square nose which she probably hated, but which actually stopped her good looks from being simply the bland glossy-magazine sort. She had slim, long hands which she kept almost unnaturally still. They ended in Rioja-coloured nail varnish and I noticed that her left hand still bore a wedding ring. She was dressed in a fitted charcoal skirt-suit and a cream silk blouse, a thin gold chain flirting with the first closed button. I smiled politely into those deep eyes and I told her I was very grateful that she had been able to spare the time to see me.

'May I ask who employed you?' Mrs Morgan said. Her voice was light and more feminine than I would have imagined. I detected a purpose behind it, however, that made me imagine her shouting at one of her assistants who was taking too long over something.

'I'm sorry,' I replied, shaking my head slightly. 'You'll understand that I won't be able to tell you that.'

'No, I suppose not,' she conceded. She didn't press me. I think she had guessed it was Sir Peter. I wondered what she thought about that.

'I called DI Gold after you left your first message,' she told me. 'I wanted to know if it was all right for me to talk to you. He said it was. He said you used to work with him.'

'That's right,' I said. 'I did.' I smiled again.

'Why did you resign?' she asked.

What is this, *The Prisoner*?

'I didn't want to end up fat, overworked and cynical,' I explained, thinking of the Chief Inspector. I thought about Luke.

'No chance of that I shouldn't think,' Charlotte Morgan said, as she ran her hands back through her hair. I found myself blushing slightly. Was she flirting with me? No. She was just trying to act natural, to keep the black event which clouded her life from gaining sway. Or was it the PR lady, trying to get me onside, wanting to deal with me as effortlessly as possible?

I reached down for my coffee and took a sip of it, thinking that it was a good job I didn't go to Agnieszka's for that either.

'I'd just like to go over a few things with you if that's OK.' I tried to sound like I understood, that I wasn't a threat to her. Like an old male friend she could tell things to.

'Fire away,' she said.

Mrs Morgan took a deep breath and got herself together. I reached down for my briefcase and clicked the latch. It's an old brown leather manuscript case which I like to think makes me look arty.

'Have the police shown you this yet?' I asked. I pulled out a copy of the picture which Andy Gold had given me, and handed it to her.

'No,' she said, taking it from me. Mrs Morgan's voice was surprised and tentative. 'No.' She looked at the post-card askance, frowning, holding it between her thumb and index finger as if it were radioactive. I saw her taking the picture in, seeing Edward behind the man.

'I spoke to them yesterday,' she managed to say, 'and they said they would come to the flat, where I'm staying, later tonight. They said they had a picture but no, no I . . . I haven't seen it.'

Mrs Morgan looked at the picture that was shaking very slightly in her hand. I suddenly realized how difficult and shocking this must be to her, to look at a picture of the man who had very probably murdered her husband, a picture taken only hours before he did so. For some reason I had assumed that Andy Gold would have got round to her straight away. Then I realized that he was in no hurry for her to see it. Edward's wife was hardly likely to recognize some guy her husband had picked up in an airport bar and taken home for sex while she was away.

Charlotte Morgan looked at the picture. Her gaze had changed and she was just staring at it blankly.

'I can't believe . . !' she said. 'It's so . . .'

I waited.

'I'm sorry, Mrs Morgan,' I said, when she didn't go on. 'Do you think you've ever seen that man?'

'No,' she said. A wistful look came over her face which betrayed a bewildered hurt.

'It seems so bizarre,' she went on, 'to think of my

husband. With a man. This man.' She put the photograph down on the table. 'And to think of what this man did to him. It's . . .' She looked for the word. 'It's surreal,' she said. She shrugged her shoulders in a way which suggested that once she thought she knew about things, but she didn't know anything about anything any more.

'You never suspected?' I asked quietly. 'I mean, that Edward may have been interested in men?'

Her face set.

'No,' she said. 'I didn't.'

'Never?'

She let out a breath. 'There was one time when we talked about it, I mean the whole gay thing, but every couple must do that at some time or other.'

'Yes,' I agreed. 'But why did you talk about it? I mean, how did it come up?'

'What?' Mrs Morgan looked a little shocked. I was sure that Edward had told her about his brother being gay. Why shouldn't he have, they were married after all? I could see her wondering why I asked the question, wondering if I could possibly know as well.

'You know,' she said dismissively, 'one of those talks.'

'And what did Edward say?'

'Well, he just said that it wasn't for him. He thought it was OK for other people but not for him.'

'And you believed him?'

'Yes. Why shouldn't I believe him?'

'I don't know. If you suspected he might be gay, for instance. Is that why you brought the matter up, because you did have an idea he might have feelings towards men?'

'No!'

Mrs Morgan was getting flustered. On the police we

were taught that when this happens the interviewee is generally hiding something. What was Charlotte hiding? I told her that I was sorry I had to ask questions like that but I was only doing it to find out who killed her husband.

'You see, Mrs Morgan,' I explained, 'it doesn't really make any sense if your husband wasn't at least bisexual. If he wasn't, then it doesn't seem likely that he would be lured to his death by a man posing as a potential partner. Either that or the sexual activity that occurred was not consensual. That would mean that the killer had deviated a great deal. Also, the police have evidence which suggests that Edward went with the man in the picture there quite willingly.'

I sat back in my chair and tried to make the expression on my face as benevolent as possible. I reminded myself of a casino bouncer who had orders to beat me up once but who, I could tell, didn't really want to. He'd looked just like that before he'd kicked the shit out of me.

Mrs Morgan pondered the facts that I had given her, trying to find a way round them but unable to.

'He must have been,' she said finally. 'I suppose he must have been but I never even thought it. I—'

I cut her off.

'Mrs Morgan, how were sexual relations between yourself and your husband at that time?'

She looked up at me. Her lips tensed and her eyes opened. I knew the police had asked her this question. I wanted to see how she reacted when I asked it. From her expression I knew what she was going to say. She was no longer flustered, she had got hold of it. She knew my tack and had set up a wall against me. She was going to protect her marriage, not let some tin-pot investigator with see-through sincerity take away her memories after a lunatic had taken away her husband. The look on her face told me that she had no idea how her life had arrived at a point wherein a stranger would be grilling her in a café, however pleasant, about the quality of the sex she had had with her recently murdered husband.

'They were fine,' she said firmly, almost daring me to go on.

I left it there.

I hadn't enjoyed asking Charlotte the questions I had. The woman had enough to worry about as it was without raking over already dead grass to satisfy the whim of a guilt-stricken Tory MP. There was something she wasn't telling me though, I knew it. It may have been something mundane and irrelevant but there was something never-theless. I wanted to know what it was but I had no right to badger her. I could tell it wouldn't have done me any good anyway. If there was something about this woman I needed to know, then I'd have to find out what it was myself.

I moved into safer waters, asking her if she knew the names of any of Edward's friends who she thought might be out of the ordinary. She said that most of the friends they had, they had in common. Except for work friends. She didn't remember Edward mentioning anyone more than anyone else, except for his regular co-pilots and the odd stewardess he used to tease her about. How they were always looking for pilots to marry and he'd loved to have met one who would have retired immediately to the family home and bred him a hoard of kids and not gone swanning off round the world on business all the time. She smiled without any humour in her face, remembering her husband's jokes.

She said, 'Maybe he should have; he couldn't have been killed then, could he?'

I ran out of questions and thanked Mrs Morgan for her time. I asked her how she was coping. She said that her company were being very understanding and that she wasn't having to deal with clients at the moment, which was a relief. She seemed glad to be off the subject of her husband and we chatted for a minute or two before she took a long look at her watch. I asked the waiter for the bill.

Mrs Morgan excused herself to go to the bathroom. When she came out she had applied some lipstick and done her eyelashes. She looked very beautiful and not a lot older than me. I caught a hint of eau de Issey as she walked past me into the hall, recognizing the scent because it was what Trish in Advertising had been wearing. As we entered the hallway the little bobbing doorman went into overdrive and had Mrs Morgan's mac on in no time. He told us that it was always a pleasure to see us there and that he hoped we would visit again soon. He held his hands together and beamed at us and I thought he was going to enquire about the kids. I smiled to myself, pressed a pound coin into his hand and followed Mrs Morgan on to the street.

Outside it had got even colder and an ominous cloud hovered over the stately buildings of Exhibition Road like a Zeppelin. I thanked Mrs Morgan again and gave her one of my cards. We shook hands and she walked off in the direction of Kensington Gore. I walked the other way, back to my car.

I wondered if she and her husband *had* been happy in bed together and decided that no, they hadn't. Her not wanting to discuss it was more than coyness. Maybe, like

Sir Peter, she didn't want to fail Edward, let him down by admitting that there had been a failure in his life, something which she thought was irrelevant, and nobody's business but hers. Perhaps she even blamed herself for Edward's murder, driving him to men after she hadn't been able to arouse him herself, and her denial of any marital problems was her way of pushing aside her own sense of blame. Maybe she was even involved in what happened to Edward, and she didn't want anyone to think that her marriage had been anything other than idyllic.

Or perhaps they had been blissfully happy and had had a wonderful love life.

But then I had another thought, one which wasn't particularly logical, and of which I was a little ashamed because it was based on an assumption which I didn't want to make. It went along these lines: why would a woman whose husband had been dead for just under three months make up her face, dab perfume behind her earlobes and walk in the opposite direction to her office at twelve fifteen on a grey morning in late October? I turned round and walked in the direction of Kensington Gore, doing up my jacket and digging my hands into my pockets. Because she always wore make-up? She hadn't with me. I broke into a light jog. Because she had an important meeting? She told me she wasn't seeing clients at the moment. I jogged faster until I was almost running.

When I got to the main road I caught sight of Charlotte Morgan walking on the other side of it, towards Knightsbridge. Almost immediately she turned into Kensington Gardens. I crossed over and kept fifty yards behind her as she walked past the round pond and across the park towards the Bayswater Road. I was worried she'd see me but she didn't look back. Crossing the Bayswater Road, she walked up Leinster Road and then turned into a small street on her right. I sprinted to the top of the street and took a very careful look round the corner. Leinster Mews. I was just in time to see one of the cottage doors being held open for her and Mrs Morgan step inside.

I sprinted back across Kensington Gardens and stuck my key into the door of the Mazda. I tried the ignition – nothing. Again – very little. Once again – more this time but my impatience made me pump the accelerator and I nearly flooded the engine. I waited. I made myself count to a hundred. I tried again. The engine took with the depth and enthusiasm of a man dragged out of a river who finally responds to the kiss of life. I pulled it out of the side street, cut into the traffic, much to the annoyance of a cab driver with a surprising command of old Saxon English, and sped past the Albert Hall. I drove through the park, back into Bayswater and turned up Leinster Road.

I sat in the Mazda at the far end of Leinster Mews keeping an eye on number 8. I booted up the camera and hoped I hadn't missed her. I waited about an hour, the camera on the dashboard, thinking that perhaps she had just popped in to collect a girlfriend for lunch or something and I was simply a sleazebag who was wasting his time.

But then the door opened.

A man stepped out. A man in a suit with a briefcase in his hand. I got a shot of him. The man looked around the mid-forties mark, maybe younger. Yes, a little younger. He had full, dark brown hair and large, steel-rimmed glasses. I thought he was just going to leave but he turned back into the doorway and a woman in a dressing gown met him halfway and kissed him. I got that too. The man kissed her back, hard, biting into her bottom lip, holding her head in his hands like he was going to shoot a basket. He grinned, a full, confident grin which told of pleasure recently enjoyed and already anticipated. The woman pulled him to her again but he broke off from her. Then he turned and walked over to a dark blue Jaguar parked at the top end of the Mews, which he got into, tossing the briefcase on the passenger seat beside him. I wrote down the plate number.

I had no idea who the man was.

The woman was Charlotte Morgan.

The door of the cottage shut. I put my camera down on the passenger seat. The Jag pulled off and I followed it out on to Leinster Road. I followed it along Bayswater and down Park Lane. I kept three or four cars back even though I didn't have to be careful because this man had no idea who I was. We drove down Grosvenor Place, past Victoria and along Birdcage Walk. Then the Jag turned into Parliament Square and skirted round St Stephen's Tower. After another right it turned into a gate which announced that it was private, with no access to members of the public. A barrier was raised in front of it and then the Jag disappeared. I stopped at a red light and looked at the gateway into which the car had gone.

It was the car park used by Members of Parliament.

PART TWO

Chapter Eight

I called Andy Gold from a phone box but I couldn't get hold of him and there was no one else I could think of who would be willing to run a vehicle registration check for me. I wasn't too concerned; I was pretty sure I could find out who the man in the Jag was on my own. I hung up and dialled the daytime number Sir Peter Morgan had given me.

Sir Peter wasn't at the Treasury, he was at Westminster today. I called the number I was given and reached his secretary and eventually convinced her that her boss would want to talk to me. I then arranged to see Sir Peter in his office in thirty-five minutes. He suggested a later time but I impressed upon him the need to see him soon, and he agreed. I hung up and then walked round to the entrance gate the Jag had driven through.

'Excuse me, sir,' I said, in broad Texan to the uniformed man on the gate. 'Could you help me?'

'If I can, sir,' the man replied. He had been sitting in his booth reading the *Sun* but he stood up and approached the window.

'I was just having an argument with my wife,' I explained. 'Shirley-Anne. You see I could have sworn I just saw the Prime Minister drive in here, in a blue-coloured Jaguar car, but she says it wasn't him.'

'And I'm afraid she'd be right, sir,' the guard said. 'Although Mr Lloyd might make it one day. No, the Prime Minister has a driver in any case.'

'So you're sure it wasn't John Major?'

'That was Graham Lloyd, sir, right Party, wrong man. And anyway, sir, John Major hasn't been PM for . . .'

'Was that who that was? Damn!' I leant forward. 'Do me a favour,' I said, taking a quick look back over my shoulder. 'Don't tell that to Shirley-Anne.'

I could feel the hangover now. It was catching me like a favourite in a steeplechase making its way through the field. I fed six twenty-pence pieces into the meter which was guarding my car and looked around for somewhere to get a quick bite to eat. I found a coffee bar and drank one of those Californian multi-vit drinks that really did make me feel a bit better – for the moment. I ate a samosa and then had one of those little Portuguese custard tart things with an espresso. London, a hundred different countries packed into one traffic jam. As I ate I wondered what the hell was going on in the life of Charlotte Morgan. I had mixed feelings about having caught her out; I was glad the case had started to move but it didn't make me happy to have my grubby suspicions confirmed. I didn't like to think of her having anything to do with her husband's death.

And then I had another thought. Sir Peter. Was I being made a fool of? I was soon to find out. I looked at a copy of the *Telegraph* which somebody had left behind, and read that Boris Yeltsin had had another heart attack and that a man with an unpronounceable name who I had never heard of before was in charge of the country. This worried me. A country with a lot of nuclear weapons should be run by someone you've heard of. I paid for my lunch and decided to leave the *Telegraph* where I'd found it. I didn't want to give Sir Peter the wrong idea.

'You're resigning?' the MP said, his mouth opening a little to demonstrate his surprise. We were sitting in his office, him in his discreet power chair backed by a panorama of the Thames and St Thomas's Hospital, and me opposite, my left foot sitting on my right knee. 'But you've only being working for two or three days!'

Sir Peter was shocked, and annoyed with me. But that was OK.

'I like knowing what I'm doing,' I told him. 'I don't like playing to someone else's agenda. I got enough of that on the force.' I settled back into the chair but didn't get too comfortable.

'I don't know what you mean!' Sir Peter's fingers spread wide apart and his head moved forward towards me, leaving his shoulders where they were.

'Fine,' I said. And I got up to go.

'Please,' Sir Peter stood up with me, 'won't you at least tell me what this is about?'

'No,' I replied. 'I don't want to tell you because you didn't hire me for that, and if you had told me that is what you wanted me to do I would never have agreed to work for you. That sort of thing isn't my line. Does that make any sense?'

'No,' Sir Peter protested.

'Fine,' I said again. 'But I don't believe you.'

This time I made it to the office door but Sir Peter took my arm before I got it open.

'All right,' he said, his voice now void of any false hurt.

'All right. I know what you're talking about but, please, let me explain.'

I sighed.

'Please,' Sir Peter said.

'I didn't hire you to snoop on my political enemies.' We were back at the desk. 'Anyway, Graham's one of us. Not that that means a damn thing these days.'

'Then why didn't you tell me about him?'

'Because I wasn't sure about it. I thought I was just being paranoid, but that if you came up with anything, well, so be it. I'm amazed it only took this long.'

'It was a fluke,' I said. 'How did you find out about it?'

'Well,' Sir Peter said, 'I introduced them. At one of those diplomatic things Ministers have to go to and hate, but which their friends and family adore. Edward was away on long haul and I ran into Charlotte in one of those ghastly restaurants in Notting Hill and asked her if she wanted to come along to the Portuguese embassy with my wife and myself.'

'And she met him there?'

'Yes. It was about eight months ago. They hit it off but I didn't think anything of it. Who wouldn't hit it off with Charlotte? She's a beautiful woman and she works in PR. Hitting it off with people is her job.'

'So why did you suspect they were seeing each other?'

'Coincidence, I suppose. Teddy and I met for lunch one day, about six weeks before he was killed. He told me that he and Charlotte were having problems. He didn't seem to think they were too serious, but he did say that she seemed quite off with him. I said that every marriage must be like that at some point.'

'I'm sure they are.'

'Yes. Anyway, it just happened that in a cab on the way back to the Treasury I saw Graham and Charlotte together on the Mall and Edward's words struck me. Oh, they weren't doing anything, they were just walking along. They could have run into each other and remembered meeting before, or Charlotte could have got Graham's number and phoned him on a work basis. But there was something about them. It was nothing blatant but it was something. Graham Lloyd is married, you know?'

'I had assumed that he was.'

'I have become adept at reading body language over the years. I've had to. It helped, of course, that Charlotte and Graham didn't know that anyone was watching them – not that they were doing anything to give themselves away. I just had the feeling.'

'So when your brother was murdered, why didn't you tell the police?'

'For the same reason I didn't tell you, only more so. I wasn't sure he was having an affair with Charlotte. I didn't want them bothering him if I was only imagining it. Even if I was sure it doesn't necessarily mean anything, and if the papers had got hold of it – Christ! I couldn't tell them and I didn't want to tell you. I wanted to see if you came up with it yourself.'

I sighed. I really love chasing around finding out things that my clients could have told me before I even started.

'There seems to be a lot of things you can't tell me. Can I be certain that's the lot?'

'Yes,' he said, relieved. 'And I'm sorry, I really am.'

'So. Are you going to tell the police about it now?'

'I suppose I'll have to.'

'Which won't hurt your corner at all,' I said. 'Will it?'

'I'm sorry?'

'Him being a pro-European, and you being as sceptical about Europe as Ian Paisley is about a united Ireland . . .'

'Now look here!' Sir Peter stood up. 'If you think for one minute that where the murder of my brother is concerned I would attempt to gain any sort of political advantage, then you couldn't be more wrong. How dare you?'

'Just to see what you'd say,' I admitted. 'You can see how I might think it. Get me to catch Lloyd in the act, maybe get some pictures off me which get leaked to the *Mail*. They're on your side, aren't they, on Europe?'

Sir Peter tried hard to suppress his outrage at my suggestion.

'If that was the case I could just have told the police of my suspicions first off, couldn't I? They would have revealed the truth just as you did, and I wouldn't have had to leak it to the papers, the police would have done it for me themselves. No?'

He had a point. Also, his anger did seem genuine. All in all I was inclined to believe that he wasn't using me in his bid to keep the jewel of Britain firmly entrenched behind her silver sea, away from nasty foreign hands. I decided not to tell him about the film I had though.

'Well,' I said, 'I apologize for doubting your motives. But if you had told me of your suspicions we wouldn't have had to have this conversation. Now, do you want to go to the police with this?'

'Yes. I think. Isn't that what you think?'

'No,' I said, 'it isn't. Like you said, the police are sure

that your brother's murder was part of a series of gay killings. For them, this will just confirm the pattern. Of course she was getting it somewhere else, she wasn't getting it at home, was she? But they will make trouble – just to do it – and somebody will almost certainly use his desk phone to call one of the tabloids and make himself a few quid. Nothing would be gained by that.'

'It disgusts me, you know, that police officers do that kind of thing.'

'You should have got Mr Howard to pay them more then.'

'It would happen anyway.'

'Yes,' I admitted, 'it probably would. I don't think telling the police would do much good in terms of finding out who killed your brother. Even if it was his wife and her lover.'

'So, what, we just leave it?'

'I'll see what I can come up with,' I said. 'If I do find anything more concrete, then we'll give it to the police. In the meantime, we can spare a few blushes.'

Sir Peter seemed relieved, either at retaining the services of yours truly or avoiding further conversations with the police. I asked him if he liked his sister-in-law and he said that yes, actually, he did. He said he would find it very difficult to believe that Charlotte had anything to do with Edward's death.

I handed Sir Peter a copy of the picture, knowing that Andy Gold had already shown it to him, and that he hadn't been able to tell him anything. Sir Peter gazed at the picture ruefully and then put it down on his desk, with a look which said that finding the man in it wouldn't actually do much for him. He wanted the man caught but it wouldn't make him happier. He sucked on his teeth, picked the photograph up again, and slid it into a drawer.

I stood up and shook Sir Peter's hand. As he walked me across his office I had a thought and I stopped at the door.

'What's Graham Lloyd like, by the way?' I asked.

Sir Peter stood holding the door handle and he looked me straight in the eye. His expression was measured and still, that very strange mixture of the deadly serious, and a wry smile, which I have only ever seen on upper-class Englishmen.

'Oh, Graham's a bastard,' Sir Peter said.

On the way back to my car I remembered that I wanted to speak to the barman at the airport so I stopped at a phone box. I called the number and a harassed woman told me that Alex hadn't come in today and no she didn't know when he would be there because he hadn't phoned her to tell her he wasn't coming, which was most unlike him and was that all because she had a bar full of customers? I smiled at the thought of the assistant manager with her polished nails cranking out cappuccinos and swearing under her breath at her errant subordinate. Thank you, I told her, that's all. It wasn't really that important. I hung up and walked around the corner to my car, beating a traffic warden to it by seconds.

Charlotte Morgan hadn't gone back to work that day. She might have nipped out after I'd seen her because she was no longer in her dressing gown when I got to the flat on Leinster Mews that she had either rented or was borrowing and she opened the door to me. As well as the clothes I had seen her in earlier she wore a look of not very pleasant surprise.

'Yes?' she said. 'What do you want?'

'To talk a little more,' I replied quietly.

'How did you get my address?' she demanded, one hand going to her hip.

'I followed you here.'

'What?'

'Earlier. I followed you here.'

I let Charlotte Morgan think about that for a second. Then I held up a roll of film. 'Now,' I said, 'are you going to let me in or should I just take this straight round to my friend Giles at the *News of the World*?'

She looked at me with horror, and at the small plastic case in my hand. I could almost see the pieces falling together in her mind and I tapped my feet until they were all in place. After a second or two Charlotte Morgan bit her bottom lip, took a step backward and opened the door.

It was a very nice place. Far too polished and expensively cluttered for my taste but then I'm the sort of person who never could see the point of buying over-priced generic articles from the Conran Shop that you don't exactly need. Charlotte Morgan, quite obviously, could see the point of that.

She was sat stiffly on the edge of a small Chesterfield while I had turned a high-backed French dining chair around and was straddling that facing her. She looked defensive, tense like a cornered cat. I looked at her and a rush of contempt filled me as I saw Lloyd again, kissing her the way he had. I calmed it down with the knowledge that I didn't have all the facts yet. I handed her the role of film which she took hesitantly, surprised to be given it.

'I'm not a sleaze hunter,' I told her. 'I want to find out

who killed your husband. I'm not going to tell anyone about the affair that you're having unless I think that it reflects upon that. The only way I can assess that is if you tell me about it. All about it. If you refuse then I'll assume you're hiding something and I'll go to the police. Do you understand?'

'Yes,' she said eventually.

'And if I go to the police, which believe me I should, then the newspapers are sure to get on to it. So. Once again, did you enjoy a happy sex life with your husband?'

She paused for a second until I let out a sigh of irritation.

'No,' she said, looking down at her lap.

'And you didn't tell anyone this because you didn't want people looking into your private life?'

'I suppose. We hadn't made love for some time but I couldn't see how that fact was in any way relevant to my husband's murder.'

'All right. Why weren't you and your husband making love?'

She looked up again. 'Because I didn't want to. It wasn't really a big thing for me. I still loved Edward. I think that I realized that it had never really been a sex thing for me. Edward was just such a lovely person so I said yes when he asked me to marry him.'

'When did you realize this?'

'Oh,' she said, and hesitated. 'When . . . when I met . . .'

'When you met Graham Lloyd.'

Mrs Morgan's mouth opened in surprise.

'Did you tell Edward about him?'

'No,' she said quickly. 'I mean, I was going to. Graham and I were both going to. He was going to tell his wife and we were going to divorce and get married. If you know what I mean. We still are.'

'Yes?'

'Yes. But it's difficult now. Graham, he doesn't need this kind of publicity, Christ knows what people might think. And Edward, he hasn't been dead long, I mean, it wouldn't be right, I . . .'

Mrs Morgan stopped speaking and began to cry. She put her head in her hands very neatly and cried quietly for a long time. She cried like she was doing something, a chore perhaps, which she had to get over before she could talk to me again. I watched her crying, the top of her head moving ever so slightly, and the animosity between us seemed to dissolve into the air. I felt sorry for her. When she stopped it was very suddenly and she sat up straight like she had before, and smiled a smile which said I'm drowning but I don't much care, and I'll do what I can before I disappear. I returned her smile and looked her in the eye.

'How did he take it? Edward? This lack of desire for him?'

'I don't really know,' she replied, thinking about it and pushing aside the remnants of a tear. 'He never said anything. Everything else between us seemed so normal. It seemed normal for me to be with Edward and living and sleeping next to him, but making love to another man. It wasn't like I didn't want to be with him, but my sex was somewhere else. This didn't seem too strange because it had never really been there with him.'

I nodded.

'But did he try to have sex with you?'

'A few times. He held me in that way, you know? In bed? But I didn't respond and he never pressed me.'

'Did he have a strong sex drive? For you?'

'I don't know. I kept thinking about that when everyone asked me if I thought he was gay. He certainly wanted to make love to me often enough but it was never like . . .' Charlotte took a breath. 'It was never like fucking. Not just that. It was more of a way to be together and communicate our affection.' She turned to the side, thinking of something, and I thought she was going to cry again.

'What is it?' I asked.

'I don't know. I still loved him. All that I ever had. But I didn't tell him, and I didn't show him, because the way that I had shown him before suddenly meant something different to me. I didn't want to fuck him. I never had and I couldn't. I wanted to find some other way to show him but it was too late then, it was too late because he was . . . He probably died thinking I didn't love him.'

Mrs Morgan looked down at her lap, where her rust-coloured fingernails were picking at the gold ring on her left hand. Her voice became small and hopeless.

'That's all I can think about,' she said. 'That's the only thing I can think about, that and what it must have been like for Teddy. When . . .'

Mrs Morgan tried very hard to stop them but her words broke up into sobs again. She pressed her fists into her face and her elbows into her sides to stop her grief shaking its way out of her. The sound she made wasn't loud, but the pain coming out of her seared the air like something tearing apart along a seam which didn't exist. I had never seen anyone cry from such a central place as Charlotte Morgan was crying. I saw my hand move up from my knee towards her, and I watched it hover for a second above the Alice band which held her hair in place.

I drew it back towards me and let it rest on the top of the chair.

I watched Charlotte Morgan crying for a long time, and I knew that I had a lot of questions that I should ask her. About Graham Lloyd. And jealousy. And her finances. And about what Edward would have done had she told him. And had she actually told him already. I knew that I should wait until she had finished her crying and ask her these things. That is what Andy Gold would have done and he would have been right to. This woman had lied to the police, she was a recently bereaved widow who, it transpired, had a secret lover. Andy would have waited and that is what I would have done too, if I was still bound by an oath which said I had to be dispassionate and clinical while exercising my duties in the pay of the public and in the public's interest.

Instead I stood up, set the chair gently aside and walked through the kitchen, and then out on to the street, with the sound of Charlotte Morgan's bewildered grief following me like a lost bird. I turned and closed the door quietly.

Chapter Nine

I drove home and changed into jeans and a work jacket which I bought years ago but which now makes me look fashionable, especially since it's faded to cream from a dark brown. As I dressed I thought about Charlotte and her lover as possibles for Edward Morgan's murder. I saw the way Charlotte had held on to Lloyd outside her cottage. I didn't let Charlotte's tears put me off; they were genuine but that didn't mean anything. Grief can be huge, but when it's joined by remorse it gets even bigger.

I pulled my boots on and checked the medicine cabinet for Advil. None. I put my camera into a bag and went downstairs to the chemist to get some.

The chemist was actually a pharmacy and one day someone will tell me what the difference is. Like optician and optometrist. Alberto saw me coming out of the pharmacy and walked out of Fred's towards me. We said hello and then he told me that someone had been asking after me.

'A young kid,' Alberto said. 'He asked if Billy Rucker ever came in here.'

'What did he look like?' I asked, thinking it might have been Dominic Lewes come to tell me to leave him alone.

'Oh,' Alberto said, 'he was black, only about fourteen.

All nerves and attitude. Said he needed to see you. I told him to call you but he said he had.'

'Well, I dare say he'll catch up with me. Thanks though, Alberto.'

'Hey,' he shrugged, 'it's nothing.'

He lit up a cigarette and I left him and walked to the car.

Another dirty table and another coffee that was surprisingly good in the café at the bottom of Calshot Street. This time it was daytime though and I was determined not to miss Dominic Lewes again. I wanted to get him out of the way so I could concentrate on Edward Morgan. I bought a copy of the *Standard* and read the back pages, my mind drifting away to gay MPs and their murdered brothers, young boys lying dead in damp basements and a woman who was tied up in intricate knots of pure misery, knots she may have tied for herself. And how unlikely it was that I'd be able to do anything about any of it. I was glad I had Dominic; something simple and easy to occupy me, nothing to do but wait and watch, and press a button.

Dominic walked up after forty minutes and stood on the other side of the street joining another lad of about the same age. I framed him and got full body shots and then close-ups of his face. He was wearing his MA1 and he looked cold, the zip right up to his chin. He leant against the window of a derelict kebab shop and then sat down on the window ledge and rubbed his hands together, before taking out a pack of cigarettes and lighting one. It seemed ironic that he was still too young to smoke. What would his mother say? I left one pound fifty on the table for the waitress who was looking my way but not indicating that she had any plans to come to the table.

Dominic didn't see me as I walked past King's Cross station and crossed the road up by St Pancras. I cut back down towards him and turned right into his road where my car was parked again. I put the bag in the boot, hoping that my camera would be safe in there for a few minutes. For some reason though, I had the feeling, which I get once in a while, that someone was watching me. I'd go back in half an hour and find either no Mazda, or a Mazda with no contents of any value inside and a broken quarter-light. I looked around, up and down the street. I didn't see anyone but the feeling wouldn't go away. I knew I was being irrational, that boots seldom got broken into in broad daylight, but I couldn't help it. I turned the key in the lock again, took out my bag and slung it back over my shoulder. I walked down the street towards the Cross, glancing over my shoulder once or twice, feeling like an idiot.

'Have you got the time, mate?'

I'd stopped in front of Dominic Lewes and the other lad. I was speaking to Dominic.

'Yeah,' Dominic replied, pushing up the sleeve of his jacket. 'It's ten to six.' He showed me his watch at the same time as telling me what the time was and I wondered why people did that. Did he think I wouldn't believe him?

'Thanks,' I said, turning to go. But then I stopped. 'Hey. Haven't I met you before?'

Dominic put both hands on the windowsill beneath

him and looked at me, squinting for a second. I could tell
he thought he recognized me. He shook his head.

'I don't think so, mate.'

'Yes, we have.' I put my bag down on the pavement. 'It
was right here!' I sounded pleased with myself for remembering. 'I bought you a sandwich, you didn't have any
money, remember?'

'I'm not sure, mate, maybe.' Dominic laughed.

'It was a while ago. I'm really good with faces, though
I can't even remember names the next day.' I smiled.

'It's Mikey.'

'Yeah, that's it.' I pointed at him and shook my head.
'You look different but I don't know why.'

At this point a car drew up and the other boy walked
over to it and got in without saying anything to the driver.
The driver was looking the other way as if nothing was
happening. A regular. The car – a big, shapeless Ford
saloon – drew off and headed up the Pentonville Road
towards the Angel.

Dominic looked me in the eyes and stood up from the
ledge. His lips pursed very slightly. He opened his mouth
and his tongue ran over his teeth, as he took a small step
towards me.

'I'll suck you for twenty,' he told me.

'God,' I said laughing, 'no. Thanks. No. But I'll buy you
a sandwich and a cup of tea if you like, if you're hungry?'

'That's all right, mate.' Dominic paused. 'No johnny.
Just my mouth and your cock.'

Dominic's eyes ran over my body and he stood even
closer to me.

'No, no. Really.' I took a step back. 'Thanks all the
same. But what about that tea, hey? You look freezing.'

I rubbed my hands together briskly. I wanted

Dominic to come with me because I wanted to persuade him to call his mother. I had last time and he'd done it, and she'd told me what it meant to her. He didn't bother answering me this time though, he just turned his head to the side and sucked his cheeks in, letting out a mocking hmm as he did so. The conversation was over. He obviously didn't need cups of tea any more, he was in control of his life now. He kept staring towards King's Cross as though something incredible had just captured his attention, thereby telling me to get lost. Oh well, I thought, I've got the pictures. I looked at the side of Dominic's face and neck and at his cropped hair, the colour of vanilla ice cream on a summer holiday.

'Your roots need doing,' I told him, picking up my bag. Then, 'Call your mother.'

Dominic's face changed for a second but he still didn't look at me. I moved off.

I had been walking away from my car when I stopped to talk to Dominic, and I kept on going that way so as not to make him think I was looking for him. I was a little pissed off. I'd done my job and would get my money, but I hadn't done everything I could have. I knew what a phone call would mean to Mrs Lewes. Maybe Bob Hoskins wasn't such a prick after all.

There was an alley on the right which I could duck down, saving me from walking all the way round the block to my car. I turned into it, stepping over a comatose drunk with an empty bottle of Imperial sherry clasped to his chest like a baby. It was beginning to get dark now and the high walls either side of me intensified the gloom, as though a dimmer switch had been turned down a notch. I walked up the alley, inhaling a wave of stale piss, kicking aside a couple of old needles and an uneaten chocolate bar. In huge red letters on the wall somebody had spray painted the words 'FUCK PIGS'. I had a sudden image of a disaffected youth committing bestiality with a Gloucester Old Spot. I smiled to myself and stuck my hands into my coat pockets.

The man stepped out in front of me when I was about five yards from the end of the alley, and he blocked the exit. He stood with his arms folded and one leg pointing further forward than the other. He looked straight at me with his head thrown back, dressed in biker boots, black Levis, a tight T-shirt and an expensive blazer jacket. One roll-up on the sleeves. He looked at me with a disgusted menace, and when I checked my stride and stopped he took a step forward. I recognized him immediately; I really am good with faces. He was the guy who came to the door on Elm Drive when I'd gone looking for Dominic.

'Who the fuck are you?'

He had unfolded his arms and was standing square in front of me. His voice was big, and it echoed off the alley walls with a metallic sound. I took my hands out of my pockets. I let my bag slide down my arm on to the ground beside me, keeping hold of the strap.

'I said, who the fuck are *you*?'

He was angry but in control. Confident. I could tell immediately that trying to bullshit this man wouldn't get me very far. So I didn't try. I didn't say anything.

'What you been taking pictures of my boys for? Why you been coming round? What you want?'

His boys.

'I'm talking to you, tosser!' A long finger stretched out towards me. 'If you're the Bill you're dead.'

'If I'm the Bill,' I replied quietly, 'you're nicked.'

He didn't like that.

'Gimme your bag. Now. Give it here.' He snapped his fingers.

I let go of the strap, keeping the bag behind me.

'Listen,' I said, fanning out my hands, taking a couple of small steps forward. 'I don't want any trouble. I'm just working for someone who wants to know that their son is still alive, that's all.' I tried a smile.

'You deaf, tosser? Are you? Well? I *said* . . .'

I hit him with a straight right arm with a lot of shoulder behind it. Unfortunately he saw it; late but he saw it. He'd begun to twist left, taking a lot of the weight out but it still sent him spinning against the wall. Before I could hit him again he came out and charged at me, grabbing my lapels, but I managed to use his weight to take him past me and into the other wall. He still had my lapels and he butted me hard below my left ear, holding on tight to me. It hurt.

I couldn't get an arm free to hit him so I rammed him hard up against the brickwork. And again. He was shaken and I did manage to get a hand free, but he lunged out at me with all that he had before I could swing at him. We both went sprawling, landing on the wet concrete side by side. We struggled, trying to get on top of each other. I heard fabric tearing. I thought that, even if he wins this fight, my opponent was going to have to lose another four hundred quid in Emporium. I managed to wedge my foot against a wall and, pushing hard, I got on top of him. His arms went up to my neck but I ignored them. I held him by his jacket and his T-shirt and I belted the shit out him, right after right after right, until his arms were on the floor beside him. I heard his nose break. I felt his top front teeth bite into my knuckles as they broke up and snapped out of the bone. I saw his eyes change their focus, from me, to his own pain, and then to something I couldn't know.

When the man wasn't moving any more and his head got heavy I stopped hitting him. I let him drop down to the floor. I pushed myself up from the ground and got to my feet, breathing hard, steadying myself against a head spin. Dominic's pimp was lying back, almost conscious. I waited, getting my breath back. His focus returned and he lay there looking at me. Blinking. His neck and T-shirt were soaked in blood and I saw that the ripping sound I heard had been the top pocket of his jacket; it was hanging on by a couple of threads. I took a breath. Then, for some reason, I leant over to pull the pocket off. Just as I reached it his hand went up to stop me and he winced. I held the limp piece of fabric in my hands. He looked devastated. I hadn't had to fight this guy at all, I should have just grabbed hold of his pocket and threatened to rip it off if he didn't get out of my way.

I pulled the pocket off and stood over the guy looking down at him. I wanted to say something to him, something cool and final. But I couldn't think of anything. Instead, something he had said to me came into my head. *My boys*.

I looked up the alley towards where Dominic was standing and I thought I saw another figure getting into a car. Another kid whose home had not been a home, who had come to find somewhere else to belong and had ended up belonging to this man here. A kid whose life was made up of so much shit that if you took it away from him he'd be lost, he wouldn't know what the fuck was going on.

'*My* boys.'

The pimp didn't move anything except his eyelids, which fluttered like two half-dead moths pinned to a board. I took a step back. I steadied myself. I looked into his soft brown eyes for a second and the fluttering stopped as he met my gaze. An appeal burst into his eyes like hold-up men in a bank, but I ignored it. Then I repeatedly kicked the man with all those boys as hard as I could in the groin until his soft eyes clouded over and he blacked out.

I stepped over the wino again. He was still smooching with the angels. I hitched my bag up over my shoulder and walked out on to the Pentonville Road. Night had fallen quickly and it was almost dark now. Dominic was gone. I felt cold all of a sudden and I shivered. I crossed the road and walked back into the café. The waitress who had served me the last two times I had been there and had seen me with my camera, looked shocked to see me. She stepped back against the counter, holding her hands by her sides. It said it all. It wasn't the blood on my face that she was surprised to see. It was me. Standing up. I threw the liberated pocket on to the counter.

'Your boyfriend'll want this,' I said to her. 'He'll need his jacket stitching.' The girl looked across at it and then quickly back at me. She narrowed her eyes. 'Come to think of it,' I added, 'he might need his face stitching too.' The girl's mouth opened into a small Oh, and her eyes widened, but she didn't say anything.

Chapter Ten

I fell asleep in the bath. I woke up when the water was cold and I got that feeling again, which I used to get when I was a child, of not knowing where I was. The eerie silence that seemed to hover in the air of my flat was not dispersed by the fact that I could actually hear things; the lazy rumble of traffic and a child crying somewhere for its mother. I lay in the water for a few minutes, getting colder and colder, staring at the toilet chain which seemed unnaturally still. I was still too, my body lying inert beneath the now grey water covering it like a shroud. I stood up, glad to break the still surface, glad of the noise the water made running off me and back into the bath. I leant across to the radiator for a towel.

It was my gym night but I decided that I had fulfilled my pugilistic requirements for the day. I turned the thermostat up and the answerphone on, and I lay on my sofa with a glass of John Powers on the floor beside me, which I immediately forgot about. I tried to go over what I knew about my case but I couldn't push the image of Dominic's pimp out of my mind. Thinking about what I'd done to him, my bones felt hollow; whatever he was there was no excuse for it. He could have been dead for all I knew. I wondered what it was that made me lose it the way I had. I kept hearing the words *my boys* over and over and then I made the connection. It was what my father had called Luke and me. *My boys* are useless. *My boys* are lazy. *My boys* are ungrateful.

No one tells me how I should treat *my boys*.

I was restless but I wasn't in the mood to do the rounds with the photo and there wasn't anything else of any use I could do until tomorrow. I thought about looking at Luke's poems but it had been a taxing day and I didn't think I could do justice to them. Instead I used the remote for my stereo to tune in to a match on 5-Live which was just entering the second half. It was Birmingham against Luton, two sides I don't have the slightest interest in, but I listened to it gladly, and to the post-match interviews. I switched to *The World Tonight* on Radio 4 and heard some politicians pretending to be stand-up comedians in, I supposed, an effort to hide the fact that they didn't have an awful lot to say. At about ten-thirty there was a click from my machine but no message followed as I had turned the volume to nil.

I turned the radio off and the TV on, sitting all the way through a film in which Keanu Reeves made great strides with his surfing technique, helped hold up banks and jumped out of aeroplanes without the reassurance of a parachute. It seemed that old Keanu had his days all filled up too. At about twelve-thirty I went to bed and tried to sleep but there were too many gatecrashers in my head making too much noise, so I took one of the Seconals that I'd asked a friend of mine to send over from New York where she was working. The Seconal felt like a spider spinning silk around my body, tighter and tighter until finally I was paralysed. When I was bound so tight, but so softly, that I couldn't move at all, the spider finished with her thread and bent down slowly to bite into me. Her poison was languorous and calming, and as her shadow covered me and blocked out the light completely I disappeared.

I woke up at eleven feeling empty and strangely removed after my flat, artificial sleep. I lay in bed for ten minutes looking calmly at the events of yesterday, from my conversations with Morgan and Charlotte to the face the waitress made when she realized what I'd done to her boyfriend. Yesterday seemed a long way away, and the faces I had seen there unreal, as if they were an implanted memory of a time I hadn't actually lived. I sat up against the wall and took a hold of myself, deciding not to take any more of those rhino pills before I went to bed. I ran through what I had to do today. Then I pushed aside the curtains to see that the day was a dull cold grey with no shadows anywhere. I got up and lumbered across the room to the telephone.

The message on the machine was from a certain Graham Lloyd. He must have tried my office last night and then looked me up in the phone book when he hadn't got me there. There was another message on from him as well, left, so the machine informed me, at 7.49 a.m. precisely. My, I thought, as I signally failed to phone him back with the urgency he requested, aren't we in a bit of a hurry today?

I had coffee and half a slice of toast and then called my office to get the messages off the work machine. Graham Lloyd had indeed left me a message at my office, not sounding quite so impatient as he had tried to reach me there first. There was also a message from Mrs Lewes asking if I'd got any news about Dominic. She asked me not to phone her, saying that she'd try me again. The final message was from Andy Gold, saying it was nothing urgent but that maybe he ought to come over and thrash out some ideas. I was surprised that he was giving any credence at all to any other theories than the one he was pursuing; gay slasher strikes again. It all seemed a lot to deal with. I thought I'd leave Andy to get in touch if he wanted to, and the MP could stew for a little while longer.

Not much longer. I was heading towards the shower when the phone rang. I picked it up with a pretty good idea who'd be on the other end. I was right.

'Rucker? Is that Rucker?'

My second ever phone conversation with a Tory MP. This was a pit bull in a Montessori Centre too but there was no leash anywhere.

'William Rucker speaking,' I said.

'Rucker. I don't know who the hell you are, but . . .' I cut him off.

'Can you hold, please.'

I put the phone down without waiting for his reply and opened my pocket diary. I'd arranged to meet Sharon later and I couldn't remember the exact time, whether it was half-six for some food before the show, or seven-thirty and we'd get something after. It was half-six. I leant over the table and picked up the phone again.

'Now then. Who do I have the pleasure of addressing?'

'Rucker,' the MP began again, 'you know damn well who this is. Now—'

'I'm sorry,' I said cutting him off again. I ran a hand over my head and tried to shake off the weary feeling I still had in spite of two cups of coffee. 'I'm sorry, but before we continue this conversation, can I ask you a question? Do you recall ever watching Ilie Nastase play tennis at all?'

That got him.

'Well, if you do,' I continued, 'you might remember him reminding an umpire to call him Mr Nastase. Not Nastase. *Mr* Nastase. It's the same for private detectives, I'm afraid.' I yawned.

'Look here—'

'No, Mr Lloyd, for I presume you are he. I will not look there. You call me, you want to speak to me. Far more, I imagine, than I want to speak to you. So I am William to restaurant owners, Billy to my friends and a firm Mr Rucker to you. Got it?'

'Don't you get—'

'I said got it, *lover boy*?'

There was a silence on the other end of the line which had the strange effect of waking me up a lot. Then, as if the first part of our conversation had never happened, Lloyd said, quite calmly, 'Mr Rucker. I think we should meet. Come to my office. No, on second thoughts don't come anywhere near my office. I'll meet you for lunch. Do you know The Flag on Carlisle Street?'

'No,' I said. 'Nor will I be there for lunch. I will, however, be sitting in The Colt on Stroud Green Road at exactly five p.m. If you'd like to join me.'

'I can't. Not at that time. Be in—'

'Fine,' I said. I tucked the receiver under my chin and took another swig of the now lukewarm coffee. 'In that case give my regards to a certain Andrew Gold when you see him. He's a police officer. He'll call on you at about six o'clock with a couple of boys in blue in tow if I'm not sitting in The Colt on Stroud Green Road at five, looking across a table at you with a G and T in your hand. All right?'

I put the receiver down and strolled into the bathroom, feeling the engines beginning to kick in now. There's nothing like being rude to someone in power when the caffeine isn't working. The phone went almost immediately but I let it ring and pulled aside the shower curtain. While I was getting drenched I wondered if all MPs had a secretary. If they did I felt sorry for Lloyd's; she probably wasn't having a very nice day today.

I walked down to the repro shop and gave Carl the film I'd shot of Dominic Lewes. Carl looked exhausted, like he'd been down in the lab all night. I felt some sympathy for him and told him that the pictures weren't that urgent and that he could take his time over them if he had to. He looked up quickly from the chit he was filling in.

'Who are you?' he said aghast. 'What have you done with the real Billy Rucker!'

After that I drove over to my office and sat behind my desk with Kojak and a bacon roll. I thought about Lloyd. I tried to work a scenario in which he could be placed. He wasn't the man in the picture but he could have hired him. I wondered if Edward had found out about the affair and had refused a divorce. Would that make Lloyd want to kill him? No, not these days, not unless Lloyd was really, *really* jealous and couldn't bear to think of Charlotte with Edward a second longer. Later on I'd meet Lloyd and maybe find out what kind of person he was.

I looked at the file and picked up the phone but was once again informed that Alex hadn't shown up for his shift that day and had not rung in with an excuse. The manager's voice was tight as a tripwire and I could hear a very persistent American woman in the background saying, 'Excuse me! Excuse me!' The manager put the phone down abruptly, without any goodbye. I couldn't really blame her.

I flicked over a few more pages until I found the statement given by Edward Morgan's co-pilot. I read how Michael James Chalkley had known Edward Morgan for two years and had often flown with him. He said he had no idea that Edward was gay. Chalkley himself was married with three young children, and had witnesses who saw him say goodbye to Edward shortly after exiting customs. One of the stewardesses also saw him get into his Saab in the car park and was then stuck behind him in traffic on the motorway, driving into London.

Originally I had decided that I wasn't going to bother with Chalkley. I didn't think for a minute that he was involved, and I couldn't imagine what I could get out of him beyond the report he gave Andy. I'd changed my mind though, because I wanted to know what sort of mood Edward was in before he was killed. If, for instance, he was miserable because he either suspected or knew for sure that Charlotte was seeing another man. I called the number Chalkley had listed, expecting a wife or a message but I got the man himself. He was in all day and yes he was happy to talk to me that afternoon if I wanted. I said that I definitely did and asked him what time would suit him. He said whenever; he was on guard duty and he wasn't going out. The screams of what sounded like a whole classroom of kids in the background told me what he meant by that.

I was glad I could get Chalkley out of the way today. I'd thought of hitting some gay bars with the pictures I had but there wasn't that much time before I had to meet Lloyd and it would be better if I had a clear time ahead to do that. Doing the rounds was still the most likely way that the guy was going to be caught, but often, when you're showing a picture round, someone will say 'Sure, he comes in here' and you have to wait until the place shuts to see if he does or not. You can't leave a message for the person to wait for you until you've finished some other business.

I copied down Chalkley's address in my diary and stood up to go. Before I could get to the door, however, it opened.

'Don't you ever bloody knock?' I asked.

'Only when I'm arresting someone,' Andy Gold said. 'And then, very very loudly.'

I sat back down and Andy must have telepathically heard me offer him a seat because he sat down too.

'Well,' he said, 'what you got?'

I told Andy that I didn't have anything more than he did.

'Nothing?' he asked, opening one eye wider than the other, not sounding like he entirely believed me. 'Not a sausage?'

'Not even a chipolata, mate.'

Andy didn't have much to give me either. He and his team had shown the picture round to everyone they'd interviewed before and no one had been able to tell them anything.

'I saw the widow,' he said, folding his arms. 'Not bad, not bad at all. Most blokes would have been more than content poking that every night, don't you think?'

I shrugged.

'If they were straight. Very nervous though, when I saw her. More so than before.'

'Probably the picture,' I said.

'Maybe. You'd already shown her it though, hadn't you?'

'Yes.'

'Funny thing,' Andy said, pretending to think. 'She never mentioned that you'd been to see her.' He folded his arms and sat back a little. 'It was me who brought it up, right at the end.'

'So?'

'So nothing. Just a little odd, that's all. Wouldn't you say? It was only a couple of hours after you spoke to her. I thought she might have said something.'

'Instantly forgettable,' I explained, 'that's me. Always been my problem that has.' Andy made a hmm sound but I didn't let him pursue it. I told him that if there wasn't anything very pressing then I had to go out. I stood up and he followed me out of my office into the corridor.

Michael Chalkley lived in a smallish terraced house in a back street two minutes away from the B-movie alien spacecraft which is Southgate tube station. He opened the door to me and led me into a small sitting room which had no carpet, and was crowded with yellow packing crates.

'We're moving,' he told me. 'Tomorrow. You were lucky to catch me.' He made some space on a sofa, and invited me to sit down.

Chalkley was a pleasant-looking man in his early forties. He had an elongated, rather sad face and had long since finished balding on top. Three toddlers, two of which I could see were twins, clung to his legs like vines and he had perfected that most impressive of feats: splitting his consciousness in two. He was paying a great deal of attention to me, as well as noting and responding to his kids' every movement and mood swing. He took his harassment, both from the kids and from myself, with an admirably stoic equanimity.

'The twins,' Chalkley explained, indicating the packing cases. 'We need a bigger place. And I want to be closer to the airport. Marion's mother doesn't want us to go, she lives round the corner, but we've decided.' He pulled the eldest child, a girl of four, on to his lap.

'Where are you off to?' I asked, suppressing a yawn. I felt slightly nauseous and detached from myself.

'Hayward's Heath,' he said. 'I've been transferred to Gatwick. I made pilot last month.'

I must have reacted to this remark because Chalkley smiled.

'It was fixed a long time before Edward was killed,' he said. 'Anyway, I don't think it works like that. You can't murder your way up the BA ladder as far as I'm aware, although it wouldn't surprise me to find out that some of our executives had done it that way. No, I've been on all the courses, this has been fixed for some time.'

I asked Chalkley what kind of man Edward was. He told me that he had really liked him, that Edward was kind and always very appreciative of those working under him.

'Some pilots can be arrogant,' he said, 'especially those who've been in the forces. Edward wasn't. The flight attendants got on with him especially well. A lot of them were very upset by what happened to him. One of the men, Jeff Downs, is gay and he felt very bad. He told me that he often went to that bar after work. He would have gone there that night but he had a date in town.'

While Chalkley sorted out the odd argument, filled some beakers with apple juice and performed minor first aid, he told me that he hadn't thought Edward was gay and was surprised to find out that he was. It didn't make him think any less of him.

'What about that last trip?' I asked. 'What mood was he in?'

'He was quite subdued,' Chalkley said, nodding slightly. 'As if there was something on his mind.'

I pictured Edward, brooding about his wife.

'He seemed better on the flight back though, and he seemed quite cheerful when I left him, although, thinking about it, there might have been something forced about it. I wanted to get home otherwise I might have gone for a quick drink with him. We often did that before braving the traffic.'

'So I understand.'

'Yes. I wish I had.' Chalkley let out a breath. 'I hardly need to say that I very much wish I had gone for a drink with him that night.'

That was all I wanted to know really, although I lingered a little while with Chalkley, asking questions I already knew the answer to or which I didn't really need answering. I accepted the coffee he offered me, and played with his kids while he made it. His eldest, Natasha, was very bright, and as pretty a child as you could imagine. We drank our coffees and then Chalkley showed me to the door. As I thanked him for his time I thought about the 'if onlys' which feature in almost every case I have ever dealt with. The 'if onlys' which haunt those who are left when someone is killed. I shook Chalkley's hand.

'Out of curiosity,' I said, 'and if it's OK to ask, why didn't you stick around for a drink with Edward that night?'

'Oh, the flight was late in. Head winds over Biscay. I wanted to get back.'

'I see. How late were you?'

'Half an hour,' he said. 'Forty minutes maybe.'

'Right. Right.'

I left Chalkley on his doorstep and walked up the garden path. I turned to shut the gate and then waved back at Natasha, who had climbed up on to the windowsill in the living room.

Lloyd lit a cigarette, blew the smoke across the table at me and took a sip from his orange juice. I'd told him it had to be a gin and tonic but I was willing to overlook the point. If I had thought more carefully when I was trying to find out who he was from the security guard at the House of Commons, I wouldn't have asked if he was John Major. He didn't look much like him. It would have been a lot more credible to have pegged him for the current Chancellor, Gordon Brown. He had a squarish, set face, full dark hair, and a head which seemed slightly too large for his body. His eyes were as dark as his suit and his teeth were as bright as the crisp white shirt which seemed a little tight round his neck. He put his lighter down beside his glass and looked at me.

'Right,' he said. 'What can I do for you?'

I'd left Michael Chalkley and driven down to see Joe Nineteen to give him a finder's fee I owed him from the week before. Joe is a West Indian former bus conductor of a very advanced though indeterminate age, who lives by the bus station at Finsbury Park. Joe often uses his connections on the London bus network to spot missing kids for me, and when he does so I visit him, which is always a

pleasure, and give him an amount of money commen-
surate with how difficult it was for his contacts to locate a
particular fugitive. He lives on his own, sitting on a stool
outside his front door in any weather but rain, and he
always has a pot of goat curry on his stove. Always. It's all
he ever eats, and if I could make it as well as he can it
would be all I ever ate too.

After a small bowlful of the stuff, I bought a copy of
the *Standard* and walked up Stroud Green Road. I sat in a
corner of The Colt on red velveteen and flicked through
the paper keeping an eye on the door. Then I took out the
picture and did a few sums. The security video had a
digital clock on it. The plane had been late in and the time
on the photo was only thirty-five minutes after the plane
had landed, which meant that Edward couldn't have been
sitting at the bar for very long before he left. The barman
had seemed to imply that Edward had been there longer
but this didn't really mean anything. I was annoyed that I
hadn't been able to get to him before the police had. If a
lazy cop thinks he knows what happened in a situation it
isn't difficult to get a witness to agree, especially when
you're talking marginally different time scales. It meant,
however, that if the man in the hat had picked Edward up,
he was a pretty fast worker. Or that he knew him. He was
his lover and had arranged to meet him there.

Graham Lloyd came in a few minutes after five and
looked around, presumably for me. Since he didn't know
what I looked like he wasn't going to see me until I
wanted him to. I watched him walk up to the bar, buy his
drink and take it to a small round table in the back of the
large room. He sat down and immediately lit a cigarette,
pulling on it impatiently. I wondered if I was looking
at a killer, at a man who had paid for the murder of a

colleague's brother and made it look like part of a series. Once again I saw the lascivious, teasing way he had kissed the dead man's wife. I wanted it to be him.

Lloyd dragged on his cigarette so hard he definitely had something on his mind. I let him finish it before going over and introducing myself.

I sat down opposite, he lit up another cigarette and blew smoke in my face.

'Is it money?' he asked me with a smile. His tone was friendly. 'Is that it? Think you can make a few quid out of me? Mmm? Well, you're wrong, I'm afraid.'

I sighed.

'And I wouldn't bother going to the press if I were you. Beside the fact that none of the Tory sheets'd touch it right now, you don't *have* anything.' His smile said he thought I was extremely dim. 'Very silly giving away the film like that. Very silly indeed.'

He sipped his orange juice. He reminded me of a headmaster I once had, who would tut at you and shake his head for ages before getting his strap out.

'I would just like to ask you a few questions,' I said.

'As for the police,' he continued, 'I happen to know the Boss. And I don't mean some paltry detective or even a Chief Inspector, I mean the Boss. I don't really think they're going to pick me up on the say-so of some failed cop who had a breakdown, do you?'

Lloyd seemed to be enjoying himself. He gave a short laugh, shook his head at my incompetence and took a last drag on his cigarette. There was a certain overconfidence in his gestures, ingrained, I suspected, by years of easing his way nicely through life. I hadn't heard anything which required a response.

'I've done my homework on you, *Mr* Rucker. I'm pleased to say that you don't have anything on me.'

'Then you don't have anything to worry about, do you?' I said. 'I'm surprised you even came.'

'I'm not worried. I simply came to tell you that if you suggest anywhere, *anywhere*, that I am having an affair with *anybody*, I will not only sue you but you might find problems getting your licence renewed. Is that clear?' He was a little more serious now.

'Yes,' I said quietly, matching his earlier smile. 'I think so. You're threatening me. Thank you for being so frank.' I moved the ashtray he was using towards him. 'However, let's not get carried away. If I tell the police about your affair with Charlotte Morgan, they will go and talk to her about it. She admitted it to me, she will to them. You will then be interviewed by certain police officers. The Queen could not prevent this; I know the officers. The crime desks of various papers will find out about this. They will know which case these officers are working on, and will be very interested in the fact that these officers are talking to you. They'll put two and two together and the answer will be one. Page one. Let me see now; "Whizzkid MP Quizzed in Gay Slasher Case". That sounds quite tasty, doesn't it?'

Lloyd was silent, biting his bottom lip. I thought I could detect a hint of grudging admiration in his eye. He shrugged. I finished my mineral water.

'As for my licence, do what you like. It's about time I got out of this racket anyway. I don't like the company.'

I stood up and walked over to the bar, giving him time to think about it. When I got back, this time with a ginger ale, he didn't look so relaxed.

'Now,' I said. 'I'm not going to the papers. Yet. Or the

police. Tell me where you were on the sixth of July, a Friday, in the evening.'

He had thought ahead. As I was speaking he took an electronic organizer from his jacket pocket. He pressed some buttons and then turned the tiny screen round to show me.

'As you can see, I was out of the country. On a fact-finding trip. Keeping some Home Office morons in order if you must know.'

'That's what it says there.'

'That is what it would say anywhere. Because it happens to be true.'

'All right,' I said.

I reached into my pocket and pulled out one of the pictures. I tossed it on to the table and watched Lloyd's face as he picked it up and glanced at it dismissively. His face told me that he had never seen the man before or was a natural liar. I didn't know which one was more likely.

'Who's this?' he said.

'You tell me.'

'I can't. I have no idea who this man is.' He put the picture down. I put my finger on it.

'He's the man who met your mistress's husband at Heathrow airport,' I said. 'And very probably stuck a broken bottle into him. Several times. Either because that's the sort of thing he enjoys, or someone paid him to.'

'Then you'd better get out there and find him, if that is what *you* are being paid to do, and stop wasting your time on me.' The veneer on his voice had now completely rubbed off. He leant forward and pointed his finger at my chest. 'I had nothing to do with this, and you don't have anything to suggest I do beyond what you thought you saw when, like the grubby little man you obviously are, you were spying on myself and the friend I was trying to comfort in a time of obvious distress for her.'

'You were being very thorough.'

'Watch it. I'll repeat what I told you just so you get it straight. It would be very foolish of you to involve me any further in this business. Very foolish indeed.'

Lloyd finished his spiel and then did something which I don't think he meant me to see. He glanced, very quickly at the door. The glance was barely perceptible but it was there. Then he focused on me, looking at me like he was the chief whip and I was a backbencher about to abstain. I sat for a second thinking about his little glance. Then I excused myself, saying I would be back in a second, and I walked into the back of the pub towards the toilet.

I walked down the narrow corridor but instead of turning left into the toilet I went straight on and pushed open a fire door leading out of the back of the pub. I was in a small yard with a circular drain in the middle and crates of empty bottles stacked against two walls. I shut the door behind me. I looked around. Unfortunately, the only way out was an alley leading up to Stroud Green Road. I didn't much want to take it but I had no choice. I walked up it and emerged on to the street as nonchalantly as I could, immediately crossing the road without turning my head. Once on the other side I stepped into a doorway and looked back over at the pub.

A heavily built man in a long, single-breasted blue coat was standing by the door of The Colt, seemingly immersed in the *Standard*. Maybe he was immersed in it. I thought about waiting for Lloyd, to see if the man said anything to him when he came out but realized that, whoever the man was, he wouldn't speak to the MP. I thought about waiting around until they both realized I was gone, and then tailing the man in the coat if he went anywhere. No good, he probably knew my car by now. Or he didn't know anything about me and was waiting for his wife to finish using the toilet. I didn't know what to do. I certainly didn't want this man tailing me, if that was his intention. I was going to meet Sharon and I didn't want her getting involved in anything. Making the decision, I stepped out of the doorway and walked back across the road.

'Have you got a light?' I asked the man, having tapped him on the shoulder. He had turned round and was looking at me impassively. Slowly, he nodded.

'Thanks,' I said.

The man reached into his coat pocket without taking his eyes off me. A thick moustache bristled above a mouth with no lips. He held up a Zippo, popped it open and struck it. I didn't move. I didn't produce a cigarette for him to light either. I don't smoke. After a second I made a small turn to the left.

'You see that car,' I said, pointing towards the Mazda parked on the other side of the road, twenty or so yards down towards Finsbury Park. 'It's mine.'

'Is it?'

'Yes,' I said, 'it is. And I'm going to get in it and drive it away now.'

The man stared.

'Are you?'

'Yes,' I said, 'I am.'

'So?'

'So nothing.' I smiled. 'Just thought I'd let you know, that's all.'

The man didn't say anything. I walked away from him and crossed the road, turning back to look at him. He kept his eyes on me and didn't move. He hadn't moved by the time I'd got the engine started either, or pulled away from the kerb. He could tell I was still watching him. I just made an amber light and as I pulled away I saw him in the wing mirror. He folded up his paper, stuck it under his arm and walked into the pub. I made another amber light at Finsbury Park, and headed up the Blackstock Road.

Chapter Eleven

As far as I could tell I wasn't tailed as I drove back to Clerkenwell. I went home, showered, and then met Sharon at The Falcon on Farringdon Road where we both had the grilled sardines. I still felt strange from the morning, and more than a little edgy from the afternoon, and I had to make a conscious effort to engage with Sharon and shake myself into the evening. I kept drifting in and out of the conversation like a hologram on half power. I couldn't help thinking about Lloyd, and as we ate I found myself wishing that I hadn't arranged to go out with Sharon that night. I always found it impossible to enjoy myself when I was in the middle of something important; I just wanted to get out and find something Lloyd wouldn't be able to smirk at. I told myself it was too late now and not to ruin Sharon's evening by being sullen with her.

We got to Sadler's Wells fifteen minutes early, bought a programme and had a quick drink at the bar. The flamenco show lasted two hours, during which I was able to pull out all the thoughts which were nagging at me and stretch them in different directions. There were a lot of directions but none was any easier to move the events along than any other. Lloyd. Was he rattled because he had something to hide, or just because he didn't want his political career to take a nosedive before it was more than ten feet off the ground? I didn't know. I thought about it and paid some attention to the show, and when it was finished Sharon and I walked over to the pub opposite. The Shakespeare, or something.

'Well?' Sharon asked, after she had set the drinks on the table and sat down beside me. I took a sip of whiskey.

'I can see why you wanted to see that,' I said.

'Oh,' she replied, smiling. 'Can you now?'

'Yes,' I said. 'You appreciate the beauty of space and movement.'

'I do?'

'Yes. Especially when enacted by a man wearing nothing but baby oil, and trousers so tight you are immediately made aware of a certain decision made by his parents soon after he was born.'

Sharon laughed. 'He's a dancer,' she said. She shrugged her shoulders, doing a good impression of one of those earnest women on the *Late Review*. 'It has to be easy to see his body. It's his medium of expression.'

'I don't think medium would be the word I'd use,' I said.

'He really was brilliant though,' Sharon said. 'Wasn't he?'

'Yes,' I said. 'He was. And just the man to have around when you've got problems with cockroaches.'

As we hunched over our little table, Sharon asked me how the case was coming. I thought of an angry MP and a man with a moustache.

'Developments,' I said.

'Really? That's great.'

'Developments which probably don't mean anything,' I was sorry to add.

Above the hubbub of a busy Friday night I told Sharon about Charlotte Morgan and Graham Lloyd, and about how I had met up with the MP. I didn't tell her about the man outside The Colt though; I didn't want her to worry about me. Or burst out laughing at my paranoia.

'Do you think Lloyd did it?' Sharon asked.

'I know he didn't,' I said. 'He told me that he was in America at the time it happened. I'm going to check that out but I don't think he'd have come up with it if it was an out and out lie.'

'Then he's in the clear?'

'No, I don't think so. He could have had it done. Paid someone.'

Sharon looked doubtful. 'Do you really think so? How would an MP know how to hire a hit man? How would he know where to go?'

I laughed, 'It's not as hard as you'd think. Or as expensive.'

'So he might have hired someone, and told them exactly how to do it, to make it look like those other ones?'

'Yes,' I said, 'he could have. I was very dubious about that when Morgan told me that's what *he* thought had happened. You see, the police don't release all the details. It would be too horrifying to read over the cornflakes. There are things which happened in Teddy's killing which also happened when the lorry driver and the schoolboy were killed, but which very few people would have known about.'

'Such as?'

'Well, the police told the press that a bottle had been used in each case, but they didn't tell them that, both times, it had been deliberately left inside the body. Thrust in so it would stay there. That happened the third time too which made me think it had to be the same man.'

'And doesn't it still have to be?'

'Probably,' I admitted. 'But a well-placed MP could find out about the details of a case if he wanted to.'

'Really?'

'If he pretended he wasn't looking, sure.' I had a thought. 'And if he knew someone high up in the Metropolitan Police then that would make it even easier.'

'OK,' Sharon said, 'he could have done it. Or paid someone to do it. But why would he? I mean, it is a bit extreme, isn't it?'

'More than a bit. But there are millions of reasons why people kill each other. In this case there's the obvious. Jealousy. He couldn't stand the fact that his mistress was sleeping with another man, even if that man was her husband.'

'Except she wasn't sleeping with him, was she? Not in the biblical sense.'

'No, but he wasn't to know that. And if he was an obsessive, a real whacko, he might have been compelled to have Teddy killed.'

'Sounds plausible. I mean that he should be a whacko.'

'Mmm. Not sure I buy it though. Charlotte told me they were both getting divorced. Divorce would be an easier way of keeping her away from her husband.'

'Yes, but we all know what middle-aged men say about divorces when they fancy someone.'

'Good point,' I said. 'But I'm still doubtful. Killers possessed by jealousy tend to do the job themselves, in fits of heightened rage which outweigh any rational sense. They don't plan it meticulously like that, getting someone else to do it in a specific way.'

'So why else would he kill him?' Sharon asked.

'The most obvious reason of all,' I said. 'Money. But I don't know anything about that yet. He might need money, or he could be as flush as the Duke of Westminster for all I know.'

'Please,' Sharon said, holding her hands out towards me. 'Don't get me on the subject of the Duke of Westminster.'

Sharon sat back in her chair and smiled.

'Teddy,' she said.

'What?'

'You called him Teddy.'

'That's what his brother knew him as,' I said.

'It sounded like you knew him. Like you cared about him.'

I thought about Teddy and I nodded. 'I do feel like I knew him. At least a little. It's strange. Speaking to his wife, his brother and his colleague, I've picked up things about him. I can tell what a good guy he was. That he had a sense of humour and was generous and thoughtful. And I see his face, every day. I have this picture of him smiling into the camera. I look at the picture and can almost see him talking to me. He looks very confident in it. Empowered, you might say. I can imagine going out for a drink with him, like his co-pilot used to do. Then I try and figure out who left him carved to pieces with his face smashed in and then rammed a broken champagne bottle in his guts.'

The pub shut, and the bar staff went from quite friendly to extremely objectionable in the space of just twenty minutes. Only in England. After the stools had been taken from under us I could just as well have called it a night but Sharon said she didn't want to go home yet and she asked me to take her to the Old Ludensian, Nicky's bar, where she had never been. I agreed without much enthusiasm and we walked down there. Friday night is never a good time to go; the place is full of suits with foghorn voices barging their way to the bar as though they're still on the floor of the Stock Exchange. Nicky was out and we couldn't find a seat and a bull-necked rugby type with a red face and his tie pulled open decided that it would be a good idea to spill half his pint down my jacket and not feel any need to apologize. Sharon told me not to do anything about it. I became irritable, and was just waiting for the next idiot to fuck me off. I should have realized that it just wasn't right for me to be out that night, and gone home. I was tired and I had too much to think about. But then Nicky came in and got us a table and flirted with Sharon so we had to stay. I compensated for my tiredness and my increasingly foul mood by drinking too much of my friend's vodka.

The upshot was that when Nicky went to help out the barmen, Sharon and I got into a fight. Sharon asked me if I'd read Luke's poems and when I said I hadn't had time she looked at me like a schoolteacher. She said she wanted to send all the poems to a publisher and the suggestion really shocked me. Automatically, I didn't like the idea. She'd gone through all his private papers to find them and now she wanted to spread his private thoughts out for all the world to see. I told her that I knew what would happen, that the papers would get into it, Luke being in a coma and all that, and then Esther fucking Rantzen would be on the phone. The whole idea was mawkish. The publishing companies would only want to do it for the publicity, not the poems, and anyway we didn't have Luke's consent.

'Maybe one day he'll do it himself,' I told her, 'but until then I just don't think we have the right.'

When I said this to her, Sharon just shook her head and looked away from me. I could tell that she had something which she wanted to say but whatever it was she thought better of it. She looked upset for a minute and it pissed me off that she should be like that just because she wasn't getting her way. I was reminded of the feelings I used to have for her, my distrust of her motives concerning my brother. I was suspicious of her again, of the way she seemed to take everything upon herself. She tried to persuade me again but I just said that I didn't like the idea. Sharon said I was being irrational, that Luke had always intended publishing a book, that it was one of his real ambitions. I didn't listen to her. If you can't understand why not, I said, then there's no use me telling you. We were on the verge of shouting at each other when Nicky came back and the subject was changed. Sharon smiled brightly and told him all about the show we'd seen. I concentrated on the vodka, each shot of which seemed to harden me inside like a varnish.

After a while Sharon went home. I managed a smile but she didn't kiss me goodnight, telling me that I didn't have to wait outside for the cab with her. She said she would call me and I nodded. When she'd gone Nicky asked me what I was so pissed off about but I told him it was nothing. He said he really liked Sharon and I was surprised by my own reaction; it was an almost physical sensation of threat. I may have taken my brother's youth away from him but I didn't have to let one of my friends take his girlfriend. Now I *knew* I was being irrational, but I couldn't help it.

'Not this one, Nicky,' I slurred. 'OK?'

'Ah,' he said, holding his hands up. 'I get it. Sorry. No wonder you didn't call Trish back. She liked you by the way.'

'It's not like that,' I said, 'you don't understand.'

Puzzled, Nicky didn't pursue it.

I stayed late, propping up the bar long after Nicky had locked the door. I was still there when the kitchen staff left and the barmen, and when Jamie said goodnight too. I sat there feeling pissed and tired and fucked off with Sharon and not really knowing why, but getting more so with each glass of smooth clear vodka. Carla, the waitress I always flirt with, saw me sitting there and asked me if I needed a lift home. I sat up a bit and said yes. Nicky interrupted to say that he'd drive me if I wanted, giving me a serious look as he did so, but I said no, it was OK. I walked outside with Carla. I said something funny and she laughed and said something funnier back. I laughed. Then, as we got into her Beetle, Carla asked me where I lived. I told her but I needn't have bothered because we didn't go there.

Chapter Twelve

The journey out to the hospital usually takes about an hour and a half but I made good time because it was Sunday. It was another overcast day, a little warmer than it had been of late, though the forecast had predicted rain for later. It was good to drive through the quiet streets, usually so jammed with angry people in their hermetically sealed shells. The city looked strangely vulnerable. It was about two thirty when I turned into the entrance of the hospital, and parked where I usually do, over in the corner near the artificial lake. I locked up the Mazda, and then Sharon and I walked towards the forbidding Victorian building where my brother had been living for the last three years.

On Saturday I'd woken up at around ten, exhausted from high resolution dreams, in a bed that I wasn't familiar with. After the inevitable brittle goodbyes I walked out on to the street, which was in Hackney, and found a minicab office. I felt like shit, and the way the guy drove the cab didn't make me feel any better. When I got home I sat in Fred's for a while, seeing if I could spot anyone taking an undue interest in the street that led to my flat. There was no one. I went upstairs and I dialled the airport, and this time managed to get through to the barman. I was oddly relieved, having had the thought that the man in the hat may have wanted to cut down on any potential witnesses against him. Alex answered the phone and said yeah, of course he remembered me. He wanted to know how he could help. I asked him if he had seen the man in the hat any time prior to the night of the murder. He said he hadn't. He did remember that the man had been there a while before Edward had shown up. I got him to estimate the time and he guessed at around three-quarters of an hour. He asked if that was important and I told him that I wasn't sure whether it was or not. It could mean that he went there on purpose to find someone. He agreed. He told me that in an airport the passengers don't normally stay at the bar for too long unless they were early for their flights. And he wasn't taking one, was he? No, I said. I asked him if he was sure that Edward and the man had sat at the bar for a long time, and explained what the clock on the security video had said. Alex laughed.

'Jesus,' he protested, 'I didn't really remember all that much. It was you guys who all told me how much I remembered. Maybe they were there for twenty minutes not forty. How the fuck should I know? If I'd known he was going to waste the guy I'd have paid more attention, but I didn't, did I? I'd have put a stopwatch on him.'

Alex had a point. I apologized for bothering him again.

There was nothing I could find out about Graham Lloyd's financial status until Monday. I wrote the rest of the morning off and gazed out the window at the dome of St Paul's, a stranger on the skyline. I spent the afternoon mooching around, unable to focus on anything. At four I went for a long walk into Soho and bought some Levis from a place in Seven Dials. I sat in a gay pub on Argyle Street and handed out a few photographs, but everyone seemed to be a tourist. I'd do better during the week, when the regulars were in. It meant that the weekend was dead as far as my current assignment was concerned. I took the bus home and then went down to the gym to work out. I couldn't put much enthusiasm into it and left early, blaming a headache which later on turned out to be a prophesy. I ate fish and chips from the Golden Fry, drank half a bottle of a cheap Chilean, and fell asleep on the sofa.

Sharon and I hadn't said too much on the journey. Sharon seemed wary of me, and I was a little nervous too. Neither of us mentioned Friday night. I turned Radio 3 on and got some very grave organ music which really underlined the heaviness of the season. Sharon was wearing jeans and an enormous sweater, with her shortish hair pulled back in a ponytail. She'd brought along some exotic-looking flowers which lay in their paper on the back seat, their sweet powerful scent like another presence in the car with us. Sharon always takes along the most pungent flowers in the shop when she goes to the hospital, reasoning that though he can't see them, Luke must be able to breathe in their aroma.

Luke lay where he always lay, in the same position, with the same expression on his face. He is in a small ward with a curtain on two sides of his bed, the foot facing the door through which we had walked. His bed is really a big, electronic lilo, which inflates and deflates automatically in given areas. It does this to prevent pressure sores, critical occlusions of the blood vessels closest to the surface of the skin, by rotating the weight on any given part of Luke's body. Luke lay with his limbs in a pronounced contraction. Due to the lack of exercise, and in spite of the daily massages he receives, Luke's body has gradually taken on more and more of a spastic appearance, his legs, arms and hands drawing closer into him as his muscles lose the habit of stretching out. It looks as though he is afraid, and is constantly trying to protect himself from something awful, but I have been assured that the position of his limbs is simply a physical reaction to his muscles' inertia. It is completely separate from his mental state.

Sharon and I took chairs either side of his bed and Hazel, one of the nurses who looks after my brother, went to find a vase for Sharon's flowers. I had actually brought along a vase a couple of years ago, one which was a lot nicer than the hospital ones, but the nurses didn't realize it was Luke's and gave it to other patients as well as him. I'd noticed it today when we'd walked in, above the bed of a frail old lady. I never saw the point of saying anything about it.

Hazel came back with a vase and asked us how we were. We both said we were fine. Hazel is a tall, very thin black woman in her early thirties. I am always pleased to see that it is her on duty when I come because I can tell that she cares a great deal about Luke. The other nurses are very good as well, but Hazel has a special quality which is hard to define. I like the way she talks to Luke, without sounding patronizing, and the filthy jokes she makes under her breath about the doctors and the ward sister. Luke would have liked that if he could have heard her. Maybe he could hear her.

Hazel put the flowers on the windowsill at the head of the bed and left us alone. Sharon smiled at Luke and took hold of his right hand which, needless to say, rested in hers without making any sort of response. Slowly, she stretched out his fingers one by one, and gradually straightened out his wrist. Luke was wearing his blue pyjamas, with the rounded collars and black piping, which I had bought for him last Christmas. The top and bottom buttons were done up, the rest open to give room to Luke's gastrostomy tube, the artificial umbilical cord which has been inserted into his stomach through an opening made a couple of inches below his breastbone. The tube feeds Luke a constant supply of amino acids in liquid form, and is preferable to a drip because a drip would send nourishment straight into his bloodstream. Luke's gut is in perfect working order and the gastrostomy tube means that it has work to do, and so doesn't suffer the wastage inflicted on other parts of his body.

The colour of the pyjamas the nurses fit him into is one of the few things that ever change about my brother. The others are the length of his hair, or the light stubble which sits on his chin from time to time. It always strikes me as strange that his hair and beard should keep growing the way they do, as if some part of Luke is unaware that the rest of him has stopped, and carries on functioning regardless, like a striker who hasn't heard the whistle. When I'd first started coming I'd asked Hazel if I could shave Luke and she had allowed it, and now I do that if he happens to need it when I'm there.

Luke didn't need shaving today though so I was redundant in that capacity. Sharon held Luke's hand, which I always feel strange about doing, and she ran her other hand through his hair and chatted to him. She told him about work, and the various things she'd been doing with her spare time. She behaved with a patience and an efficiency which made me feel clumsy and unimaginative. I thought it was good the way she was with him, and I wondered what she talked to him about when I wasn't there. We both focused our attention on Luke, and Sharon did most of the talking. I could talk quite well when I was on my own with Luke, but was happy enough for Sharon to be in charge while I was there with her. I'm sure he would much rather listen to her.

As Sharon chatted away I studied Luke's face, and tried to decide if he was looking any older since he had been here. He looked thinner certainly, drawn, and his skin was very pale, but I wasn't sure if I could see any age on him. As often happens when I sit there watching him, I couldn't help imagining him in ten years' time. Twenty, thirty. Lying there as time passed him by, growing slowly into the body of an old man, a slower body, a body which had grown weary without having done anything to tire it. I couldn't imagine it. I couldn't imagine coming here every week or so for the rest of Luke's or my life, bringing along the baggage I had acquired, the sights and sounds and experiences, the children maybe; all the things Luke may never have, because he put himself in a position of danger so that I would not be in it. I couldn't imagine growing older, and watching Luke's parody of ageing growing older alongside me.

Sharon chatted on and I said the odd thing now and then. The ward was warm and Sharon pulled her sweater over her head, her full breasts pressing upwards against a fitted, ribbed T-shirt. The contrast between the young, vivacious woman and her inert fiancé was startling, and I had to make myself remember what they had looked like before, fighting together on the sofa, or dancing salsa at the Mambo Inn. Imagining that made me think of that night and I asked Sharon if she remembered it, how Luke and I were too English to ask anyone other than her to dance, and how we had had to keep whisking her away from overly amorous Latinos. Sharon said of course she remembered. And then a private memory crossed her mind and she looked back down at Luke. A wistful breeze blew across her features and she squeezed Luke's hand harder. As she set his hand down, however, the wistfulness was blown away by something stronger. She sat back in her chair, letting out a long, slow breath.

Sharon seemed to have gone somewhere and so I started to tell Luke about my case. I didn't tell him any of the details, just that it was paying well and that I might be able to get away sometime, do some skiing after Christmas. I told him how Forest were doing, and how he had better get well because they needed all the support they could get at the moment. I talked about going back to Australia with him, up to the Northern Territories this time. I told him that Sharon had recently made me go to see a Spanish porn show with her, and then told him that his acting agent had phoned recently to ask how he was doing. Apparently, she still got the odd enquiry after him. I told Luke that it really was about time that he got off his arse and started working again; his public were demanding it.

While I was speaking I hadn't really noticed Sharon. I turned towards her and saw that she wasn't looking at Luke but at me. Her expression was blank, her eyes narrowed slightly and her mouth open as though she couldn't quite believe something. I thought she was going to speak to me but suddenly she stood up and walked out of the door without a word. She didn't look round, at either Luke or myself. I called after her but she had already gone. Hearing me call Sharon's name, Hazel gave me a quizzical look from the other end of the ward.

I stayed with Luke another ten minutes. I didn't know what Sharon's problem was but soon became restless thinking about her. I tried to imagine how this all must be for her but because it was completely different for her than it was for me I couldn't. In some respects it was far easier for me. I wondered if Sharon had met somebody recently, a man she couldn't bring herself to go out with, or who she was going out with but was feeling very guilty about. Maybe that explained it. The thought was unpleasant to me, more so than it ever had been and I wondered why. It was probably seeing Luke lying there in his featureless limbo, imagining Sharon with another man. I thought about Sharon and the other man going out for a long time. Getting married maybe. Coming here together to see Luke. Or maybe Sharon would make the decision that she couldn't come at all any more.

I said goodbye to Luke, and found Hazel to say goodbye to her too. I went to look for Sharon in the cafeteria, but it was empty except for a young man in a white coat reading a fat paperback over a cup of coffee. I found her on a bench by the lake. Her hands were folded into the sleeves of her sweater. I sat next to her and prised one of her hands out, holding it between mine, rubbing it. I'd wanted to cheer her up but it wasn't sadness that I saw on her face. It was more like contempt. Contempt mixed with anger. I let go of her hand, which was as cold and unresponsive as Luke's had been on the few occasions I had ever taken hold of it.

'You OK?' I said, after a second or two.

'Yes.'

'Yes?'

Sharon let out a breath and turned her head away, towards a muffled-up old man who was being led slowly around the lake by a middle-aged woman.

'Sharon,' I asked her, 'is there something you want to tell me? I mean, if there is, you can. In fact, I want you to.'

Sharon turned, and looked at me.

'I mean it,' I assured her. 'You can. Really.'

She nodded to herself. She thought for a second and then looked at me with hard, measured eyes.

'Billy,' she said, 'what do the doctors say about Luke?'

The question threw me. She knew what they said.

'They say he's in a PVS.'

'And what does that mean?'

'Well, they say that he has no control of any of his physical faculties, but that they are uncertain as to any level—'

'Billy,' Sharon said, cutting me off. There was an edge to her voice. 'What do they say about recovery? About the chances of Luke waking up again?'

It was my turn to look away. 'The whole subject is open to debate,' I said. 'I've read about it. Occasionally someone is misdiagnosed and—'

'How occasionally? How occasionally is that, Billy?'

'Christ,' I said, 'I don't know. But it happens. And the doctor says that Luke isn't suffering at all. Not at all. So I see no reason why they shouldn't keep him alive, just in case, you know. It happens, it does . . .'

'Oh Billy,' Sharon said, her voice full of anger, 'I can't stand it! I can't stand it when you talk to Luke as if he's going to get better. I can't bear it!'

'Sharon . . .'

'Trips to Australia, going to see the football, oh God, Billy, it's so stupid of you! It's so stupid! He's never going to go away with you, or act again, or watch Nottingham bloody Forest. He's not. I wish you wouldn't speak like that. Every time you do it's like a wall is put up in front of me. It's killing me, Billy! It really is.'

I was shocked. Sharon was looking at me with some-thing approaching hatred. Her eyes filled and her mouth trembled but she held on to it. I didn't know what to say.

'I don't understand . . .'

'Billy,' Sharon went on, ignoring me. 'You don't have to turn his machines off. You don't.' She took a breath. 'Because he's dead. Luke's dead. He is. He is. He's dead now and you just keep on pretending he isn't. We meet up all the time and you just pretend Luke couldn't make it, that he'll be along next time, that he's got a cold or some-thing! But he hasn't got a cold. He's dead.'

Sharon's eyes filled up completely this time and I put a hand on her shoulder, but she shrugged it away as though it was painful to her. She moved further down the bench. I moved closer to her but she pushed herself off from the bench and ran into the trees. I saw her stop on the other side of the man-made lake and sit against a tree with her head in her hands. I couldn't hear her crying but it was only a small tree Sharon was leaning against and the rocking motion she was making disturbed the last of the flame-coloured leaves clinging to the thin, dark branches, leading several of them to lose their hold and float down to the floor around her. I turned my eyes away from her, to the ducks diving in the dirty brown water.

My brother wasn't dead. I understood why Sharon said what she had but she was wrong. I wasn't going to get mad with her, or think badly of her, but I couldn't help her either, not if that was the way she was choosing to deal with it. I felt sure now that someone else was involved. I was disappointed that killing Luke in her mind was the only way Sharon could deal with his presence in her life.

But then, I had always known how practical a person she was, how she dealt with things decisively before they took control of her. It was her way of getting on with her life, of not allowing what happened to Luke to claim her as well. I knew that. But I saw her as ruthless, the way she could decide to end something like that, to shut out my brother. I pictured her set face as she had walked out of the ward, not even turning to look at Luke.

I found myself thinking of Peter Morgan. I wondered if he had told his wife about employing me. I wondered what she had said. Leave it. Just accept it. Accept what happened, however bad it was. Don't make it worse for yourself by living in the past, raking over things you can't change. Maybe that's why I felt such sympathy for him, because he couldn't do this. Because he had lost his brother like I had and all he was left with was an image. The only difference was that the image he had was of blood, and sharp glass, and semen, while mine was of a greying young man who was still alive but equally motionless, whole but completely severed from himself. Present, a hundred yards away, but lost. Lost as a kid on a street corner.

When she was calmer Sharon walked back towards me. Her face was set hard again. We got into the car. We drove back into London with a pregnant silence joining the remnant of scent left from Luke's flowers. The roads were busier now, and it was slower going. As night fell I realized that I hadn't put the clock in my car back the night before. I did it with one hand as I drove along, feeling sad that it would be dark so early from now on. I made that point to Sharon but she didn't answer me. I turned the radio on, but every channel sounded tinny and annoying so I gave up on it. Once or twice, I glanced at Sharon in the passenger seat, but she kept her gaze fixed at nothing through her side window and wouldn't look at me. After the third time, I didn't look over again.

I pulled up outside Sharon's flat in Ladbroke Grove. It was residents' parking but as it was Sunday I was fine. I didn't have to leave the car there long however. When I went to undo my seat belt Sharon reached out a hand to stop me.

'I think I want to be on my own.'

'Right,' I said. 'Right.'

Sharon waited for a second. She looked at me for a long time, studying my face. Her look was one of complete self-control, the way you look when you've made a decision no one can talk you out of. A decision which has made itself.

'Billy,' she said, in a measured voice. 'I'm sorry for shouting at you. But I have to change things. We both have to. We keep going round the same circle. I need . . .' Her voice tailed off.

I didn't say anything. Sharon took my silence as a rebuke and said, by way of a wounded justification, emphasizing each word:

'I'm not very happy, Billy.'

Her voice accused me. I started to speak but Sharon was out of the car before I could say anything. I fumbled for my seat belt but I was already too late to catch her. I gave up and watched her run over to the block of converted flats she lived in, then fumble for her door key. *I'm not very happy*. What the fuck did she think I *was*? I watched her open the door hurriedly and let it swing behind her, keeping sight of her as she ran towards the stairs, until the door closed. I wondered how long it would be before I saw her again. When the door clicked shut I stared at it for a second and then I was aware, suddenly, of the lingering scent from the flowers which had been on the back seat and were now in a cheap plastic vase a foot above my brother Luke's head. The scent was cloying, insistent. I opened my window to get rid of it.

So, I thought, I'm dead too.

A light came on in her flat. A figure walked towards the window and drew the heavy curtains against the oncoming night. And me. I reversed up and pulled the car out into the street. I managed to scrape the side of a BMW parked too far out from the kerb, and its alarm went off, an outraged scream like a chisel rammed into my head. Fuck it. I drove back across London to Clerkenwell.

My flat was empty and I didn't want to be there. I went down to the Old Ludensian, and Nicky shut the place early because I was the only customer and why waste the electricity? We sat at the bar, the tables stacked high with chairs casting twisted shadows from the streetlights on the pillars and the whitewashed brick walls. Nicky didn't ask me about Carla so I didn't tell him. We drank a few beers. I'd meant to tell him about what had happened at the hospital but found myself not wanting to. I wound up telling him all about Teddy Morgan and then about Dominic Lewes.

We got talking about the whole gay thing. Nicky confessed to me that he had actually had a fling with a guy on Rhodes, where he'd gone after breaking up with a girl-friend. I was surprised; Nicky had the most heterosexual life of anyone I knew. He told me that he had never felt that way about any other man, but still found himself thinking about the tall American from Kansas whom he had fallen for. He said that the whole thing had confused him at the time and still did, especially when he started getting serious about a girl. He looked troubled, and suddenly embarrassed.

'You needn't worry, by the way,' he assured me. 'He was blond.'

I laughed and told Nicky that I was shocked and offended that he had never considered me as a sexual partner. Then I wondered if I would ever, *ever* meet anyone whose life was simple and straightforward, who could live happily in mind and body. I wished that we could somehow find a way to circumvent the body, the power it has over us to make us miserable. To trap us, like Luke was trapped, or Peter Morgan was; unable to live in his body, making only brief, clandestine sorties. What it would be like if we could either be free of the body or else free of the guilt we feel at some of the demands the body makes. I wondered what it meant that I spent hours in the gym, causing myself pain, trying to get my body to obey my commands. I wondered what it would be like to have the need to do that, not to yourself, but to others. To have power over other bodies.

Nicky and I drank another beer and sat in silence for a while. A car drove by, sending the shadows from the stacked chairs running across the walls like a hoard of demons. I left Nicky to his thoughts and went home to mine.

Chapter Thirteen

On Monday I got to my office before nine, had two slices of toast with coffee and waited for the mail. There was a time when the mail came before you even thought about getting out of bed in the morning. Now you have to wait for it.

I wrote a list of things to do. I left two messages for Sir Peter to call me and then typed out a letter to Mrs Lewes. I told her that her son was physically fit and seemed to be living in a house which had electricity and was heated. I told her that he had dyed his hair, which would explain his appearance in the pictures I was sending. I didn't want her thinking I was sending her photographs of somebody else's child. I slid the letter into a hardback A4 envelope, addressed it, and resolved to pick the pictures up from Carl later in the day. I wrote a letter to a man who owed me some money but then tore it up when a cheque from him was included in the mail, which arrived at about half past nine. It was accompanied by a letter addressed to a Mr J. Brinsford, the previous occupant of my office who, I knew for a fact, had emigrated to Sydney four years ago. It was from the Renault people who valued him highly as a customer and wanted to offer him the chance to test-drive the new Renault Megane. The only other letter was a bill for business rates which, unfortunately, was addressed to me.

Once I had dealt with the mail, thoughts of Sharon drifted into my head. They made me feel weighted down and slow, as though someone had replaced my blood with mercury. I began to run through the events of the previous day, pausing and rewinding, seeing her set face, feeling her shrug away under my hand, hearing the sound she made as her tears fought with her words for space. I had just got to the point when she ran off towards her flat when the shrill tone of the phone brought me back to the present. It was Morgan. He sounded excited and worried at the same time until I assured him that I hadn't called him for anything important.

'I need a favour,' I told him.

'Anything,' the MP replied. People seldom mean that.

'It's not a lot but you're the only person in the Commons I know.'

'I'm not in the Commons today, I'm afraid, I'm at the Treasury.'

'That doesn't matter,' I said. 'What I need to know is how to get hold of the register of Members' outside interests.'

'Ah,' the MP said, raising the pitch of his voice, 'you want to see if I'm involved in the arms trade. Or if I earn so much you can put your fee up. Well, I'm sorry to disappoint you but once you get to be a Minister you have to give up any other jobs you might do, and since our great humbling I haven't had time to line up any plum directorships. Yet. Come back in six months.'

There was a lightness to his tone which I hadn't heard before. I liked it. 'Sorry to disappoint,' I said. 'But it's not you I'm interested in, I'm afraid.'

Sir Peter said that it would be easier if he got his assistant at the Commons to photocopy the relevant page for me; I could pick it up from his office there rather than going rooting through the register myself. I also asked if he knew Graham Lloyd's address and he said he didn't but that it wouldn't be too difficult to find out. He would get his assistant to include it with the photocopy I was to pick up. I wondered if that was a good idea, letting his assistant see how much I was interested in Graham Lloyd's background, but Sir Peter laughed.

'No,' he assured me. 'It's all right. Thomasina's not what you'd call quick on the uptake. No, and to be perfectly frank I've never had a parliamentary assistant who was. I get them foisted on me by my constituency association. They tend to be the daughters of the ladies who organize the garden party fund-raisers which keep us afloat, the ladies who can get me thrown out on my ear any time they like. Pretty girls, all MPs' wives before they're twenty-five. It's perfectly all right, I assure you.' He stopped to think for a second. 'I'd worry if I was on the other side though. The Labour lot get brilliant assistants, LSE interns on their way to the *Guardian* or *The Economist*. He laughed. 'They're normally a damn sight quicker on the uptake than the idiot MP they're working for.'

I picked up a sealed brown envelope from Thomasina, who was indeed very pretty and dressed in a Chanel suit which must have cost about twice her monthly salary. Somehow, I didn't think her current job was her chief source of income. I walked back to my car and sat behind the steering wheel, using my nail to tear the envelope open, and then emptied the contents out on to the passenger seat.

Under Graham Lloyd's name was a list of three companies, none of which meant anything to me. They soon would though. At the bottom of the sheet was an address only five minutes' drive away over Vauxhall Bridge. As Lloyd had a London constituency I assumed that this was his only house but I made a mental note to check. I stuffed the sheet back into the envelope and pulled out into the traffic.

I actually drove over Westminster not Vauxhall Bridge and then down the Kennington Road. The square Lloyd lived in was on the left and I pulled into it and cruised round looking at the house numbers. The square was a little Georgian oasis in a dismal area of high-rises and big trunk roads wheezing carbon monoxide over small utility shops protected by steel meshes. Planted straight inside it, and ignoring the insistent groan of traffic, you might have thought you were in the middle of a prosperous town in the shires; the square was tree-lined, full of Volvos and Mercedes, and there was a rustic-looking pub in the corner. It seemed an ideal place for an MP to live.

The houses all had big, smartly painted doors with large brass knobs on, the kind that sit in the middle of the door and which you use to pull the door shut after you. The doors were either red, blue, or in the case of number 12, bright yellow. I stopped the Mazda outside number 12 and looked at the house for a second. Lloyd seemed to be doing all right if he could afford to live there. The house had three floors and wasn't broken up into flats as far as I could see, and there would be a sizeable garden out the back. I wondered if Lloyd's wife was in. I wondered what she would say if she knew that the man sitting in the conspicuously old and dirty car in the street outside was investigating the possibility that her husband, who was definitely involved with another woman, was also involved in the brutal murder of a fellow MP's brother. She'd hold her Marigolds up in horror.

I decided that it would serve no purpose telling Mrs Lloyd who I was. I'd only come because it was close, and I wanted to see the style to which Lloyd had become accustomed to living in. I pulled away from the house and drove back round to the Kennington Road, which was the only way in or out of the square. As I waited for a gap in the traffic I noticed the street name bolted to a brick wall, and only then appreciated the irony of Lloyd's address. He lived on Cleaver Square. Close. Close enough.

I drove back up the Kennington Road but didn't turn off towards Westminster. I eventually crossed over Southwark Bridge and headed up past Bank. The IRA have made this area virtually impossible to park in but I knew of an extortionate car park near Spitalfields Market where I left the Mazda, very glad I was on expenses. Thinking of the feeling that I'd had the other day at King's Cross I made sure it was all locked up and then walked up past Liverpool Street station to the City Road.

Company's House is a big building but not as impressive as you might think it should be, bearing in mind that within it are details of every business in the land. I had been there several times before and went straight to the reference section where I chose a table. I sat down and pulled the various pieces of paper from the envelope Thomasina had given me, laying the top one down on the table and putting the others back. I pushed the envelope aside and looked at the parliamentary register's entry for Graham Lloyd MP.

Carlson Holdings. Consultant. Part time.

Chalmers and Broge. Parliamentary Consultant. Part time.

The Buckner Group. Directorship.

On the table I was sitting at were two terminals. I moved in front of the nearest one to me and gazed at the screen which was displaying a menu of options. I moved the blinking green icon down the list to 'Company Search' and pressed 'Enter'. I then typed in 'Carlson Holdings' and hit 'Enter' again. The screen changed to one headed by the title 'Carlson Holdings PLC', with a list of information underneath.

Carlson Holdings was a very big company dealing in bonds and derivatives. It had a turnover greater than that of some small countries but only employed a hundred and fifty people. I took down the address and the phone number. I repeated the procedure for Chalmers and Broge and was told that it was basically a lobbyist company. They had only twelve full-time employees and their turnover was infinitesimal compared to that of the holdings company. Then I typed in 'Buckner Group'. The Buckner Group was also a small company, but it was involved in what the computer very unhelpfully termed 'Investments'. It didn't say what sort. The company was less than two years old and no figure was given for its annual turnover. It was based in Maidstone and the computer didn't tell me how many people worked there. I took the address and phone number down and then packed up my envelope and headed back to the lobby, where there was a public telephone in a conveniently soundproof booth.

'Hello, Personnel.' The voice, a young woman's with a bad cold, sounded bored. 'Juliet speaking.'

'Yes, hi there, Juliet,' I said, 'it's Fulton here from Accounts.'

'Who?'

'John Fulton, I'm sure we've met.'

'Oh, hello, Mr Fulton, sorry, I was a bit confused. The switchboard said it was an external call.'

'Christ, are the phones still doing that? Wondered what that noise was. Anyway, we're having a problem with some invoices. MP fellow, name of Lloyd. Graham. Wants to know why we haven't paid him for some work he did, when we think we already have.'

'Bloody cheek!' Juliet was quite appalled. 'Should spend more time running the country if you ask me rather than working on the side all the time the way they do.'

'Now then, Juliet. Anyway, can you give me a list of the days he's worked since this time last year, then we can clear this up.'

'OK, Mr Fulton. I'll phone you back. It'll take me a while, I'm not used to this new system yet.'

'I'd rather hold if you don't mind, Juliet, got to get this sorted.'

'Righto.'

I waited five minutes and I was afraid I was going to run out of change for the phone, but Juliet eventually came back on the line.

'Right,' she said, sniffing. 'He worked a total of thirty-six days since November the first last year. OK?'

'Wonderful. Thanks, Juliet.'

'Thanks, Mr Fulton.' She paused a little nervously. 'See you on the third.'

'The third?'

'At the ball, silly.' She giggled delightfully.

'Of course! Save the last dance for me.'

I went out for more change.

'Accounts. Alan speaking.'

Alan sounded like he also had a virus. Must be something going round the office.

'Yes, hello, Alan, Fulton here, Personnel. Got put through the switchboard for some reason.'

'Sorry, who?'

'Fulton. Now listen, Alan, Juliet and I are having a spot of bother down here.'

'Oh,' Alan said, 'how is Juliet?'

'Fine, Alan, she's fine. Except the Chief's in a stink, wants to cut back on freelance expenditure. So, we need to know some wage figures before he can decide which consultants to call in for the budget thing.'

The budget thing?

'All right, who were you thinking of?'

'Lloyd, Graham. MP I think. Your new system tell you that, can it?'

'Don't talk to me about this piece of shit.'

'Now then, Alan.'

'Just a mo there.'

Alan was a whiz with the new system whatever his reservations about it. He was back in no more than a minute.

'Seven-fifty the day,' he said.

'Thanks, Al. Most helpful. See you on the third.'

'The third?'

'The ball, stupid.'

'Oh God, yes. Yes.'

He paused for a second and lowered his voice.

'Fulton, you wouldn't happen to know if Juliet was going, would you?'

So, Lloyd was earning twenty-five grand p.a. from Carlson Holdings. I couldn't get anything out of the secretary I spoke to at Chalmers and Broge who immediately asked me if I was a journalist, and when I tried the Buckner Group all I got was an answerphone. It didn't matter. The twenty-five from Carlson plus whatever thanks a lobby firm give to a well-placed politician, *and* however much he made investing through the Buckner Group meant that Graham Lloyd was well enough off. There was also the salary I was helping to pay. He wasn't quite the Duke of Westminster but he was doing all right. It was disappointing but I hadn't realistically thought that I'd stumble on a motive as obvious as that. Graham Lloyd certainly didn't need to kill anyone for their wife's money. Oh well.

So he had nothing to do with it. I didn't totally dismiss the idea, but I could no longer see a reason why Lloyd should kill Teddy Morgan. The affair was just a coincidence which for various reasons neither he nor Charlotte Morgan wanted to let on about. Teddy may have known about the affair but he didn't sound like the sort of man who would stand in the way if his wife wanted a divorce, and so need removing. Lloyd had no motive and was in the States at the time of the murder. The man outside The Colt must just have been a man outside The Colt.

Even if he wasn't, the fact that Lloyd had hired a man to keep watch on a detective cum blackmailer who was very possibly out to fuck his life up, didn't make him a murderer.

The killer had to be the man in the baseball hat but I was still bothered by the idea. I just couldn't figure why he had let people at the airport see him, let alone stroll in front of a security camera with the victim. It just didn't seem very clever compared with the other murders. It meant that Sir Peter could still be right about a copycat killer riding the fame of another man, but the cat was not Graham Lloyd.

I ate lunch at a nearby Prêt à Manger and read the sign which said you could call either of the two bosses any time if you had any complaints. I had none, so I didn't, but I thought it was good that you could do that if you wanted to. I wondered how many calls they actually got. I wished you could do the same thing with British Telecom. Or British Rail. Phone the Chief Executive when your phone was cut off after you've paid the bill, or there was engineering work on the line when you'd been specifically told there wouldn't be. They'd get a few calls. I also wished you could phone whoever it is that organizes things so that airline pilots get carved up in their own homes, by someone who was looking increasingly likely to get away with it. Or who decides that people should have lovers in comas and not be able to deal with it any more. Or deal with the person who reminded them of it. It would be good to talk to that person. Very good. Or, rather, it would be good to talk to that person and for them to give you some answers.

I drove home and picked up the pictures of Dominic Lewes from Carl. I sent them off to his mother. I changed out of the suit I was in. I pulled on a pair of jeans, a T-shirt and my work jacket, and I spent the rest of the day walking round pubs asking if anyone had seen either of the men in the two photographs I was carrying.

Chapter Fourteen

In fact, I spent the rest of the week doing that. It was all there was left to do, and if it weren't for Graham Lloyd I would have got on to it much earlier. I went from pub to café to pub. When you're working on your own you just have to keep searching in the most likely places, hoping that the right person shows up. You have to leave a trail of messages for someone who may never see them, or want to contact you even if they did. There was a man out there looking for gay men and I had to go to the places he was likely to find them and hope our paths crossed. I could almost feel him out there and I wondered if he could feel me, my presence, searching for him. I hoped he could. I wondered all the time if I had already spoken to someone who knew what was going on. It annoyed me to think that I had very possibly been as close as two feet to the truth, that it resided in the thoughts of someone I had interviewed, right there, locked away behind a mere inch of skin and skull. I thought how far away and inaccessible people can be, even when you're sitting next to them. I remembered being a child, thinking that everyone must surely be able to see my secrets, the dark things I wanted.

I made a list and walked up and down various parts of London with the two photographs in my pocket. One was of Edward Morgan and the other was of the man who had probably killed him. I started in Islington, at the Edward VI near the Angel, and The Hart in Canonbury. In each pub I left a copy of the video-still behind the bar. I went to The Moorland Tavern and across Highbury Fields to The Cooper's Arms off the Blackstock Road. These were the gay pubs nearest to Edward's house and I tried them to find out if he had popped in any of them recently, either because he was a regular or because he was curious. Much to the chagrin of several of the men I talked to, he hadn't been seen in any of these places. Neither had the man in the baseball cap.

This kind of work can be very boring indeed but the fact that it was pubs I had to go and sit in meant it wasn't so bad. I'd chat to the barman for a while and then ask him if either Edward or the other man ever came in there. Others around the bar would notice the pictures the barman was peering at, and they would often come over to have a look at them themselves. If not, I took the pictures round. Once I had assured them that I was not the Old Bill come to arrest them for kissing in public (yes, it happens) they were usually very co-operative, and happy to help me.

In every pub I went to, at least some of the people recognized the picture of Edward, but it was only from the newspapers which carried the same one a few months ago. You would normally expect news stories, however lurid, to fade from the memory, but the people I was talking to had a very good reason to remember Edward's face. There was a respectful, even reverential hush whenever a group of men gathered round to take a look at the pictures. I could see them imagining what it must have been like for Edward, many of them knowing that it could have been a picture of them that a private detective was showing around the gay pubs and bars of London. One man, sitting in a chrome-filled café on Camden High Street, even said it, and seemed to age ten years as he did so: there but for the grace of God go I.

For the first three days I walked into a lot of pubs, met a lot of people but didn't get anywhere. It was frustrating, but patience is the primary requisite of my job and I didn't mind it too much. I know it's a bit of a cliché but gay bars are almost always a lot more friendly and easy to be in than most of the regular ones. People were polite and helpful and I believed them when they told me, either from behind a bar or in front of it, that they would keep an eye out for the man in the hat and would phone me if they saw him.

One guy said, 'He's like a virus amongst us, something which will kill you if you don't look out. He preys on loneliness and youth, the need to be with someone, feel another person's skin next to yours. You need to give love and he's waiting until you do it so that he can take your life. He's like AIDS. Except how will I know how to protect myself against him?'

I gave him a copy of the picture to keep.

'Remember his face,' I said. 'That's how.'

'And you're sure that's him?' the man asked hopefully.

'No,' I admitted. 'No, I'm not sure.'

'Well then,' the man said. He took the picture anyway.

Because I couldn't think of any other way of exploring the option that Edward had been killed by someone trying to fit it into the pattern of the other murders, I plugged away with the photo. My job had become as simple as it normally is: I had a face to find and all I had to do was look. I went to Clapham, Hampstead, Brixton, Westbourne Park, Notting Hill Gate. I spent hours sipping pints and chatting to people. I got hit on a few times and whenever I did I couldn't help thinking of Nicky and his American. I revisited places I had already been to and I had to get Carl to run me off some more copies of the picture, I had handed out so many. Some people said that the police had been round already. They laughed amongst themselves, remembering obviously uncomfortable coppers who they could just tell felt like mice in a snake's nest. They were easy to spot because they couldn't even bring themselves to pretend they were gay. I found it sad to think that they cared more about being mistaken for a poof than they did about finding a maniac before he could kill someone else.

I worked hard but only got one hit. A middle-aged man, in a pub on Old Compton Street, said he thought he may have seen the man, but then changed his mind quickly. I thought he might have changed it on purpose, in fact I was pretty sure he had, and I got quite excited. I asked the man if he was sure. Yes, he was. He told me he had to use the toilet and when he didn't come back after five minutes I could have kicked myself. He'd done exactly what I'd done to Lloyd. The fire escape was open and when I chased out of it on to Dean Street all I could see was a few hardy souls sitting outside a café and a waiter sneaking a fag break in a doorway. I wondered why he had legged it, why recognizing the man had caused him to panic. Was he scared? He didn't look it. Ashamed maybe? I made a mental note of his face in case I ran in to him again. I never did. None of the other patrons of the pub had seen him before.

Sitting in various pubs, bars and cafés I sometimes thought about Lloyd, and tried again to see if there was anything I'd missed out concerning the charming MP. I racked my brains for a way to get to him, to connect him with the man in the hat. I couldn't think of a way. I could, of course, let the police know about his affair, and I did resolve to do that when I ran out of anything else to do. It was, after all, the only thing of note I had managed to find out. It wouldn't do much good though, I knew. If he was innocent it would just cause a lot of embarrassment and if he was guilty it wasn't really much in the way of evidence against him. All it would do was cause him grief, which I wasn't too concerned about, but it would cause Edward's widow a whole lot too.

I called Sir Peter, having forgotten to check up on Lloyd's alibi, and he confirmed that Lloyd had been away when Edward was killed. Sir Peter's cheerfulness had vanished, a temporary blip on a downward slope, and my lack of progress didn't cheer him up any. I told him what I'd done and he insisted that I had to go on until there really was nothing more I could think of doing. I felt there was something masochistic about his fervour, as though he was punishing himself. I told him that I needed another cheque if I was to continue and he was more than willing to send me one. He sounded very depressed and I got the feeling that finding his brother's killer was all that he could think about now. He then told me something which proved that I was right. Sir Peter Morgan was resigning from the Tory front bench and retreating to the relative safety, as he put it, of the back benches. He might even chuck it all in completely, he said.

Spurred on by Sir Peter's unsettling determination I took a day off from the bars and pubs and interviewed some of the stewardesses Edward had flown with. Apart from glowing descriptions and in one case a flood of tears, I didn't get anything out of them. I spoke to the steward

Michael Chalkley had told me about and he said that he did go to the Pavilion Bar now and then, and he sometimes met men there. That meant that it could well have featured as a potential pick-up place for the killer, even though it was risky. But how, I wondered, would he have known about it? It certainly wasn't in the *Time Out Guide to Gay London*.

I thought about talking to Charlotte Morgan again but I knew it wouldn't lead anywhere, not if I couldn't find the man in the hat. One lunchtime I got a call from Andy Gold, and he met me at Mike and Ally's café for lunch.

Andy looked very tired, and unusually subdued. He picked at his sandwich and only made a half-hearted attempt to get me to tell him the information he suspected I was keeping from him. We chatted about old times, cases we had worked on together. He told me that he was sick of police work. He had been taken off the gay killer case and reassigned to something even more nasty, if that was possible. Somebody, other than their parents, was meeting young girls from school, apparently offering them modelling contracts, and then taking them for photo shoots. He may have taken some pictures for all the police knew but what he did then was almost too disgusting to imagine. There had been two so far and one lucky escape.

Andy said, 'It's not the bodies. They don't get me any more, they really don't. It's the family. The dad looking bewildered, the mother hysterical, a little sister who'll stay lost in the middle of her head for ever. The photo on the mantelpiece. And worse, we never learn. Something happens and we fix it and then there's something else that happens which we haven't thought of. There's always something else, some new way some poor fuck's going to cop it. Thinking ahead is too expensive, it pisses too many people off without apparent just cause. All we do is clean up after the shit's already been shat, then spray pretty-sounding words around to kill the smell. What's the fucking point of it?'

'Don't ask me,' I said. 'I left, remember?'

Andy gave me a set of keys to the Morgans' flat in Canonbury, and that night I took the short drive over there. Teddy's Rover was still in the garage, as was Charlotte's car. She hadn't been able to bring herself to go back there, even for that. I noted the scrapes of paint on the Rover's wheel arch and the slight dent in the side of the Golf. I walked through the garage and into the apartment the way I assumed Teddy and his guest had gone. The apartment was dark but for the orange light of a lamppost spreading in through the open curtains. I closed the curtains, flicked a switch and walked into the middle of the living room.

The flat was very large for two people. The floor was Norwegian pine and the walls were an off-white broken up by modern prints and the odd original. There was a Chesterfield sofa, a coffee table and two armchairs. The place was far more to my taste than Charlotte's mews cottage had been and I wondered if actually she was borrowing that from a friend, or had rented it complete. I liked the simplicity of the place, the roomy feel to it. I felt perhaps that my flat could look like a miniature version of it, if I ever got round to making that trip to Ikea.

I checked out the bathroom and then the bedroom. The forensics people had taken away the bedroom carpet, the bed, and all the sheeting so there was no sign of the events which had taken place there. There was a faint smell though: someone had closed the windows a little too early, and it's not the sort of smell you could ever forget once you'd encountered it. It was faint, the tart iron of blood mixed with that of old sex, and excrement, and something else, something indefinable but very present nevertheless. It was the smell, not just of death, but of violent death.

I stayed in the flat for a while, poking around, opening cupboards, not really knowing what I was looking for. I found a box containing four bottles of champagne and thought of the forensics report I'd read. I listened to the silence which seemed to ring from the walls, the indiscernible echoes of vicious blows and terrible screams. I sat back on the sofa and closed my eyes and tried to picture what had happened to Edward, patching together everything I knew about him and his last day alive, filling in the gaps with movements that I thought were the most probable.

I saw him at the airport. I saw him at the bar and then on the way home. I saw him smile. I saw him sitting where I was sitting now, with another man by his side. I managed to put together a scenario, complete with dialogue, one which I knew was plausible enough but could never be exactly right. Even if I had got the broad facts, and put them in roughly the right order, what I saw was only guesswork, a model which I had built simply to help me. Only two people ever knew what really happened in this flat. Only they really saw it. I was looking for one man so that I could ask him, but even if I found him he was hardly likely to tell me. And as for the other, I was sure that he would have been more than willing to speak to me if he could, but he would never be able to tell me. This flat, which was so full of his things, his clothes in the closets, half-empty bottles of after-shave, a brand new tennis racket, seemed so full of him I felt like saying, 'Teddy, who killed you, who was it?' The clothes and the scent and the tennis racket could make no answer to me.

I knew that sitting there moving different figures through my mind was just a fiction, but for some reason it seemed to help. It struck me that Edward's killer, in spite of the apparent frenzy of his actions, was someone perfectly in control of himself. He had waited until he was in the bedroom. Going into the bedroom is the last thing you do with someone. It was the last thing Edward had done. They had apparently been in the bath together, the man must have been itching to kill Edward then but he hadn't. He was a man with composure, a man able to deny himself something until the exact moment when it would give him most pleasure. It was this, I knew, which was making it so difficult for either the police or myself to find him.

Sitting in Edward's flat, and thinking of the person I felt I now knew, depressed me immeasurably. This easy-going man had, as far as I could tell, inspired only affection in all the people I had spoken to. I thought about his killer again and got a physical pang of hatred for him, for his cynicism, for his shrivelled and petrified heart. I wanted to catch him far more than I had done before, talking to his brother over the crème brûlée. I left the flat and knocked on the doors of some of the neighbouring flats and houses. I spoke to a few people who had nothing to tell me, no suddenly recalled flashes they hadn't relayed to the police. No one had seen anything or heard anything. The people were all unwilling to talk to me, annoyed that I had come round to remind them that they lived next door to the house where such a horrible thing had happened. One old man even looked at me suspiciously. He made the point that murderers often came back to the scene of their crimes. He closed the door a little once he had thought of this, and glanced back into his hallway. I got the feeling that as soon as I had gone he would phone the police. I didn't want to get Andy into trouble for giving me the flat keys so I got in my car and drove home before I could find out.

I dropped the keys off to Andy and went back to my round of the pubs with renewed determination. All that week and then the weekend too, and then Monday and Tuesday. I didn't do anything else or see anyone. Elbowing themselves into the spaces between the thoughts I was having about Edward Morgan and his death, were thoughts of Sharon. I hadn't seen or spoken to her. I left her a message which she didn't return, and I stopped myself at the last minute from leaving several more. It was obvious she didn't want to see me. I asked myself how I hadn't seen this coming, and then realized that I had in a way. It had been ages since we had been to see Luke together. Sharon never wanted to, saying it was better if we went on our own because that way he got more visits. It was me who suggested we drive out there together last Sunday. I kept seeing Sharon's face, remembering the times we had gone to the movies together or she had sat across from me at my table sipping wine, her teeth stained, her hair the colour of old Condrieu. I thought about going round to her flat, talking to her, trying to find out exactly what she thought, trying to make her see that she didn't have to abandon any hope that Luke would recover in order to get on with her life. I didn't go. I worked hard instead. I didn't really know what to say to her. I probably wanted to tell her she should live her life as a celibate, tragic heroine, stoic at the bedside of her fallen lover, waiting for the magic day when he would wake from his sleep and finally marry her. I couldn't say that so I didn't say anything.

To keep myself from brooding I hiked round London trying to catch a killer. The weather had turned from irritable to petulant, and then from that to sullen and miserable. It seemed dark all the time and London was dull and quiet, the streets clenched as people braced themselves for three months of freezing winter. The last of the tables disappeared from outside the cafés, the tennis courts and parks were emptying. The doorways which had held recognizable, sleeping forms in the summer, were now filled with mounds of old clothes and blankets which could have covered any number of people, or no one. Faces were tighter, bodies more tense, and there were less people hanging around to ask questions of. London itself seemed to hold on to its secrets tighter.

I had grown colder too. I kept myself to myself and got more and more depressed about both Sharon and Edward Morgan. I tried not to admit it but the case was going nowhere. No one had seen the man in the picture and in any case by now he had almost definitely changed his appearance completely. It was especially frustrating because I had become convinced, for no concrete reason that I could think of, that there was more to this than simply the latest instalment in a series of never-to-be-understood acts of savagery. There was, I knew it, but getting close to it was like trying to hold the shadow of a man who's left the room. I had nearly gone through the entire section of the *Time Out Guide to Gay London*, and once I had finished that I knew that there wasn't going to be anything else I could do to quell the doubts which were nagging at me like an ulcer. I trudged on, telling myself to think of the money, but after two and a half weeks of increasingly dull and aimless leg-work I had just about decided to give up on it.

But then one night I took the car down to the gym and did some training. Sal told me that she definitely hadn't seen the man in the picture I had given her a week and a half earlier. I went in with Mountain Pete. I watched a cocky boy who thought he was Naseem Hamed and noticed a look of fear on the face of another boy holding a big orange coat, who wasn't sure if he wanted to get into the ring with either of his friends, who were both a bit bigger than he was. I got in my car. I went to see Nicky, who I'd not seen for nearly two weeks, and then I went home to my bed, drifting off into sleep to the bitter honey of Nick Drake's ballads of death and longing.

And then a voice on my answerphone woke me from my dreams and I went to stand in the cold outside a freight depot behind King's Cross station, where the owner of the voice joined me and pointed a sawn-off shotgun at my head.

PART THREE

Chapter Fifteen

He was not, as far as I could tell, someone I'd met before. But he could have been. He'd stepped out from behind a trailer and I could barely make him out. What I could see was that he was tall, with a right arm strong enough to hold the weapon steady in one hand at arm's length. He was wearing what seemed to be jeans and a waist-length leather jacket.

And a baseball hat.

I didn't move. The night was very cold but suddenly I couldn't feel it. The man was backed by the blackened brickwork of the Victorian freight depot. He held the weapon steady as he took a step forward, his left foot dragging slightly as he did so.

'What the fuck do you want?'

It was the second time somebody had asked me that question recently. I still didn't have much of an answer to it. I was thinking what sort of a chance I'd have if I tried to bluff him out and get the gun off him. Not much.

He didn't seem upset that I hadn't answered his question. As he took another step forward his foot dragged again on the wet tarmac.

'Turn round.'

I didn't move. Turning round didn't seem like a wise

thing to do. I tried to find some spittle in the back of my throat.

'Listen,' I said, trying to sound casual, 'there's no need for this . . .'

'Shut the fuck up and turn around!' The voice was angry, nervous, not the sort you want with a finger behind it pressed against a trigger. I decided I may as well do what he said. He was standing far enough away that if I lunged for him he'd just blow my chest apart before I could reach him, and near enough that if I turned and made a pattern he couldn't easily miss if he wanted to blow a hole in my back.

Slowly, I edged round to the right until he was out of my frame of vision. I moved round some more and focused on the streetlight fifty yards across the road on York Way. I remembered speaking to a prostitute once, standing underneath that very lamppost. Why the fuck wasn't she there now? Why was there no one on the street at all? My throat was completely dry; I thought about it, but I couldn't have begged him if I wanted to. I did want to, and I would have if I'd thought it would have done any good. Why the hell not? But it wouldn't. I wondered if I would hear the shot. I wondered if I would even feel it. My stomach began to lurch, and then to tremble like there was a sparrow stuck in there. I suddenly became aware of an odour, a strong smell of aftershave. I couldn't tell which type. Through my fear I remember thinking, hey, that doesn't smell too bad.

I heard the foot scrape again. Then the entire freight depot fell on my head and the streetlight multiplied and spun around my eyes for a dazzling moment until every-thing was blackness.

*

When I came to I was inside.

Somehow I could tell this even though a thick canvas bag had been placed over my head and tied tightly round my neck with what I took to be a short length of rope. My hands were tied too, behind my back but not secured to anything. I was on a cold concrete floor. My head rang and I nearly threw up, which would have been a mistake given the bag. I could feel a cut on the back of my head where the butt of his gun had connected. I tried not to move, seeing if I could hear anything before my assailant knew I had woken up. He must have been watching me though and there's really nothing you can do to prevent the change in your body when you come into consciousness. I heard him stand up and push a steel chair aside violently which shrieked to a halt across the floor and then tipped over. I found myself pushing my feet against the floor, backing away from the sound that was coming towards me.

A hand grabbed my jacket and pulled me up. It then pushed me back and was replaced by two hands which jarred my back against the wall hard, three times in a row. I didn't resist except to try to keep my head from connecting. On the third time I was winded and started to cough violently. I was released and I kicked out, trying to get lucky where I thought his groin would be. I think I got the side of his leg and received a heavy, steel-capped toe in the ribs for my trouble. I curled up in pain, closing my arms on my sides, expecting more.

I heard the man step back and then take a few steps. There was a metallic sound and then another one much closer to me as the chair was set down and the man sat on it. There was silence for a second.

'I didn't think you were too bright. If you try anything else I'll blow your fucking bollocks off one by one.'

His voice was more controlled now, and mocking. It came to me muffled through the bag and my headache. I thought I caught a trace of North in it, Leeds maybe, from a long time ago. It was a white voice.

'Now then, Mr Rucker, I'm not very happy with you.'

'I guessed that.'

'Showing such a terrible photo of me around. It's a very poor likeness. I don't look very good at all.'

'You could let me have another one.'

'No. I've decided you're not going to be handing out any more photos.'

I heard the snap of a shotgun barrel as it was opened and shut again quickly.

'Not bad what you did to that flash coon Rollo though, I must say. I heard that some dentist somewhere is gonna make a nice few quid out of him. He'd wet his knickers if he knew I had you like this. He'd stick this fucking thing up your arse and you'd die with a smile on your face.'

The chair moved backwards and he came towards me.

'Me, I'm far more conventional.'

He gripped my jaw and forced the end of the gun barrel hard into my left eye, pushing my head back against the wall.

'What you know about me, hey?'

'Nothing.'

'No?'

'If I did I wouldn't be here like this, would I?'

'Maybe not. Maybe I'd be inside, hey, Rucker?'

'Maybe.'

'See, I know your name. Do you know mine?'

'Yeah, it's Cliff fucking Richard.'

He put his free hand round my neck, pushing it back and closing his fingers at the same time. I struggled for breath. I tried not to move too much, not knowing how much of a hair he kept his trigger on.

'It would be so easy,' he said. 'No one saw me come here, no one will see me leave.'

'My answerphone,' I said. 'Your voice is on it.'

'Clever. But it's not as if it'd make any difference if they did catch hold of me, would it?'

I didn't answer. He was right. He could kill ten more people and if they caught him for it he'd go away for exactly the same amount of time as if they caught him now.

'What have the Bill got?'

'Nothing,' I said. 'No one has anything.'

'Except the picture. You been pretty free with that, haven't you?'

I didn't answer that either. I tried to get my hands free without attracting his attention to the fact, but he'd done a pretty good job with them. I felt the grip on my throat relax and his body move back a little. The gun was still in my cheek and he pressed it in harder. I heard an assured click as he pulled the hammer back. I waited. I wouldn't hear the shot. I wouldn't feel it either.

We stayed like that for a long minute, the inside of the bag heating up more and more, the silence cut only by my own breathing and the small movements of the thick canvas. I wondered why he didn't just get it over with.

'Scared, Rucker?'

I was.

'Wish you'd stayed at home?'

I did.

'Wish you'd not gone round getting a bunch of shirts all excited with my pretty picture.'

I wished that too.

'Well, it's too fucking late, mate.'

He didn't say anything for a long time. I stayed in the present, I didn't think about anything profound. My mind didn't go anywhere. It turned off. All I could feel was fear, and pain great enough to force a way through it. I felt his hand round my neck again, this time at the back, pulling the rope tighter. I began to choke and I tried to struggle, realizing that he was going to do it that way. No noise. My struggling wasn't very effective but nevertheless he released the rope a bit, still holding it tight.

'No more pictures,' he said. 'Understand?' I was surprised. I tried to nod. He pushed the barrel even harder into my face. 'You're very lucky,' he said, in a voice that told me he was shaking his head. 'Very lucky indeed. I've heard you know certain people. If I hadn't heard that I wouldn't be telling you this. You'd have your brains splashed against this wall like some piece of modern fucking art.'

The way he was ramming the back of my head against the wall it felt like half my brain was smeared against it as it was. Sal, I thought, bless your cotton sweatpants. But surely she wasn't enough to stop him, was she? I didn't know. Right then I didn't care.

He still had hold of my jaw. He dug his fingers in and I could tell that his face was only a few inches away from mine. The face which had smiled at Edward Morgan, which had fooled a lorry driver, which had stood above the body of a schoolboy before its owner had ground a broken bottle into the remnants of the face it was looking down at. I got the strange sensation that somehow I had been in the state I was in now ever since I had started this case, ever since I had started handing out those pictures. The face was right in front of me but there was something in the way of me seeing it.

His hands relaxed and he moved away.

'You won't be lucky twice,' was all I heard him say.

Then the freight depot came down again.

I lay for a long time without trying to move. I had no idea how long I had been out this time but my whole body ached. I was dizzy with the thundering pain which was straining to burst my skull open and this time I did throw up. I gasped for air, finding it difficult to get the pieces of vomit out of my mouth, the thick canvas of the bag being sucked in every time I took a breath. I coughed and retched madly for a bit, panicked that I was going to suffocate, and then I made myself calm down and breathe through my nose. I listened for any sounds other than the ones I was making myself. I couldn't hear anything other than the slow movement of a car cruising down York Way. I lay still for a second, straining to hear if he was still there, waiting for me to try and get up. The place had an empty feel and I decided he'd left.

I was lying on my front, and I tried to turn over on to my side so that I could hook my hands under my feet. I winced at the pain in my side where he had kicked me and decided that he must have broken a rib or two. I rolled over on to the other side and managed to get my hands in front of me.

I undid the rope around my neck first and pulled the bag over my head, getting vomit in my eyes and in my hair. The air tasted good. I looked into the darkness and then scrunched the bag up and used the outside of it to wipe myself down quickly. I then moved my hands back and forth to create some slack and managed to pick at the many knots enough to be able to pull my left hand out. I loosed the slack on my right hand, threw it aside, and rubbed my wrists with the flats of my palms. Then I looked for a way out. I struggled to stand up, did it too quickly, and threw up again, a heave of bile which sent darts of agony spearing through my ribs. This time it was on the floor in front of me.

There wasn't much light in the place. I was surrounded by huge shapes which I took to be piles of boxes and container crates. I leant against one, waiting to make sure that I wasn't going to heave again. My stomach calmed down. I still couldn't see much. I fumbled around for a light switch without success. I bumped into the chair which the guy had been sitting on and realized that he must have been using a torch. He wouldn't have wanted any light to show from outside. The bag he'd used on me was heavy-duty canvas and I wouldn't have been able to tell if he'd been keeping me in broad daylight.

Eventually I found the door and managed to slide it open. I couldn't stop it making a loud, wrenching noise. I could see a huge, broken padlock hanging off it where he'd broken in. I stepped out cautiously into a courtyard. I was at the back of a building, with a dim security bulb casting deep shadows. I was nervous. I pulled up my sleeve and could just make out that it was now almost five thirty. There was no sign of the sun. I hesitated a second or two but reasoned to myself that if my attacker had wanted to kill me he wouldn't have waited until I was outside, with room to move, but would have done it when he had me tied up and blindfolded. Nevertheless, I looked cautiously round the corner before moving out into the space at the front of the depot. A sudden throb of pain in my head nearly took my legs away and I had to use the wall for support. Fuck it, a Brownie could have taken me out now if she'd wanted to. I pushed myself off the wall and walked awkwardly into the open space, towards the trailer which the man in the baseball hat had been hiding behind.

The trailer held no more unpleasant surprises for me. I passed it and walked out towards the street. The street-light was still there but this time there *was* a girl standing beneath it. I walked towards her, holding my head, and she must have thought I was a drunk the way I was moving.

'You got any money?'

She was frail and rather old. She wasn't attractive in any sense I could see. But then again, I wasn't exactly in the mood, no matter what she looked like. There would be men who were.

'Did you see a man,' I asked, pointing behind me, 'come out of there. Wearing a hat?'

'Fuck off,' the girl told me. I was too tired to argue with her.

My car was still where I'd left it. When I got to it I suddenly panicked, worried that he might have gone through my pockets for either my car keys or the money he'd told me to bring. The keys were still there but there was no money of course as I hadn't taken any with me. I wondered if he'd had a look and been disappointed. I didn't care. I just wanted to get home.

For a second I considered not driving. Two bangs on the head would rule me out as far as any medical expert would have been concerned, but there was no way I'd get a taxi anywhere. I got in and turned the key and nothing happened. I nearly began to cry. I waited and nothing happened again. I was about to stumble out, open the bonnet and take a look when I realized that I was on a slight incline, facing down towards King's Cross. I put the Mazda in gear, used both hands to release the handbrake and let her move forward. When she had picked up a bit of speed I pulled my foot off the clutch and the engine fired. I drove home very carefully, feeling like someone had installed the most powerful stereo in my car and turned the volume up to maximum. It was all bass, and my head was the only speaker.

I couldn't think about this. I just wanted to get into bed. As I drove along, pictures and sentences kept surfacing in my brain, but I just focused on the red lights and the road ahead and making sure I used the indicator when I turned right or left. I didn't want to get stopped. I got home slowly but without any trouble only to find that someone had taken my parking space. I parked in a delivery bay two streets away. I locked the car and walked down Exmouth Market to my flat. It was cold again and I shivered into a tunnel of wind, pulling my coat tight round me. I was tired, and as I got used to the throbbing in my skull my cheekbone began to hurt where the gun had been rammed into it. That pain was sharper and more defined and strangely comforting. The image of my bed was almost too much to bear now and I hurried myself along, holding one hand up to the cut on my cheek. It was wet with blood and I was surprised by that. My bed called to me; the sheets were still twisted round my form, the pillows packed together with a nest for my head. I'd take three Advils, get in, and all this would be a very bad dream.

My outside door was open. It was an inch ajar. Did I forget to lock it? I didn't think so but then I wasn't in the best frame of mind to remember a detail like that. I had been in a hurry. But when I looked closer I saw the lock had been forced. There was splintering on both the jamb and the door itself.

I pushed the door open a slice and peered up the stairs. Darkness. My hand moved towards the hall switch but I pulled it away. I listened. Nothing. I couldn't believe I'd been burgled. Maybe the man in the hat had set it up with some kids as a further warning that he could get to me. Maybe it was a fluke, a bizarre off-chance. What about Lloyd's goon? I stood, looking up the stairs, holding my breath, trying to figure out what was going on. I was vaguely aware that I was doing it to put off going up there. What if he'd changed his mind? What if he was up in my flat, sitting on my bed with his sawn-off shotgun in his hand? I still didn't really know why a man who had shown absolutely no compunction in killing at least three other men had let me go. What if he'd decided he didn't care who I knew?

I pushed the door open some more and stepped into the short, narrow hallway. I tried to remember if any of the stairs creaked at all. I stood at the bottom deciding what to do. Call the police? I didn't know. He couldn't have been up there, an idiot could have seen the state the door was in. What if nothing had been taken, what if he'd just done the door, done it himself after leaving me unconscious to show that he knew where I lived and he could break in when he felt like it? I'd look stupid if I called the police. I'd feel stupid.

I put a foot on the bottom stair. It didn't make any very loud noise and neither did any of the steps above it.

At the top of the stairs I saw that the door to my flat-proper had received the same treatment as the street door, only this door wasn't ajar but wide open.

I stopped again, peering into the darkness and up the stairs inside the door, which lead up to the studio. Again I couldn't hear anything. Again I had the same doubts and questions. I was afraid. No rationalization of the circumstances could quench the childish terror in me and my stomach started to flutter once more. I stepped forward and gripped the handrail, preparing myself for another meeting with a murderer, or the kind of mess I had witnessed in a lot of houses but never my own. Furniture everywhere, spray-can graffiti, drawers out, a turd or two among the debris. I walked up the stairs slowly.

I stopped in the doorway.

There wasn't a murderer in my flat. By the light of the anglepoise lamp by my bed, which I had left on, I could see that no one had ransacked it either. Or taken anything. My flat was exactly the same as I had left it, the drawers in, the furniture upright, and the walls still clear, with only the numbered Salgado print to decorate them. The only thing different was my bed.

On my bed lay a young man. He was naked, on his back. His arms were stretched up behind his head as though begging someone not to shoot him. He was covered in welts, cuts and bruises, and his stomach had been torn open. He had had his penis severed, and it lay on his chest, shrivelled up small, covered in blood like a newborn rat.

Chapter Sixteen

I stood in the silence of my room, my eyes pulled down to the body on my bed. I had a sudden flash of my brother, lying in what was left of my car, covered in blood. All of the pain I felt melted away and I found that I could neither move, nor take my eyes from the sight which had stopped me far more suddenly than any bang on the head. I felt a constriction in my chest and realized that I had stopped breathing, not wanting time to advance another second from where it stood now. I could taste the bile at the back of my throat and, when I did draw breath, the air was sickly sweet and so thick I could almost feel it against my tongue.

The boy was lying on top of my duvet with his face covered by a pillow. The duvet was drenched with his blood, especially beneath his belly, which was gouged open to its innards, with the skin pulled back to show his organs like an anatomical model. His torso and both his legs had been hacked at too, deep wounds running down the insides of his thighs from his groin to both of his knees.

The boy was a mess. I forced myself to take a step forward. And another. I found it difficult to take in what I was seeing. The smell grew stronger. The centre of my chest burned. I walked round and stood to the side of the raised futon. The lamp burned away happily. On the floor there was the bottom half of a wine bottle lying parallel to the boy's head. From the label I could see it was one of mine; it was the Grange, the Grange '86 which had cost a fortune and I'd been saving. The rug was stained deep red beneath it. I bent down to look closer but I didn't touch the bottle.

The top half of the bottle was rammed into the boy's throat. It was wedged in place between his chin and his breastbone. The pillow covering the boy's head was resting on top of it. The boy's head was propped forward by other pillows to create the pressure sufficient to hold the bottle in place. I could see behind the sides of the pillow; an ear, the side of a head. I put my hand on the pillow.

I didn't want to do this. I took my hand away and then I put it back. I took a breath before pulling the pillow off and setting it down on the floor next to the wine bottle. Then I turned my head back slowly and deliberately to look at the top of the bed.

I saw what I expected to see.

The boy was staring at a place high up above the door I had come through. His eyes were open but his mouth was shut, like he was watching a film at the cinema. He looked calm and unconcerned about what had happened to him. Only a little surprised. He looked casually unaware that he had half a broken bottle stuck in his throat, like a bank manager with his tie in his pint. His face was untouched. It was completely unmarked, the clear, simple features contrasting with the rest of his body which was covered in either slash wounds or the blood from them. I looked down at the face for some time, the full lips, the strong, dark eyebrows. He was looking away from me and I remembered how he had turned and looked away from me before. I bit into my bottom lip. On impulse I bent over and I ran my hand through the short, cheap vanilla ice-cream coloured hair. The vanilla went straight to the roots. I closed his staring eyes and walked over to the telephone.

I picked up the receiver and dialled three nines. I started to tell the girl that I needed the police but stopped when I heard a sound. It was the petulant whine of a siren, backed by an engine working too hard. It was close. It was getting closer. I told the girl to hold on, put the receiver on the table by the phone and walked over to the window. I made a hole in the blind. I was in time to see a squad car turn hard into my street and then I heard it screech to a stop outside my building. I heard two doors slam and hurried footsteps. I heard the footsteps stop at the bottom of the stairs.

I was in a flat with a corpse and I was covered in blood and vomit. Someone must have seen something going on, one of the postal workers from Mount Pleasant maybe, and called it in. Or else . . . I turned to the door and was suddenly confronted by Dominic. That thing on his chest. I wanted to cover him, take that bottle out of his throat, but I knew I couldn't do that. I waited for the sound of feet on the stairs and wasn't long in getting it.

I wanted to speak to them before they came running in and saw what there was to see in my flat. I hurried over to the door and got halfway down the first flight of stairs. I stopped before they turned into the door at the bottom, so that they wouldn't think I was trying to leg it. I wanted to tell the officers what they were going to see, to make sure they were rational and controlled about it. I wanted to tell them before they found it themselves. I wanted that to be on record.

I called out.

'Up here.'

A tall figure appeared at the door.

'There's a switch, just to your left. On the wall.'

A hand reached out and pushed the timer and the small bulb popped on. There were two of them, both about my age, a man and a woman, both staring up at me. I told them what was up in the flat behind me and that I had come home to find it. They both looked shocked, nervous. I told them they had nothing to worry about from me and that I wouldn't make any trouble. The WPC broke the silence by telling me to step back into the flat. She took a step towards me. I didn't much want to go back in there but I agreed.

I sat in the far corner, at the table, while the WPC made a brief examination of the body. The PC stood square in the doorway, glancing round anxiously at the windows in the front and the skylight to his right; any possible exits. Both of the officers were very efficient and neither of them made a scene or produced the torrents of vomit I have witnessed on similar, far less gruesome occasions. The PC was almost immediately on his radio reporting what he had found, asking for assistance, and I knew that very soon there wouldn't be a whole lot of room in my flat. By now, both officers were glaring at me, trying to decide if I really was going to cooperate with them and not try anything. Their faces told me that they didn't have any doubt as to what had happened here before they'd arrived.

I held my head, which was starting to thud again, the

contents of my room threatening to move on their own, to spin and merge into one another.

'You found him like this, is that what you're saying?'

Involuntarily, I followed her glance to my futon. It brought me back a little. 'Yes,' I said.

'And did you touch anything?' The WPC went to stand halfway between myself and Dominic. She should have called me Sir. But I understood the extenuating circumstances.

'No,' I said. 'Nothing. The pillow, I pulled it off his face.'

'Why?'

'Wouldn't you have?'

'And you live here you say?'

'Yes.'

'Where had you been before you came back?'

That was all the small talk I could manage. I held my head in my hands and ignored the question and then the others they pummelled me with. They gave up and the WPC asked her colleague whether or not we shouldn't all be waiting outside. The PC said better not but didn't give a reason. The three of us waited the ten minutes it took before anyone else arrived. I spent it keeping my eyes away from Dominic, fingering the blue folder my brother's poems were in, which had lain on the table for almost a week. I even pondered taking them out but the WPC looked nervous.

'Please don't touch anything,' she said, with an edge in her voice which she didn't bother trying to conceal.

'Sir,' I mumbled. I put the file down.

When the next car drew up and cut its siren the PC walked down and did the same thing I had, briefing the officers on the way up. There were two of them, both plainclothes, one very big, almost a kid. The other was a man I vaguely recognized, a tall, thin man with a very small head and a face which was so pinched it looked like a clay model. The elder one looked shaken but the younger one tried his best to look cynical and unconcerned, disgusted by the moral implications of the events only. They were followed in by four uniforms, each one taken aback like a row of dominoes. The elder plainclothes sat down opposite me and asked me a few simple questions which I answered, and then some harder ones which I did not. He cuffed me and then he led me past Dominic Lewes, who would soon be photographed by someone other than myself, and down into the street, by which time there was a total of four marked and two unmarked cars blocking the road outside my flat. I could see a space, a space in the row of cars where mine had been parked, but which had been occupied when I'd come back from the depot. I tried to remember the make of the car that had been there. An Escort. I thought it was an Escort.

I was pushed through a small, official crowd of sullen faces, all full of either curiosity or contempt, towards the top of the street. The morning was still dark and there was only the odd postman about to see me taken past the newly erected cordon and bundled into the back of one of the marked cars. It took less than five minutes before the car had arrived at the station on Carlisle Street.

Chapter Seventeen

It had been a long night. It turned out to be a long morning too. It was obvious that I was exhausted and having difficulty focusing but they didn't let me sleep. I wouldn't have done either. I was left to stew for twenty minutes and then the officer who had cuffed me came in with his younger colleague. The colleague looked like a big farm boy, strong enough to pull a tractor, and I hoped it didn't get nasty. I was feeling bad enough already.

A medical officer came in and took scrapings from underneath my fingernails as well as hair samples for matching and possible DNA profiling. I was asked to remove all my clothes and these were taken from me. They would be analysed for blood and semen traces, as well as for stray hairs or pieces of skin which did not belong to me. The medical officer then examined my body for cuts, scratching and bruises; plenty of which could be found. He paid particular attention to my groin area, taking swabs from my penis and removing more hair. The two officers sat in disgusted though joyful silence throughout, both with their arms folded in front of them. I was given a pair of jeans and a sweatshirt to wear but no shoes, socks, shorts or any underpants.

The medical officer expressed the opinion that I should see a doctor, both for the superficial wounds to my face and head, but also for suspected broken ribs and concussion.

'Let the bastard suffer,' the young man opined, but the doctor was sent for.

I asked for a lawyer and gave the uniformed officer minding the door Mike Williams' number.

'Shame his office isn't open yet, isn't it?' The older man stood up and brought his chair over to face me at the desk. 'Don't mind if we start without him, do you?'

It didn't matter what I minded. In fact, I was glad to get on with it; I wanted them to get an officer round to the freight depot on York Way to find evidence of what had happened to me there. With any luck there would still be the bag with my blood in it. That's if they got there before some idiot chucked it out. They might even get some prints off it if I was lucky.

I went through the events of the evening from going to the gym, and seeing Nicky, to getting the phone call and what had happened after that. I didn't know whether or not to mention the fact that I'd known Dominic Lewes but decided I should. There were files in my office that could link me to him. I told them how I had photographed him and beaten up his pimp who was apparently known as Rollo. I told them that the man who had beaten me up had mentioned his name. I told them that a Ford Escort, five or six years old, had been parked outside my flat but had gone by the time the police arrived. It was my opinion that its owner had killed Dominic, left his body in my flat and then waited outside for me to come home before making a call to the police. All of this was noted with clearly displayed scepticism.

I was beyond tired and it was now my ribs which were giving me the most trouble. Discovering Dominic's body in my flat had taken my mind off the painkillers I had intended taking and I asked if I could have some.

'The doctor will be here soon, sir,' the older man said with a smile.

The doctor didn't come for another hour, and only then because I refused to answer any more questions until he did, and took to groaning quietly. Not wanting a cell mortality on their records the two officers let the doctor into the room and he bandaged my head and my ribs and put a dressing on my face. He sent for a nurse and an hour later they stitched up the wound on the back of my head. The front of the head is harder, the doctor informed me. He was told not to give me anything that would send me to sleep. He didn't give me anything.

All I had to do was sit it out. Both the pain and the interrogation. I was nervous, but the physical evidence would say that I had been at York Way as I had claimed, and the police would find no forensic evidence on Dominic Lewes to say I had killed or indeed been any-where near him. The ravings of the two officers, taking it in turns to play bad cop and bad cop, sailed over me. I gazed round at the dull grey walls, at the flimsy table, perfect for sweeping aside in dramatic temper tantrums by detectives who have seen too many reruns of *The Sweeney*. I drank three cups of lukewarm gun oil and as the tiny window announced the coming day, I waited for the appearance of my friend the Chief Inspector. The Chief liked to take a personal interest in the bigger cases, and I'd have to go through it all with him anyway so there was no point saying a great deal to these two. I tried to make some sort of sense out of what had happened, how everything had got tangled up together, but I could hardly make the table sit still let alone figure something which seemed totally incomprehensible. What did Dominic Lewes have to do with what I was doing for Sir Peter Morgan?

The Chief didn't come at all that day. They let me have two hours' sleep and Mike Williams came at around ten. He wasn't a criminal lawyer but he was glad to help and would know who to get in if it looked like I was going to need anyone special. I told him that I didn't need him around for the interrogations. He asked me if he should demand that I be sent to a hospital but I said no, it would only slow things down. I kept expecting Andy Gold to show up but then remembered he'd been taken off the case. I kept expecting him to show up anyway, because we were supposed to be friends, but then remembered that friendship can be an embarrassing concept for a police officer, especially if the friend in question is a suspect, a likely candidate for serial killer.

Milson and Clarke went at me all afternoon but I didn't tell them anything that I hadn't before. They tried to pick holes in my story, especially the York Way episode which I had no witnesses to, but when what you are telling is the truth your story tends to stand up – if you ignore the deviations and stick to the facts. It pissed them off, I could tell, but they still thought they probably had me. They asked me where I was the night John Evans was killed, where I was when James Waldock had been butchered and what I had been doing the night Edward Morgan had taken a man back to his flat. I couldn't tell them of course, not without looking at my diary, and they got a lot of pleasure out of that. They even sent for a baseball hat, which they put on my head, gazing at me in profile with copies of the picture I had been showing round in their hands. They photographed me and I assumed that they would be showing my picture round to the people they had interviewed already.

I tried to remember how long forensics people took. I was more than three years out of date but I did know that a case like this would get top billing. I figured that if the Chief wasn't here then the report wasn't ready yet; he wouldn't waste his time if there was a chance that forensic evidence would prove it one way or another. Milson and Clarke were just to soften me up, to keep me awake and my head hurting. I remembered what a good detective the Chief had been, what a calculating, heartless, vindictive bastard. Even if he knew I had nothing to do with it he'd have let Milson and Clarke have a go at me, to see if I knew anything else which might be useful to him.

At seven that night I was taken from the holding cell to an interview room and was eventually joined by Ken Clay, the Chief Inspector of Islington Police. He came into the room quickly, accompanied by a humourless, sour-faced DC I had never seen before. He pulled the chair opposite me and sat on it, his thighs running over the sides like a cake rising out of a tin.

'Well, Billy boy, we have been busy, haven't we?'

Clay's face was a huge, fleshy maze of broken vessels and his hands were too; matching mounds of unbleached tripe. He had placed a folder on top of the table and he pulled the contents out of it. He leafed through the fifteen or so pages briskly, his fingers clumsy, not built for such close work. He put them down and then smiled, giving me a flash of lurid red gums above yellow teeth stained with black.

'All of it. From the beginning. Don't leave anything out.'

I took a breath and went through it, from first meeting the MP, to trying to get a picture of Dominic Lewes, to the night before last when I'd been beaten up and come home to find a corpse in my bed. I didn't tell him about Charlotte and Lloyd but not for any other reason than belligerence. I'd let him have it if it looked like he was going to guess there was something missing. Clay's face was a livid mask.

When I'd finished, he sat back.

'You beat up a pimp and then the boy you're after winds up starkers, without his cock, in your bed, after someone sees you threatening a young lad with a knife and forcing him into your doorway.'

'What knife? That's crap, that's absolute crap.'

Clay laughed. 'Glad I'm not you, Billy.'

I took his point but tried to ignore the mocking, self-satisfied tone. 'Who is he, the caller?'

'The caller preferred to remain anonymous.'

'What about the pimp? Have you found *him* yet?'

'He's relaxing downstairs.' Clay was pretending to be affable. I was surprised he was letting me ask him questions.

'He's still got a bit of a face on him. Claims he was mugged, doesn't know anything about any boy prostitutes or private detectives.'

'He was in Dominic's house, I saw him.'

'I know, I know. I believe you there, Billy. There. Just giving him rope to hang himself. You know the score.'

He fumbled for the top sheet of paper on the table and managed to pick it up. The DC sat up a bit.

'Now then,' he said. 'What have we got?' Clay's

sarcasm was stronger than his aftershave. 'A corpse in your flat, not *only* that of a boy you were looking for but *also* connected to a job you've been doing for a bereaved MP; exactly the same MO as that used by a serial killer the MP had paid you to look for. Curious. We've then got a flat door which has been broken into, very probably by your good self to make it look like someone else did it. Not very convincing. And . . !' Clay looked over at the DC and then at me. 'Thanks to Dr Burg at the forensics lab, we've got something a jury would be very interested in. *Very* interested in indeed.'

Clay leant forward. The DC sneered. They both stared at me with a look I recognized; that of detectives who had something. What? What forensic evidence? I began to get an uncomfortable feeling in the pit of my stomach. Did he mean fingerprints? It was my flat for God's sake. Blood on my clothes? Maybe, but it was mine and I had already accounted for it. Hadn't they checked the freight depot? What else could they have? I figured they were just fishing, but I didn't like the look on them.

I waited for it. Clay cleared his throat and read from the page.

' "On examination of the back passage no semen was found although traces of Nonoxynol were evident as were two hairs which, under examination, did not match those of the victim. They probably arrived there during the anal intercourse which accounts for the presence of the Non-oxynol. The hairs are both compatible with those usually found in the groin region." ' Clay paused and the DC sat up even straighter than he had been doing. Clay pointed his chin at me.

' "Microscope analysis of the hairs, and of those taken from the suspect in custody, shows that the hairs are of the same colour, width and type as the suspect's pubic hair, though only a DNA match could prove they came from the same person. At this stage I would *guess* at a likely positive outcome. The samples have been sent to Cambridge and I will advise when the results are in." JM Burg MD.'

Clay put the paper aside and raised his eyebrows. A muscle twitched in my jaw which could have been seen a mile away. I looked Clay in the eye.

'They were in my bed.'

Clay shook his head slowly. He spoke softly. 'They were up his arse you mean. They were way up there.'

'He shoved them up there, he . . .' I stopped speaking. There was no point, I was just falling into his trap, getting angry. A well of doubt rose from my bowels.

'They were found on my bed,' I said as calmly as I could. 'They were found by the killer and placed in the corpse to deflect suspicion from him on to me. The whole thing is a set-up to do that.' I tried to sound sure but Clay was right; evidence like that was always compelling in the hands of the right prosecution brief. Crying 'frame-up' always sounds like clutching at straws. Clay didn't say anything, waiting for me.

'I would hardly be likely to do him in my own flat, would I?'

'You could have got carried away. Butchering young boys isn't exactly logical, wherever you do it.'

'What about time of death?' I said.

'A couple of hours previous to discovery, maybe three. You could have done it easily.'

I turned my head away. A dead kid in my bed with my pubic hair inside his body. Caught red-handed, on the scene, after a tip-off. Mike Williams, I thought, I hope you know someone good.

'I wasn't there, I told you.'

'Yes, yes, York Way and the Big Bad Wolf.'

'Did you check it?'

'You were there, Billy, I'll give you that. Prints on the door handle like you said and a bag full of puke. Some blood. But there's nothing to say at what *time* you were there. What I think is you went there earlier, before picking up the arse and—'

'A girl, a whore on the road. I spoke to her . . .'

'Got a name? An address? Might be difficult to find her.'

Clay put down the sheet and picked up another. He started to read it, not seeming particularly interested in me. He was strangely subdued and I didn't know why. He would usually have gone after something this good like a bull through a gate in springtime. My mouth was dust. Clay let out a sigh. Then he shook his head and smiled.

'Such a shame,' he said, turning to the DC. 'It would have been very convenient.' He looked back at me. 'Not that I would have wanted to see a distinguished ex-colleague like yourself go down, mind you. No.' He paused and glanced back at the A4 sheet before putting it down. 'I fibbed about the time of death I'm afraid. It was earlier. Burg is sure it wasn't much after seven and it can't have been earlier than six-thirty because the boy was seen going into the Mcdonald's in King's Cross at that time. He was a regular and a lassie there recognized him.'

I took that on board. I was in the gym. Pete. Sal. Witnesses.

'Why did you check the Mcdonald's?' I asked. I was

relieved, curiosity moving into the space being vacated by panic.

'You've to thank Burg for it. If I were you I'd send him a bunch of flowers.' Clay pushed the pile of papers towards me and I picked up the top one and looked at it. 'There was a Big Mac in his stomach, or at least a small part of one. Burg patched it from the mayonnaise. You'd already told us the lad worked the King's Cross area so we checked the restaurant.'

I scanned the page trying to find the part I wanted. I couldn't. 'Where was the rest of it?' I asked. 'The burger?' I had a horrible feeling that I knew what the answer would be. Clay's smile made me feel slightly sick.

'Removed,' he said.

I saw a gaping hole of blood and intestines. Clay read from the sheet again.

' "Only a small part of the food was found, which had been chewed but had not begun to be digested, indicating that it cannot have been present for more than an hour at most. It is my opinion that the rest of the burger, assuming that all of it was consumed by the victim, was removed by the perpetrator to avoid an accurate assessment of the time of death. This theory is compatible with other evidence, specifically the slashing open of the stomach and the disturbance of other local organs." ' Clay pursed his lips and nodded to himself again. 'Clever fellow. Burg too. I'm not sure every stiff stitcher would have spotted that. He says he suspected something like it when he saw how the stomach had been carved up, and that's why he looked so closely for the food. There wasn't much of it left by all accounts.'

I caught a picture of two bloody hands scraping the contents out of Dominic Lewes' stomach.

'It means, of course, that your movements can be accounted for.'

I shut the picture out.

'Like I said. And the hair, I mean, he put it there. You can accept that, can't you?'

'Maybe. Or you could have fucked him before he met his maker. We might do you for that. Sex with a minor.'

I ignored that. 'But how did he get the kid into my flat? I'd gone back after the gym, he wasn't there then, after Burg says he was killed.'

'You're sure of that?'

'I'd have noticed,' I said.

Clay paused. He liked having me on the hook. He didn't want to let me go lightly, simply because I was the wrong fish.

'He was killed somewhere else,' he admitted finally. 'The body was moved. He'd been strangled. There was very little shit on your sheets which would not have been the case had he been done there. The blood patterns were wrong too, the major arteries didn't spurt the way they should have if his heart was beating. The boy kind of just leaked. All that gory stuff in your place was cosmetic. He carried the boy up there and *then* had his home anatomy lesson.'

'He was hoping I was out.'

'Or he was waiting outside till you *went* out.'

I thought for a second.

'Or he knew I was unconscious and he did it then,' I said. 'He was having a go at me and all the time Dominic's body was in the boot of his car.'

'Possible,' Clay admitted. 'Possibly so.'

Clay looked wistful. I'd seen him look that way before. It was the distant, all but faded ghost of compassion, conjured up by a vision of Dominic Lewes. He shook it off with a laugh.

'By the way, we had a look in your office, to see if we couldn't link you with the lorry driver or the other rent boy. Or Morgan. We found the keys in your flat. Your office diary said you were in the clear but we checked anyway. Some dodgy bar owner we weren't sure about and then a lawyer bird called Sharon. She backed you up.' Clay laughed again. 'Your office is not what you'd call impressive, is it? You doing well in the private sector, Rucker?'

Having established that I was no longer in the frame Clay asked me questions about the man in the hat. I told him that he might be from the North, and that he had practically admitted being the killer. He'd said it didn't matter if he killed me, he would go away for the same stretch anyway. Clay asked me if I'd seen enough of him to add to the picture image; apparently there's now a computer program that can do stuff like that. I told him that, unfortunately, I had not. I told Clay about the Escort. Whoever it was had obviously been waiting in it, and when I came back he called in a report about a young kid and a man with a knife. Clay said he'd already put it out on the wire.

I sat back in the chair and stretched. An hour or so had passed. Clay asked me about Rollo and I told him what had happened, that the Morgan thing and looking for Dominic were completely unconnected.

'They're not any more,' Clay said.

I asked if Clay had grilled Rollo on the man in the hat. Clay said he had but he'd pleaded ignorance. They were going to have another go at him. Clay said he thought that was the best bet for now, the closest they were to him;

Rollo was someone he knew of even if Rollo didn't know him.

I relaxed some more, allowing latent exhaustion to begin to spread into my bones. I was waiting for Clay to tell me I could go home. But he didn't. He put the sheets of A4 back into the file and sent the duty officer out for tea. He also turned the tape recorder off.

'Right then, Rucker.' Clay made a movement with his hips and his whole enormous frame shivered forward in the chair. 'What have you got?' I was about to reply but I was cut off. 'And don't give me any shit. You're close. The guy in the picture picked on you and then this bumboy winds up in your bed after you've had a go at his daddy. Not for the first time he's been there I don't imagine but this time he's dead. You're close, I know it. So give it to me.'

I shrugged my shoulders. He'd done this the wrong way round. If he'd said this when I thought I would be facing twelve indignant citizens having to explain what my pubic hairs were doing in the anal passage of a murdered fifteen-year-old rent boy I might have tried to answer. Now, I didn't have to say a thing.

'Tell me about Lloyd.'

That surprised me. How did he know?

'Lloyd?' I said.

'I've had Mother Teresa on my back. He says that a certain former detective from my division had been harassing a prominent and respected MP.'

'A different matter,' I said.

'Like fuck it is!'

'And harassment is a bit strong. I just wanted to chat.'

'About what? What did you want to chat about?'

I shrugged.

'TELL ME WHAT YOU *CHATTED* ABOUT!'

Clay continued to ask me that question, or tributaries of it, for the next hour, at a steady increase in volume. He also wanted to know what Dominic Lewes had to do with Morgan and simply would not believe that I was working on two things at once. He mentioned terrifying terms such as 'withholding evidence' and 'perverting the course of justice', but I knew the law. I didn't know the link between the two things myself, and I still couldn't think of a reason to tell him about Lloyd and Charlotte. There wasn't much the police could do other than lean on Lloyd and hope for a very unlikely confession. They had to catch the man who had beaten me up. Without him they didn't have anything.

He got tired eventually.

'You better find out what's going on, Rucker, and you'd better tell me when you know, or I'll make some big shit for you. We're checking that gym story of yours again and if it looks like you might not have been there exactly when you said, you'll be back in here quicker than piss down a drain. Hear me?'

Clay left in as much of a hurry as he'd arrived. A sergeant came in. My clothes were returned to me and I put them on; all except my shirt which would have to go in the nearest bin. I was allowed to keep the sweatshirt they had given me. I was made to sign for everything and was offered a lift home, which I initially declined. I didn't know whether or not I wanted to go home. I wanted to think about it over a curry but then I realized that I had no money on me. I changed my mind about the lift and told the sergeant on the front desk that. He said I should take a seat and wait.

It was now ten thirty and I was shafted. The adrenalin

which had kept my system in operation for the last thirty-six hours had drained away and all that was left was a deep lake of fatigue, along with a diminishing pain in my head and on my face, and an increasing pain in my ribs. I didn't rate the chance of sleep too highly though. It would have to be on the sofa in my flat, or on the sofabed in my office, and anyway the whirl of questions which had been stirred by the events of the last day and a half, but kept in the back of my brain, had begun to spin right out into the front of it.

Who broke into my flat? How did Dominic fit in? Lloyd, was Lloyd involved? It seemed ludicrous to think so but I couldn't think of anything more plausible. But if he was, why carry on after doing Edward? To fit me up? Really? Or *was* it all the same guy? How had the man got the picture with my address on the back? Was he in one of the pubs I went to? Did I speak to him? Had I spoken to the killer, been friendly, given him information to help him find me? Find Dominic?

And how the hell was I going to find any of this out?

When the boy in blue came to give me my ride he was plainly pissed off at having to do so. It was a course in crime detection he'd done, not the Knowledge. I ignored his attitude and told him where I lived. I'd decided to go home because I had some cash there which I could pick up and then cab it down to the twenty-four-hour greasy spoon on Theobald's Road before deciding where to sleep. At least I hoped I had some cash. My flat had been broken into by a psychopath *and* given the once-over by a team of detectives. Was it likely? At least I could change out of these clothes and pick up my cash card or a chequebook.

The car stopped at the top of Exmouth Market. I

walked down towards my flat, wondering if the police had left it open or fixed the door jamb for me. I wasn't looking forward to going in there. I wondered how much clearing up they'd done. I was tired, hungry, and in no small amount of pain. As I got closer I saw the light from Fred's Café on the right and I wondered if it was still open. It was quarter past eleven and I knew it would be but there wouldn't be any food on. They'd probably do me a sandwich if I pleaded but I wanted something hot. I walked past the café and was about to turn down towards my flat when I heard the door swing open. I glanced round as a figure hurried out of the door towards me. My heart bucked in my chest on impulse and I turned, backing away, pulling my hands out of my pockets.

'Billy!'

Sharon stood in front of me. I let out a breath. She went to put her arms around me, but stopped when I winced. She looked at me for a second, holding on to my arm, and then held a hand up to my face, lightly touching the bruising beneath my left eye.

'Oh, Billy,' Sharon said. Her voice was a mixture of worry and relief. It sounded good. Her eyes reached up for mine. Sharon rested her hand on my shoulder.

'They called me,' she said. 'I came but they wouldn't let me see you. I've been here all day. I was so worried.' Sharon's hand moved across my bruising again. She moved her body closer to me. The pain I was feeling, and the exhaustion and the latent fear, all seemed to rise up and out of me like the soul from a dead man's body. All the misunderstandings, the problems we'd had, went too. There wasn't anything left, nothing but the face in front of me, and the pleasure I felt seeing it there. I moved forward, filling the small gap between us, and Sharon's fingers closed round my neck.

'Oh, Billy,' Sharon said.

And then there was fear greater than when a shotgun had been pointed at my head.

'I love you. I love you so much.'

Chapter Eighteen

We stood in the street and we kissed for a long time. After that we just stood holding on to each other. I didn't want to let her go. I didn't want to not be holding her, I didn't want to deal with what we were doing or what would happen next. I felt hollow and weak. Eventually Sharon started to shiver with the cold and I released her and watched her run back into Fred's for her coat which she had left on the back of a chair.

Later, in her flat, we made love, gently at first because of my ribs, but then with a fervour which brooked no mitigation for pain or injury. Sharon was so familiar to me but her body was so strange; I found it odd that the woman I knew should have this great store of sexuality, a physicality which was as much herself as the Sharon I had known had been. Her full breasts, her nipples, her belly, her sex, the flushed look on her face when I entered her. This was not a woman I had known, not a woman I had even suspected. It was as though, when I helped her undo the buttons of her blouse, I hadn't expected to find anything underneath. What I did find was exhilarating, a nakedness so complete I was winded by it, a fist clenching desperate fingers round my heart.

I hadn't thought about anything, not even in the taxi over to West London during which we had sat, hands tight together, not speaking a word. Neither of us had said what was going to happen or spoken about the future. Sharon had led me up to her flat and then into her bedroom where we'd kissed for a long time before Sharon pulled away, her face solemn, her hands going to the bottom of my T-shirt which we pulled over my head. My ribs were bandaged and Sharon carefully undid them and then kissed the bruising there and held her cheek against it. When we were both naked we just sat looking at each other, the slightest sad smile on her lips, my bones light but my stomach heavy. I felt like I was about to throw up. Sharon moved under her duvet and I joined her beneath it, merging into the warmth and a smell which was so familiar but richer than I had ever experienced it. We held on to each other and Sharon drew me inside her almost immediately, her hand cold on my cock, her sex full and so wet I moved straight into her. We made love slowly, hardly moving, unwilling to surrender our skin to even the shortest moment of not touching. We came with our mouths locked together, Sharon's teeth biting into my lower lip.

We had both been completely silent, and now we lay together, Sharon clinging to the side of my torso which wasn't bruised, both my arms around her neck and shoulders. We still didn't speak, and there were still no thoughts in my head. There was just the smell of her and the feeling of her body next to me. Time was a closed warm space, a static world, a pressure cooker of sensation and emotion. It didn't have an outside to it; nowhere it had come from, nowhere it was going to.

We made love again and this time it was wild and uncontrolled as we let our emotions unleash themselves. I bit into her beautiful skin, making marks which would stay on her, and she did the same to me. The pain I felt seemed part of a greater, more powerful sensation, a tunnel of feelings which I'd never known I needed but I needed more than anything. We didn't speak to each other, not like we had spoken in my flat, or over dinner or in a bar. But there were words. Embarrassing words, sex words not love words. We tore at each other and pulled the other back close, we moved into different positions, our hands never satisfied, clawing, prying, our mouths moving constantly in an effort at completeness. I wanted to touch all of her with all of me, I wanted to have her in every possible position all at the same time, to turn her inside out and fuck her that way too. I wanted to do something which could never be undone, something which could never be just explained away, causing a slight blushing or a looking to the side. Something close to terrifying. I held on to her and scoured her body with my three-day beard. I felt her nails in my back, her teeth in my bottom lip, more, harder, my cheek, my stomach. I couldn't tell where my body ended and Sharon's began. It was stunning and uncontrollable and I never wanted it to end.

But it did end. We lay together, exhausted, feeding madly on air, our tears running down each other's faces. I moved on to my back and we lay side by side, Sharon's hand covering mine. Almost immediately I was asleep, but it was a sleep in which I was cut off from though aware of the room I was in and the body I was lying next to. My body just went somewhere, to a place of rest and perfect calm, where it lay detached from me in an ambient limbo. It felt like bathing in an enchanted pool. And then I floated back to a more connected sort of consciousness, a greater presence in the room, with Sharon there lying on her back with her eyes closed, her breasts rising and falling in a steady motion.

The duvet had long since fallen on to the floor and Sharon was naked. I could not accept or fully believe the actual fact of that. I looked at her body and found myself feeling guilty about doing so, as though I shouldn't be looking at her. I desperately wanted to touch her breasts, to hold them and run my hands down over her belly and entwine my fingers into the golden triangle of her pubic hair. But I was scared to, I was afraid of being so familiar. I didn't know why, given what we had just done, but the feeling would not go away. With her eyes closed I felt like a voyeur, seeing something I shouldn't, but I just couldn't keep my eyes from running all over her, boring into the places they had never had access to before. It was exhilarating. Had I always wanted to do this? I was suddenly aware of my own nakedness. I was naked. I was lying in a bed, naked, next to Sharon.

Sharon's eyelids pulled open and fluttered slowly like a moth's first wings. When she saw me watching her, her face creased into a smile which caused tears to well behind my eyes. I felt so good. So good. I looked into her eyes but couldn't stop my eyes darting back to her body. She saw this and we laughed together and she did it too, very obviously looking at me, checking me out. Beneath her gaze I began to grow hard again, but I wanted to be calm for a while. I used a fingernail to push some damp strands of hair from her cheek and moved closer to her. I ran my fingertips over her face and she closed her eyes and smiled. I stroked the side of her neck and then her shoulders. The feeling of her skin was tattooed on my fingers. I ran my hand over her left breast and then the right.

When my thumb began to play with Sharon's right nipple she moved away a little and, bringing her left hand up to her breast she covered it. She looked uncertain. Sharon's right nipple had an extra curve to it, a half moon added beneath the aureole. The half moon was raised from the skin and was just the same texture but separate from the rest of the nipple. It was as though someone had double stamped the nipple on to her, and the second time had been slightly out of kilter with the first. I was surprised that she had moved away from me.

'God,' Sharon said. She blushed, trying to pass it off. I was looking at her but she broke my gaze. 'I forgot about that.'

Sharon's voice was now the one I was used to hearing but it sounded strange, wrong; it didn't seem to belong here, where we were now.

'It doesn't matter,' I said.

'It's like an extra nipple. Not a whole one but kind of.' Now Sharon sounded self-conscious, either because she was nervous about what she was saying, or because she was finding it odd to be talking at all. 'I've had it since I was a child.'

'I like it.'

She shook her head.

'You don't have to say that.'

'I know. I like it. It's magical. It makes you . . . unique.' I smiled and moved closer. I didn't want to talk.

'It makes me self-conscious.' Sharon looked away for a second. 'It's why I don't go topless at the beach; people can't help looking at it.'

'That's not what they're looking at.'

'Ha. It is though. It's why I didn't that time when we went away. I could tell Lisa thought I was being square.'

She meant the time Luke, Sharon, myself and the girl I was kind of seeing at the time had gone to Crete for a week.

'I thought it was because of me.'

Sharon reddened a little more.

'Maybe that too,' she said.

I moved closer to Sharon and gently pulled her hand away. She didn't want to let me. I moved even closer until my face was right next to her breast. I stroked her nipple again and kissed it. Slowly I ran the tip of my finger all round it and kissed it again, tugging softly at it with my teeth.

'It's beautiful,' I said, and I meant it. It was fascinating. It felt good in my mouth. Sharon didn't answer. 'I'm not saying it to make you feel better. You don't believe me anyway, I can tell. But I mean it.'

'I should have told you though,' she said. 'I have done in the past. But I didn't think.'

'I'm glad you didn't think.'

'It must have been a bit of a surprise though.'

'No,' I said, 'it wasn't.'

'Billy . . .'

'It wasn't a surprise, Sharon. I mean it. I . . .' I moved up the bed and looked into her face. The next words came out of my mouth without me thinking about them. I immediately wished I hadn't said what I did but if I hadn't it would have only been putting off the inevitable.

'I knew about it,' I said. 'I mean it wasn't a surprise. And I like it, I do.'

Pain moved swiftly over Sharon's face like the shadow of a hawk. She smiled seriously at me and kissed me, running her thumb along my eyebrow, but something in the air seemed to change. The room grew suddenly colder. I tried to find a word to say but there wasn't one.

I wanted to tell Sharon that Luke hadn't told me about it in a bad way, a guys' way, he had just mentioned it once. I wanted to reassure her of that. I think she would have known it though. She wasn't upset that he'd told me, I was sure she didn't begrudge the things which Luke had spoken to me about. Including her. It was just the lurch in the stomach as time jerked back into gear. The space was broken. It was Luke. It was the fact of him.

Sharon bent over and retrieved the duvet and I helped her pull it over us. She turned her bedside lamp off. We lay together and kissed occasionally and tried to smooth away the thoughts that were rising back up to the surface of both of our minds. We both knew what they were. We lay there in the semi-dark and I pretended to be asleep but my eyes were open, staring blankly at the long, cream-coloured curtains covering the Georgian windows. I wasn't tired any more. My body, though without proper sleep or food for days, and carrying the signs of a beating, felt heavy and good, but my mind nagged at me to turn to it, to consider the living knot of thoughts which twisted inside.

I pushed the thoughts aside but I couldn't sleep. Sharon's head was resting on my chest and I tried not to move but she could tell I wasn't relaxed and her eyes opened to mine. Even though I could barely make out her face I could read there everything Sharon might have wanted to say to me. I looked into her darkened eyes for a second or two and then sat up a fraction.

I couldn't stay there. Sharon lifted her head and I moved from beneath her and pushed myself up from the bed. I slid over to the edge and stood up, immediately crouching down to my trousers, my sweatshirt and the rest of my clothes. I sat down again and dressed slowly with my back to Sharon, balling up the bandage and stuffing it into the back pocket of my jeans. When I was finished I turned back to her.

Sharon looked at me for a while without speaking. Then:

'Must you?'

I nodded. Sharon's face was unreadable as she turned slightly and nodded back, looking down at the duvet.

'I understand,' she said. I tried to smile. 'It's weird for me too.'

'I know it is.'

I left a second and then I leant over to kiss the top of her forehead. I'd meant a gentle kiss, but she took hold of my head and pressed her lips hard against me, surprising me with the frankness of her passion. It was a message, a clear statement. It was scary and I could feel an edge of hardness in her kiss which set a corresponding one up within me. I pressed my lips back against her before breaking off. I stood up again from the bed and looked down at her. She started to get up but I told her not to worry. I knew my way.

'There's some money in my purse,' Sharon said. 'On the table in the living room.'

'Thanks,' I said.

I walked into the living room and found the purse. I borrowed some money from it and called a cab. It didn't come for twenty minutes, during which time I sat in the living room on the edge of the sofa, staring at the carpet. When the door buzzer sounded I looked up at the entry phone and then at the closed bedroom door. I could almost feel Sharon's body, fitting into mine, her wrist resting on my hip bone. I thought about ignoring the cab and going back in there but suddenly the idea of being with Sharon, there, in her bed, filled me with an incomprehension which was something close to horror. Kissing her. Fucking her. Her sucking me, my tongue moving down between her legs. It was too much, it was way too much. I stood up, pulled the front door open, and walked into the hallway.

Chapter Nineteen

I woke to the sound of someone's voice, far away, a voice which sounded like my own voice but how could it be my voice? I was here, not somewhere else. I was confused. I rolled over, pushing aside the pillow that my head was under.

It was my voice. My answerphone was telling somebody that I wasn't in my office at the present time. The message ended and there was a long series of blips, followed by a woman's voice.

'Mr Rucker, this is Charlotte Morgan. I was wondering if you could call me. I would very much like to speak to you . . .'

I managed to prop myself up on the sofabed and reach over the table to the phone before Charlotte had finished speaking. My ribs bade me a fond good morning as I picked up the receiver.

'Mrs Morgan,' I said, 'hello. Yes. William Rucker.'

I pressed my elbow into my side. There was silence on the other end of the line for a second, before Charlotte Morgan spoke.

'Can you come and see me?' she said. 'At home? I've taken the day off but we could do it this evening if you wanted.' Now that I was more fully awake I realized that

there was a bitter tinge to her voice. She sounded chast-
ened and small.

'I'll be an hour,' I told her.

I stood up from the bed and kept my left arm close against
my ribcage. I felt groggy and slow, and my head ached.
My muscles had all closed in on me, like I was wearing a
straitjacket which was a good size too small. The floor of
my office was cold. I wondered what time it was and
turned the clock on my desk round. Midday. I heard footsteps in the hall and the distant sound of a typewriter. I
pulled the sheets from the bed and stuffed them into a
cupboard which had always smelled of turps and paint
and still did. Careful of my ribs, I put the bed up, pulled
my jeans on, and found a clean T-shirt in the bottom
drawer of my filing cabinet. I scratched my head, touched
the stitches there and opened my office door. I wandered
out into the corridor.

Ally's face dropped in horror when she saw me. In the
mirror behind the counter I could see that the left side of
my face was a sick yellow colour, sitting on a sweet purple
like the skin of a swede.

'I know,' I said, acknowledging her shock. 'I didn't
shave this morning.'

Ally poured me a coffee and held her hand out to my
face. Women did that; what the hell good did they think it
would do?

'The police were here,' she said. 'They asked me questions and they were in your office.'

'I know.'

'I made them let me watch them, so they didn't take
anything.'

'Thank you,' I said. I was surprised at Ally's concern for my property.

'They used your phone a lot.'

'I'll send them the bill,' I said.

Ally asked what was going on. I told her that when I found out she'd be the first to know. I asked her if anyone else had been round.

'No,' she replied. 'Only that other policeman, the one who was here before. Your friend. He came a couple of hours after the other ones.'

The way Ally told me this made me think she was hiding something; probably the fact that Andy had made an embarrassing pass and she didn't want to say what a tosser he was because she thought I was tight with him. I suddenly remembered Andy's strange willingness to come over to my office to discuss Edward Morgan rather than meeting in his natural habitat, the pub.

'What did he want?' I asked. It can't have been me, he knew where I was.

'He wanted to know if anyone had been looking for you.'

'Right,' I said.

I carried the cup into my office and sat down at my desk with it. I wanted some space, a little time in which to think, but the number on the answerphone bugged at me. I took a pen and then pressed the play button. Five messages. The first was from the day before yesterday; a man enquiring about my services. I wrote the number down but didn't think I'd be calling him. I had a little too much on. Then Nicky wanting to know if I was out yet and what was going on. Sharon, the same thing, her voice concerned but efficient. The fourth person who'd called me didn't leave a name, but it was a voice I recognized.

'Rucker. I hope you get this message. I hope you got the

message I was trying to give you the other night. I hope I made myself clear because if you didn't get the message I'll have to come back and make sure you do. All right?'

It shocked me to hear his voice. I wanted to keep the message, to save it, as if having that would bring me closer to him. His voice sounded tangible, like I could hold it. Like I could hold his voice to account.

The final message was from Charlotte Morgan, and it cut out suddenly where I'd picked the phone up.

There was a pile of letters which I had ignored last night as well as the messages. I picked them up and went through them. The Direct Line people wanted to know if I, Julian Brinsford, wanted to see how much money I could save on motor insurance. The *National Geographic*, a rates reminder, and a white envelope with neat hand-writing and a Doncaster postmark. I tore it open without thinking and pulled out a single piece of blue notepaper stapled to which was a cheque drawn on a building society account. The letter was dated 10 November and it must have been posted the day before I had gone on my fool's errand to York Way.

Dear Mr Rucker,

Thank you for the pictures you sent me of my son. It is such a great relief to know that he is all right. I'm afraid to say that he has not called me, but there was a call the day before yesterday which my husband answered but the caller rang off. It may have been him. If you see him again, please could you ask him to call me.

A cheque is enclosed. Thank you once again.

Yours sincerely,

Diane Lewes

I read the letter over and then looked at the cheque, pulling it free. I left the letter on the desk and dropped the cheque into the waste-paper bin. I couldn't really cash it, could I? Certainly, I had found her son, and sent the pictures of him to her which the contract between us had required. But then I'd killed him. I'd killed him by finding him. I'd killed him by taking a murder case and not clearing my backlog first, by involving him in something he should never have been anywhere near. I didn't know how I had done this, but I didn't have any doubt that I had.

I looked at the address Mrs Lewes had written in the top right-hand corner of her letter. There was a phone number with it. My hand reached over to the telephone but I knew I wasn't going to call her. The police would have told her that Dominic had been murdered. They wouldn't have told her where his body was found, not yet, not without charging me. I wasn't going to call her; what the hell would I have to say? I pulled open a drawer of my filing cabinet and looked for Dominic Lewes' file but it wasn't there. The police must have taken it. I dropped the letter into the drawer and pushed it shut.

I tried to think how Dominic had become involved. Someone had seen me taking his picture or talking to him. Who? Rollo. The other kid. The waitress. A little old lady. The girl in his house when I went to call there and asked if he was in. She'd called him Mikey. Who told someone about it? Which one of them? And who did they tell, the man in the hat? Lloyd? I didn't know. Anything was possible, but nothing seemed anywhere near likely. Had Lloyd tried to fit me up? Maybe, but if he had he must have known I would have fingered him; it was no way of keeping his name out of the papers. And why would he? What then? Was it part of the man in the hat's warning, knowing that I wasn't likely to go away for it? Perhaps. It was risky though. Wouldn't he have just tried giving me a kicking first to see what effect that had? If he was willing to take the risk of killing Dominic and leaving him in my flat, surely he would have risked just killing me. I scoured my mind for answers and for small pieces of information, something I knew or had seen but had overlooked. There was something, I was sure of it. A picture which had struck me. I remembered a feeling I'd had, when I'd gone to see Dominic, a feeling that someone was watching my car. There was that but there was something else too, I knew it. But I couldn't dredge it up.

The phone rang. I picked up and it was Sir Peter Morgan. He sounded tentative and apologetic. He'd heard what had happened to me but he didn't know all the details. He knew that I'd been beaten up and arrested, that a boy had been murdered and left in my apartment. One of the officers had phoned him and warned him off employing me.

'I understand,' I said. 'And don't blame yourself. When you take a case you have to accept what might come with it.'

I thought that would be all but Sir Peter said that in spite of the police he still wanted me to carry on.

'You're close,' he said. 'You must be. To whoever killed Edward. I'm very sorry about the boy but nevertheless it shows that you had found something out. Getting attacked and then having someone try to frame you. You must carry on.'

Again, there was an obsessive quality to Sir Peter's voice. I told him I'd think about it. I had some people to

talk to and I'd decide what to do after that. I didn't want
to carry on. I wanted to go and lie on a beach. I rang off
and thought about what Morgan had said. Clay thought it
too; I was close. I didn't feel close. I felt like I was playing
blind man's buff and I kept bumping into the furniture.

I pulled on my jacket. Apart from the fact that I'd
been officially warned off, I was in no state to go and see
anyone; the T-shirt I was wearing had a tear in it and I
hadn't showered, shaved or eaten properly for days. Apart
from the food though, I didn't care. The way my face was
arranged a suit would not have made me look any better,
and a shave would have been as cosmetically effective as
a window polish on a written-off Renault Megane. I would
still look fucked. I called a cab, asked them to give me
twenty minutes, locked my office and walked to the café.

Ally made me a sandwich which I ate quickly,
washing it down with more coffee. I walked down to the
forecourt and waited for the taxi by the front gate. The
taxi took me down past Regent's Park and along the Mary-
lebone Road before eventually pulling into Leinster
Mews. When I got out to pay him the driver couldn't help
himself.

'That's some shiner, mate.'

'Yeah.'

'Don't tell me; I should see the other guy, right?' He
laughed.

'If you do,' I said, 'call the police. He's a serial killer.'

The cab pulled off and I walked down into the small
street. I could see Lloyd, kissing Charlotte goodbye,
getting into his car. The day was surprisingly warm for
mid November. I saw that it had rained last night. Small

stones gave a little under the soles of my boots and a freshness blew across from the park.

Before my hand could reach the door knocker of number 8, the door opened to reveal Charlotte Morgan. She was standing in a pair of jeans and a fitted black sweater which looked to be cashmere. She didn't have any make-up on and the difference between the way she looked now and the way she had before, in Agnieska's, was startling. She didn't look any worse, just different. She reminded me of Helen Mirren when she's playing a housewife rather than a successful career woman. She did look older though, and tired.

'Mr Rucker,' she said. 'Thank you for coming.'

Charlotte Morgan showed me into the small kitchen and invited me to sit at the table while she poured us both some coffee. I took a sip and waited as she took a chair herself. She studied my face.

'It wasn't the police?' she asked. 'Who did that?'

'No,' I said. 'Not them.'

'They were here.'

'I imagined they would be.'

'They showed me a picture of you. I told them that you had been to see me. They wanted to know if I had ever seen you before but I said that I hadn't. They wanted to know what we talked about.'

Charlotte looked nervous.

'Did you tell them?'

'No,' she said, 'I didn't. Not everything, no.'

She took a sip from her coffee and then looked down into the steam. I watched her and I remembered watching her before, in the other room. But this time she wasn't crying. There was a cast to her face which told me that whatever pain she felt was now enclosed within herself, locked up well away from the surface. She looked thoughtful and determined. Her look was a more effective cover than any amount of make-up.

Eventually, a bitter smile broke into her features and she glanced up at me.

'I want to thank you,' she said.

'Thank me?'

'For not telling the police. I thought you had when they phoned yesterday. I thought that's what they wanted. But it wasn't.'

'I still might have to tell them. I probably will.'

Charlotte Morgan nodded.

'I understand,' she said. 'But it doesn't matter now. I might even tell them myself.'

Charlotte put her cup down and leant forward on her elbows. Her eyes were looking at me but they were focused on her own thoughts. Luke had once told me of an acting exercise where you have to split your level of awareness into different layers: the distance, the immediate surroundings and then to a place no further than your own mind. That's where Charlotte Morgan was now.

'I saw Graham last night.'

I'd guessed this was coming.

'After the police were here. I'd been trying to see him for days but he was always too busy or something just came up. I knew what was going on but I wouldn't let myself believe it.'

I waited. I think she wanted me to say it. 'And he ended your relationship?'

'He said that it was too complicated, that things had changed. He said his wife was ill. He said all kinds of things. I didn't really listen to him. I didn't respond very well, I'm afraid.'

'I'm not surprised. It hasn't been easy for you.'

'Yes it has!' I was surprised by the ferocity of Charlotte's denial. 'It has been *so* easy for me. I wasn't killed. I didn't have a wife who was being unfaithful, unfaithful with a worthless bastard. I didn't have a wife who went to her lover the night she found her husband's body.'

Charlotte's focus had changed. It was levelled directly at me now. She finished off her thought: 'I didn't have a wife who was cold, who drove him to try and get some affection somewhere else.'

I let Charlotte take hold of herself. There was no point contradicting her. She ran her hands back through her hair and pushed them together in front of her like she was praying. Her hands touched her chin.

'Charlotte,' I said, 'why are you telling me this?'

She had regained her composure very quickly. I could see her censuring herself, reminding herself to keep it in. There was a notepad on the table beside her which she took hold of, and opened to the first page. She took a breath.

'A few weeks ago,' she said, looking down at the pad, 'Graham wanted me to invest in a concern of his.' My mind went to a computer screen in Company House. 'It was called the Buckner Group. Basically it's a vineyard in Sussex.'

'And did you?'

'Well, I was very interested to begin with. I am a very wealthy woman as you may already know, and it sounded like a good idea. Last summer was the best one ever, and with new techniques and cross-bred varieties of grape, England is becoming a viable place to produce wine.'

'Then why change your mind?'

'Well, it was my accountant really. He was always against the idea. He told me that investing in a vineyard is the best way to become a millionaire; if you're a billionaire.'

'Nice.'

'Yes. I brushed him off but he did some research which I hadn't asked him to do. He was my father's accountant. He's my godfather actually.'

'And he came up with some dubious figures.'

'Yes. Not in the vineyard in question but in two others that the Buckner Group owned. They're close to bankruptcy as a matter of fact. They owe over a hundred and fifty thousand to various people.'

'And you told Lloyd this?'

'Yes. He tried to whitewash me but I am a businesswoman after all. I told him that it just didn't make sense. Not for either of us. It would just be throwing good money after bad.'

'And did he get angry?'

'Yes, he did. It was our first argument. That was three weeks ago. Since then his passion for me . . . well, shall we say it began to cool a little.'

The bitter smile returned, but it was accompanied again by the look of determination. She shifted in her seat.

'Last night,' she continued, 'when he finally ended it, it got me thinking. He obviously wanted my money all along but did he want it so badly that he had my husband killed to get it?'

I looked hard at her. What was this, jealousy? Revenge?

'Divorce would have done that though,' I said. 'He would still have got your money.'

'Yes, he would, though it would have taken longer. Maybe too long, *and* he would have had to marry me. More importantly, there wouldn't have been as much. I collected a substantial sum from the life assurance policy Edward had taken out.'

'I see. He may also have figured that a recently bereaved widow would not be too financially aware, not too careful about investing her money with the lover who had promised to marry her.'

'Yes,' Charlotte Morgan agreed, 'he may very well have thought that. When he put the idea to me I was initially thrilled. For some reason I thought it was his way of committing to me, as if we were joining up all of our eggs into the same basket. And if that *was* his thinking he was right. If Miles hadn't been my accountant and willing to go the extra mile for me I'd have willingly given Graham my money. Even before we were married.'

Charlotte sat back. She picked up her cup but didn't drink out of it, holding it in her left hand with her right hand supporting her elbow.

'Do you want to tell this to the police?'

'I don't know. For some reason I wanted to tell you first. I want you to talk to him about it. I want you to let him know that I'm aware of what he was trying to do. Whether or not he killed my husband. Will you see him? I'd gladly pay you.'

'I have a client. Besides, why should he meet me? He's already warned me off once. What have I got on him?'

Charlotte stood up without answering me and walked into the living room. When she came back into the kitchen there was a packet in her hand. She set it down in front of me. On the front of the packet were the words QUICK PRINT'. I pulled the flap open and took out a set of negatives and seven black and white photographs.

'I had them developed,' Charlotte explained. 'At a one-hour place. Risky, I know. But I was curious. Graham told me to throw the film away and I told him that I had but I didn't. I didn't have a photograph of him, you see. Not even one. I didn't have one of us together. I know it's not the usual shot of a happy couple, and I hated you for taking it, but I wanted to keep it.'

I laid the pictures out on the table. Two were of the car, clearly showing the number plate, and one was of the front door of the house. Another showed Lloyd coming out of the door while another showed him in Charlotte's arms, kissing her, his hand up to her forehead. There was no doubt as to who the man in the picture was, and there was no doubt as to the nature of the kiss. The final two photographs pictured Lloyd walking to his Jag and then getting into it.

Charlotte put her finger on the picture of her and Lloyd.

'It's funny,' she said, straightening it out towards her. 'It's such an intimate picture. It's touching. It's odd to think it was taken by a snoop. No offence meant.'

'None taken.'

'It reminds me of that photo in Paris, you know, of the lovers.'

'Robert Doisneau. It's on every schoolgirl's wall.'

'That's the one. "The Kiss". Look at Graham,' she said. 'He looks like such a tender man. He looks so concerned, so involved.'

'Yes,' I agreed, 'he does.' She was right. It was a

surprisingly good shot and it really did convey a youthful, uncomplicated passion.

'To look at this,' Charlotte said, her lip curling down in disgust, 'and then to think of him. The way he has been on the phone, evasive, slippery, and the way he was last night. I was just trouble, an annoyance to be brushed aside without any fuss. You wouldn't know it was the same man. Here he looks, well, he looks like he's in love.'

'The camera always lies,' I said. 'That Doisneau shot was a set-up.'

I asked Charlotte if she wanted to go to the police. She said she didn't know. She didn't know if she could handle the publicity which we both knew would follow.

'At work,' she said, 'it would be impossible. I'm in PR. It would hardly help the image of the company.'

'Do you care?'

'I don't know. But I do know what the tabloids would do to me.'

I could see the story myself. They would crucify her, or at least the ones she hadn't sold her story to would, out of spite if nothing else. The Widow and the MP. Suspect MP and the pilot's wife. If Morgan was in the frame someone would be bound to speculate about whether she was in there with him. If he was innocent the mud would still stick to her for her infidelity, and if he was guilty no one would ever be completely sure she wasn't a part of it.

'I think I want you to handle it. Please. If it was Graham who did it then I don't care, I'll tell it all. But if he didn't I can't see the point. Can you?'

'No,' I agreed. 'Except the police will roast you if they find you've been holding out on this.'

'I don't care,' she said. 'And I won't hold out, not if you

think they'll be able to do anything you can't. But can you try first?'

'Yes,' I said.

I thought about showing Lloyd the photographs. I would enjoy that.

'And, Mr Rucker,' Charlotte said. 'I really do want them to catch whoever killed Edward. You know that, don't you?'

I looked at her.

'Yes,' I said.

I scooped up the photographs and handed Charlotte the negatives.

'Keep them somewhere safe,' I said.

She showed me to the door and walked me to the end of the mews, on to Leinster Road.

'Charlotte,' I said, as I held my arm out for a cab. I wanted to ask her the same question I'd asked Sir Peter Morgan about her. 'Do you really think that Graham Lloyd can have had anything to do with what happened to Edward?'

'I don't know,' Charlotte replied. 'It sounds so out-landish. But then if you'd told me two months ago that he was screwing me for my money and would drop me as soon as he either did or didn't get it, I wouldn't have believed that either.'

Chapter Twenty

Cleaver Square was quiet. I sat in the pub, by the window, with a pint of bitter which tasted so good I had to stop myself having another, which would have led me to needing to stop myself having another one after that. I was sitting in the corner, by the window, and I stayed there until I saw a blue Jaguar drive past slowly and then park. No other car followed it. I waited another five minutes, stood up and took my empty pint pot back to the bar. Then I walked out into the street.

I'd called Graham Lloyd from the phone in the back of the pub. I was pretty sure he wouldn't want to talk to me so I told his secretary I was a policeman and gave her an imaginary warrant card number which was in fact the phone number of a woman called Sue, which someone else had written in biro on a beer mat next to the phone. When he realized it was me on the line Lloyd was very unhappy indeed and proceeded to mouth off some legal-sounding invective until I told him about the photographs I had. He shut up. I informed him that I would be going to his house on Cleaver Square and would be there in about an hour. I was then going to show the photographs I had to whoever opened the door; whether that was Lloyd himself, or his wife, was his choice.

I crossed the square thinking that, apart from its

location, I couldn't imagine many more elegant spots in the whole capital. I walked past a green door and then a red door and up to a yellow door. The door, when I approached it, looked to be newly painted and I wondered if actually it had been a red door originally but with Lloyd hoping to rise in the Party he'd thought it politic to change it. No. In that case it would have been blue. Daft theory.

A young girl opened the door. With her Scandinavian accent and the fact that a small child was hammering both of his fists against her legs I assumed she was the au pair. Would she be interested in the photos? I didn't get a chance to find out. Graham Lloyd appeared from a side room.

'Ah,' he said, moving his hands like a lollipop man to indicate which room I was to go into. 'Please, this way.'

The child, surprised and pleased to see his father at such an unusual time, made a beeline for the door in front of me.

'Not *now*, Thomas. Go with Kristen.' Kristen picked the boy up and he had just begun a sustained bout of wailing at the fact when Lloyd closed the door behind me, shutting the noise out.

Lloyd made no comment about the state of my face. Maybe that's why the kid had started crying; he thought I was Frankenstein's monster come to kill his daddy.

'Please, Mr Rucker. Have a seat.'

We were in a large room which looked like the cross between an office and a study. It was all old-school Chesterfields but there were two computer terminals that I could see, as well as a fax machine and a small photocopier. I relaxed into an armchair. Lloyd hesitated above me. He seemed uncertain of what line to take, how to deal with me. He was friendly, but brusque at the same time.

Looking at him, in his public schoolboy only ever been to one tailor in his life outfit, I couldn't help wondering what it was that a stylish woman like Charlotte Morgan had seen in him. There must have been something though, and it wasn't necessarily on show for me to see. Maybe if he took his glasses off. His glasses were not stylish. He can't have been high enough up yet to warrant the attention of the spin doctors.

It was after 3 p.m. and a pale winter sun was sloping through the Georgian windows, resting on an empty wineglass like a broken yolk. Lloyd plunged his hands into his trouser pockets and rocked back on his heels.

'So,' he said. 'I am to understand that Charlotte kept the pictures you took. Yes? Or you had another set?'

I shrugged. 'What does it matter?'

'No. You're right. It matters that you have them. You won't mind me asking to check that, I presume.'

I fished in my coat pocket and handed him the packet. He stood back from me and leafed through the pictures quickly. His face clouded but then he smiled.

'She really is very beautiful, don't you think?'

Again I shrugged.

'You can understand why I fell for her, can't you? Anyone could. But you must also understand why I had to end it. After what happened.'

' "What happened"?'

'Yes.' Lloyd shook his head. 'Damned unfortunate. I know Morgan of course. Fine man. Very fine indeed.'

Lloyd walked over to the far wall. I was surprised by his relaxed manner. He hadn't mentioned our previous meeting, our hostility to each other, me and my swift exit. It was like a mad aunt, walled up in a room downstairs somewhere.

Lloyd stood thinking. He opened a small cabinet and drew out a bottle of malt and two tumblers. He walked over and sat opposite me, resting the bottle and the glasses on a low coffee table.

'I suppose she hates me,' he said. 'I don't blame her. But how was I supposed to know all this was going to happen? A discreet affair, that's what I thought was going on.'

'Charlotte says you talked about marriage.'

Lloyd looked uneasy. 'Well, I won't deny it. I was blown away, to begin with at least. That never happened to you?'

Oh yes, it had happened to me.

'But then I realized that it couldn't go on.'

'No?'

'No. It wasn't fair on her as much as anything. She was beginning to need me, I was a crutch to her. I knew I couldn't keep it up for ever so I broke it sooner rather than later. Before she couldn't do without it. I don't blame Charlotte if she's feeling bad. She really is having a very awful time.'

Without asking me if I wanted one, Lloyd poured me out a good measure of Scotch, and pushed the glass along the table towards me. He then filled the other glass but didn't pick it up. He sat back in his chair, still holding the bottle, stroking the body of it as though it were a big, fluffy cat, and he was Donald Pleasance. His hands looked like two, independent creatures, and for a second I was almost mesmerized by them. Reluctantly, I took my eyes from his hands, and the bottle they were lovingly caressing, and rested them on the MP's face.

Lloyd was trying the reasonable approach. His bullying sarcasm hadn't worked on me before so he thought he'd try to get me on-side with a bit of discreet male 'you know how it is' bandinage. I picked up the tumbler and took a sip.

'Scotch OK for you?'

'Actually,' I said, looking up, 'I'd prefer wine. If you have any.'

Lloyd looked mildly irritated but went to stand up. 'Of course. Red or white?'

'Either,' I replied. 'As long as it's English.'

Lloyd stopped, and sat back down. He bit into the side of his cheek and looked at me. He nodded to himself, as though he'd just worked something out.

'You don't care about infidelity, do you?' he stated.

'Not a lot.'

'No, I didn't think so. When you first approached Charlotte I thought you worked for a newspaper. I thought I'd have to write you a little cheque in the end. But then you told me you didn't have any evidence.'

'I didn't.'

'No. And now you do, but you don't care about our affair. It's not a cheque you want, is it?'

'No.'

'Not even if it were a rather large cheque?'

'It wouldn't make any difference. It isn't me who has the evidence, it's Mrs Morgan.'

'Yes, but she's not going to expose herself, is she?'

'Maybe not. I don't care either way. As you say, I'm not really interested in infidelity. I just want to know who killed an MP's brother. Oh, that and who left a boy prostitute on my bed, with his cock cut off, gutted like a trout at Billingsgate Market. And made it look like it was me who did it. I really am interested in finding out who did that.'

Lloyd put the bottle down on the table and picked up his glass without drinking from it. He certainly was a man who liked to build up to things.

'In that case, why are you here?'

I laughed.

'You want me to explain? You were having an affair with a rich woman whose husband was murdered. The company you own is up shit creek and as soon as the woman decides not to give you any money you dump her. Tell me, where the hell else should I be?'

'Looking for a killer. Do I look like one?'

I thought about what a worried gay guy had told me, sitting in a Soho coffee house.

'As much as any killer I've ever met,' I told him.

'OK,' he said. 'I dispute the facts you have given me. My company is not up shit creek, and neither did I either begin or end my relationship with Charlotte Morgan because of money. But if that is what you think I can understand your interest in me. Tell me what I can do to assure you of my innocence.'

'Show me your diary,' I said.

Lloyd reached into his pocket for his electronic organizer.

'No,' I said, 'the one on the desk.'

Lloyd stood up and walked over to the heavy oak desk where the fax machine sat next to some loose papers and a large black book with 1998 written on it in gold letters. I stood up too and took the book off him when he turned round. I walked over to the photocopier.

'Now wait a minute.'

'Fine,' I said, dropping the lid of the machine back down. 'Then I'll take it with me.'

'You have no right . . .'

'None at all,' I agreed. 'All I've got is pictures.'

Lloyd let me take copies of his diary. I thought about asking him for his company records but I was pretty sure that Charlotte Morgan's accountant would be able to tell me everything I wanted to know about them. As I used the machine I could feel Lloyd bridling next to me. He was finding it hard to stick to the tack he had chosen. He wanted to get rid of me, to stamp on me like a cockroach on the floor of a Cibar kitchen.

'Is that all?' Lloyd said, when I had finished collating the pages and handed him back his diary.

'For now. Unless you can think of anything else you can do to show me how innocent you are.'

'Shouldn't it be the other way round?'

'Usually,' I replied, 'but not in this case. The more you can tell me, the less you'll have to tell the police.'

'There's nothing more,' he said. 'Really.'

'That's a shame,' I told him. 'Because if I don't find anything else to either put you away or keep your nose out of it, then not even Mother Teresa will be able to keep your name out of the papers.'

'Mother Teresa?'

'Forget it,' I said.

There wasn't any more I could ask him. I walked over to the door and opened it. Lloyd followed me to the front door and got to the handle before me.

'Don't you want these?' he asked, handing me the photographs. The sarcasm had crept back into his voice, making him sound no older than his son.

'They're only copies,' I said.

'Nevertheless.' He handed them to me like they were hard-core porn snaps and I was trying to sell them to him. 'I don't want them lying around.'

'No. I don't imagine that you do.'

He held the door open and at that moment his son flew down the stairs, crying 'Daddy! Daddy!' and holding his arms out to Lloyd. The child grabbed hold of Lloyd's trouser leg but the MP ignored him.

'For God's sake, Kristen! How many times must I tell you? Keep Thomas upstairs during the day! How many times?'

I walked through the door and down the steps. I didn't wait for Lloyd to finish reprimanding his domestic staff to say goodbye to him.

Chapter Twenty-One

The taxi was already on the Clerkenwell Road before I realized where it was that I was going. Back to my flat. I hadn't been there for three days and I didn't know what I would find there. The cab got snarled up in traffic on the Farringdon Road so I got out and walked up past Carl's Repro shop, with a feeling of trepidation which I couldn't explain. It wasn't as if I was likely to find any more mutilated bodies lying on my bed. I could not, however, dispel a certain edginess as I walked into the small road and fished my spare keys out of my pocket.

The outside door had been mended, but this didn't surprise me because I shared it with another flat. There were only small signs that it had recently been broken into. The key turned in the lock quite normally and the door opened.

I stepped into the hallway and turned on the light even though I could see well enough. I walked up the stairs. When I got to the top of the first flight I could see that my door had not been mended. Nor was there any no-entry tape or police-aware stickers to indicate a police presence. The door was slightly ajar and I thought great, why don't you let the whole fucking world into my flat. I not only wondered if I'd still have the cash I had, I wondered if I'd still possess a stereo and a TV. I walked up the stairs into my living room.

Only the futon was gone. The space where it would have been yawned with its absence. The wine stain on the rug next to the space was larger than I remembered it, and more distinct now that it was in the daylight. Why the hell had he chosen my Grange, the finest wine ever made in Oz, one of the top ten made anywhere? What was wrong with the Sainsbury's Côte du Rhône? I wondered why the police hadn't taken the rug. They should have, they might have found something in it, a fingernail or a small piece of dirt from a shoe. I knew then that Ken Clay hadn't visited the scene; he would not have overlooked it. I folded the rug carefully and found a bag from the deli to put it in. I'd call Clay and tell him, and then enjoy the thought of what he would then say to the two alleged detectives who had been in charge of searching the place.

I spent about an hour in the bath, refilling with hot when the water started to go cold. I let stress and pain seep out of my body, and I let thoughts and questions seep into my mind. I tried to let them in slowly, one at a time, so that they wouldn't merge into one another.

There wasn't anything else Lloyd could have told me, except that he was the perp and he was hardly likely to do that. Was he desperate enough to be involved in this? It seemed, from what Charlotte Morgan had told me, that he was very good at hiding his real reasons, painting a coat of veneer over what he really wanted. If I was the police what could I do which would help me get to him? I could talk to his colleagues in the Commons, see if they remembered any changes of mood in him, if he had ever mentioned his financial troubles. I could talk to his partner in the Buckner Group. Both those things would probably only reveal motive, which I already had. Money. Someone might however have seen Lloyd with an unusual person, someone not dressed in a suit. Wearing a baseball hat maybe. It wasn't likely, I didn't peg Lloyd for being that stupid, but if he was a first-time employer of contract muscle then he just *might* have been careless.

Other thoughts came to me, which I processed and mainly discarded. Then some other thoughts came which could not be separated, but whirled around in no sort of order. They concerned Sharon, and what we had done in her flat, the significance of it and what markers and signs we had set for the future. What, if anything, it had determined. I wondered if what we had done meant what I had not even dared think it would mean, when I was so caught up in the painfully brilliant moment of her that there was no way I *could* think. Simply, I wondered if what we had done was right or wrong, if it was the future or something to be shocked at, appalled, something to be buried in the dark bog that we call experience. A scary place, full of sprites and foul gases, never to be returned to. I lay in the bath, staring at the ceiling, lying still, not even moving my eyelids.

I got out of the bath and dried myself gingerly. I pulled on some jeans, a T-shirt and sweatshirt. I sat at the table and made a few calls. The first was to Ken Clay and I got his machine. I told him that it might be worth sending some men round to the Commons with the picture, to do a discreet bit of canvassing. I said that it was unlikely but that someone there *may* have seen the man. I called a futon shop that I'd seen on Calthorpe Street and asked them for some prices and whether they delivered. I couldn't be bothered hunting around for anywhere cheaper so I asked them to send me one in the middle of their range. To my surprise they said they could do it before six, if I was at home. I told them to go ahead. I gave them my credit card number and wondered if I could charge the whole thing to Sir Peter Morgan, claiming it on expenses.

I put the phone down and took another look at my flat. Apart from the futon there was something else wrong with it, something else changed or missing. I looked around but all the major things were still there: my TV, my stereo, the four bottles of wine in my rack. My Salgado print. I even checked my loose cash and bank cards and was surprised to find that they were all where and as I had left them. I sat back down at the table. Maybe I was imagining it. I brushed my doubt aside and went to put the kettle on. Then I realized. I went back to the table again but the blue folder containing my brother's poems was not there.

I'd gone to open it when I was waiting for the cavalry, and the WPC had told me to leave it. They must have thought it was important and taken it in. That would have been on her suggestion; if the two idiots who'd been round earlier hadn't thought fit to remove a rug stained in the course of the crime they were hardly likely to seize on a collection of verse the suspect had casually turned to. I wanted the folder back, and was suddenly panicked. Was it the only copy or did Sharon have another? I hadn't even looked inside it. What if they'd lost it, or thrown it out? I dialled Clay's number again. I expected his machine but this time I got the man himself.

'Only if you give me what you have,' he said, after I'd told him what I wanted. 'Otherwise I'll keep them here and use them to bring a little culture to the place.'

I hesitated a second. A little bit couldn't hurt.

'Graham Lloyd,' I said. 'I sort of like him for it. Or, rather, I like him more than anyone else.'

'The one Mother Teresa . . .'

'A *maybe* maybe,' I said. 'But only for Edward Morgan. Maybe Dominic Lewes.'

'And?'

'And that's it. That's all I have. Really. That's why I suggested you take that picture to the Commons.'

'On what grounds do you suggest? Your say-so?'

'Make some up,' I said. 'Tell them he's been mugging MPs on their way home. That'll make them remember if they've seen him or not.'

Clay paused. 'I'll think about it.'

'Right. What about the folder?'

'Oh, that. I had DC Milson go through that with as fine a toothed comb as his mind can supply. I don't think he got much out of the experience. I didn't know you were so creative, Rucker.'

'I'm not,' I said. 'Are you going to let me have them? They're not important, I promise you. You can take copies if you're not sure and give me those.'

Clay thought for a second.

'OK, Rucker, they'll be on the front desk.'

'Thanks,' I said. 'Oh, and Ken, don't be too hard on Milson and the other chap.'

'Clarke.'

'Yeah, Clarke, that's it.'

'Not hard on them for what?' Clay asked.

'You'll see.' I put the phone down.

I was relieved. I thought about the folder and wondered how come I had never got round to looking in it. Didn't I want to read Luke's poems? Of course I did.

Didn't I? I'd have got round to them sooner or later if events hadn't got in the way first.

I spent the next hour going through Lloyd's diary. I looked at the dates on and around the day Teddy Morgan had been murdered. They didn't tell me much. There was an appointment with a man called Harvey, although whether that was a Christian or surname it didn't say. I wrote the name down and made a note to check it. I wrote down a few more names as well, knowing that Lloyd wasn't the type to write 'Contract killer, 11 a.m.' in his desk diary. I'd get him to tell me who the names referred to, check up on them, and then if there was a name that didn't match – who knows.

The futon came. Two guys carried it up the stairs and to my surprise it was fully constructed. When I remarked on this I was told that it was a showroom model, the only one they had in stock. I was glad. The two men wanted to know where they should put it and I told them to set it down where the other one had been. They did so and I thanked them and they left.

The futon was pretty much the same as the old one, with a black cover and an easy-fold mechanism. The actual mattress seemed to be thicker but I put this down to lack of use. I stared at it for a second and then tried out the mechanism to see how smooth it was. It was fine, and the sofa-shaped object changed easily into a bed. I stared down at it. Dominic Lewes stared back at me. I changed it into a sofa again.

I looked round my flat. The futon had always been where the futon was and the table had always been where the table was and the wardrobe where I keep most of my clothes had always been where that was. Was there any reason for it? Maybe if I moved the table to where the cupboard was, and I moved the cupboard to where my old futon had been, I could put the new futon where the table was now. There was a small enclave that fitted the table quite well but it would fit the futon even better. And having the wardrobe over there made sense because where it was now seemed to dominate the room and who wants to look at a wardrobe? If I moved the table there it would get more light and that way I could use the plug socket to the left of the wardrobe and it would also mean I wouldn't need the extension lead to the phone which stretched right across the middle of the floor.

And I wouldn't have to share my bed with the ghost of Dominic Lewes. His blood soaking down into me, his face saying that he wasn't at all surprised that he had been strangled and torn open, not after the life he had had, not after some of the other things which various people had done to him.

I changed the flat round. By the time I had finished it was dark. I kicked myself for forgetting to phone a locksmith. I turned the stereo on, quite loud, and turned most of the lights in my flat on too. I left and walked down to my car and was amazed to find it without a clamp even though it was still in the delivery bay where I had left it three nights ago. I'd have to remember that. It started nonchalantly, as though I'd only been out of it five minutes to buy a newspaper, and it took me to the station where I had recently been incarcerated. I picked up the folder, left Clay the rug with a note, and got back in. I pulled off and swung the car round the one-way system, intending to go back to my round of the pubs. Old Compton Street, where the man had recognized the picture.

Instead I thought of something else. The one-way

system took me closer to King's Cross. I parked on one of the streets behind it. Elm Drive. I parked outside number 23. There were no lights on. I got out of the car and locked it. I walked up to the door and knocked. There was no answer. I pushed open the letter box and looked through it but I couldn't see anything.

I walked up to the top of the street and then back down a small alley, counting off the houses. When I got to number 23 I had a quick look round and then hopped over the fence and into the back garden. The garden was a small yard, with an overflowing dustbin which, by the smell of it, had been there some time. I walked up to the back door.

The door pushed open beneath my hand. I found a switch and was surprised when light came out of a single bulb dangling from the ceiling. I listened, but couldn't hear anything other than a leaking tap. I walked around the house. It was obvious that no one was living there. The whole house was miserable and cold with huge blotches of damp in the corners of the bedroom walls like sweat-stained nylon. Strange smells brushed past me like malignant ghosts. In one bedroom I found, lying on the floor next to an old mattress, a train timetable. Apart from the mattress it was all that was left in the room. His clothes and his other effects must already have been bagged and sent to his parents. They wouldn't have wanted a train timetable. I picked it up and saw that it showed times from London King's Cross to Newark North Gate and then connections from there to, among other places, Grimsby Town. A young man thinking about going home. He hadn't been thinking it for some time though; the timetable was out of date.

I flicked through the pages. Maybe the timetable had

just lain around for months and Dominic hadn't bothered to chuck it out. Perhaps he didn't realize he still had it. Or maybe he kept it on purpose, and looked at it now and then, when his head was somehow higher than the shit which surrounded him usually and which was slowly pulling him down into it. Maybe he looked at it now and then and wondered if one day he would ever make use of it. It was like a St Christopher, a small, desperate, useless talisman of hope. I decided that one day soon I really did have to speak with his mother, and when I did I would tell her about it. It might provide some kind of comfort to her to know that once in a while her son did think of home.

I had another idea. I left the car where it was and walked towards the Cross. I turned right. I walked past the spot where I had spoken to Dominic, past the alley Rollo had stopped me in. I crossed the road and peered through the window of the café at the bottom of Calshot Street, and then walked round the back. A gate was open. I glanced in and saw a small backyard with an old Biffa skip and some stacked crates. The back door of the café was ajar and I could see into the kitchen where a pair of dark hands was chopping a shiny mound of liver. I slipped into the yard and stood in shadow behind the skip, with my eye on the door. I waited.

She came out after about forty minutes, with a cigarette already in her mouth and a Bic going up to light it. I moved behind her slowly and pushed the door shut, making as little noise as possible. She turned at the sound.

'What . . .'

I didn't let her get any further. I grabbed hold of her wrist and pushed her backwards into the hard wood of the fence which surrounded the yard. A streetlight lit her face and I saw her recognize me. She tried to scream but I forced her back further by grabbing hold of her neck.

'Who else did you tell?'

She shook her head desperately but she didn't make any noise.

'Who the hell else did you tell about me watching Dominic?'

I loosened my grip a bit.

'I don't know Dominic.'

'Mikey. Mikey. Who did you tell?'

'No one . . .'

'You told Rollo. You told him and he was waiting for me. Someone else knew. Who the fuck was it, who did you tell?'

'No one. I swear. I never. Please.'

'Where's the girl who lived with Mikey?'

'I don't know. I never went there.'

'Didn't Rollo live there?'

'No, he just went for the money. Please, you're hurting me.'

I pressed my thumb harder, up into her chin.

'Who did you tell?'

'I didn't, I swear I didn't.'

I let go of her throat and put my hand over her mouth. I fished into my pocket and pulled out one of the pictures that were still in there.

'Who's this?'

'I don't know. I can't see it.'

I held the picture more into the light.

'I've never seen him, I . . .'

'Tell me about Rollo. How long have you been seeing him?'

'I'm not, I'm not! He just used to come in.'

'You knew what he did?'

'Not at first. Oh, listen, I screwed him a couple of times. He's got a really nice place, that's how I know he didn't live with those kids. When I heard about that boy it was terrible. He used to come in for Coke.'

'And the girl he lived with?'

'Yes, sometimes.'

'What was her name?'

'I don't—'

'What was her fucking name!'

My hands went up to her throat again.

'Emma, I think her name was Emma.'

I released her. I stood back. Her hands went straight up to her neck, and she rubbed it, breathing deeply. Her eyes narrowed and I could tell that she was scared. But not of me.

'You bastard,' she said. Her voice was small and full of hate. I left her there and walked back to the station.

I spoke to Ken Clay, who made a point not to mention the rug I'd left him, and I sat with a guy on their computer imager. I gave a description of Emma and he pressed the right buttons until something close to the face I had seen through a crack in the door of number 23 Elm Drive appeared on the screen. It's amazing what a memory the mind has for faces, if someone is trained to give it a hand. Clay said he'd get the picture and the name to the boys in blue first thing and it wouldn't be long before Emma turned up. I didn't ask him if he would give me a copy of it. I'd had enough of showing pictures around.

Clay wasn't angry with me any more, not now I was giving him stuff.

'What about the waitress?' he asked me.

'Pick her up,' I said. 'She might tell you who the bastard is eventually. I don't think she knows though.'

'Rollo neither,' Clay said. 'We've got him on a dealing charge, raided his place and found the usual.' There was a glint in Clay's eye which told me that 'found' might not be the right word. 'We've offered to forget about it if he'll give up the man in the picture and I can tell he wants to. He's either scared or hasn't got it.'

'The man said he knew him. Or at least knew who he was.'

'Everybody knows Rollo. He's a flash one, spreads it about. This other chap keeps himself to himself it seems.'

'Yes, but if he knew Rollo, maybe he's in the same line of business.'

'Maybe,' Clay said.

I left Clay to it and walked back to my car. I was glad I'd thought of the girl in the house Dominic was living in. Emma. She might know something. I'd let the police find her though. I didn't think it would take them long. I wondered if she'd tell them anything, or just clam up like Rollo. I remembered her sick face and her flat eyes.

I was exhausted. I thought of but immediately canned the idea of going down to Nicky's for a beer and drove home instead, to my newly arranged flat and to my newly installed futon.

Chapter Twenty-Two

In the next few days I went through the names in Lloyd's diary. I got him to tell me who they all were and each one of them checked out the way he had said they would. Other MPs, colleagues at both the lobby company and the Holdings firm as well as a couple of old friends and his brother. Harvey turned out to be Harvey Lawrence, Lloyd's only partner in the Buckner Group. I called him and pretended to be a potential investor. He seemed very pleased to hear from me and didn't even ask where I'd got hold of his name. I arranged to meet him in two days' time which would give me a chance to set up a meeting with Charlotte Morgan's accountant first.

But I never got the chance to meet either of them.

I wanted to talk to Dominic's other friends, the other kids on his patch. One of them must have seen him go off with the man in the hat that night. Andy phoned to tell me that the police had found Emma but she hadn't seen Dominic since the night before he was killed. I wanted to speak to the kid I'd seen Dominic with the night I'd had the run-in with Rollo. I was pretty sure I'd recognize him. I'd seen him and Dominic talking; they looked like friends. I set myself up in a pub this time, on the Pentonville Road itself, which was not as near as the café was but close enough that I could still tell if there was anyone standing about for business without having to get my zoom out and make a show of myself. The pub was dark and smoky and smelled of piss. It had a smallish stage which was occupied by a bored stream of readers' wives style strippers. The pub's clientele was made up exclusively of men but I wasn't the only one not bothering to pay attention.

The spot across the street was completely empty for the first day that I sat there watching it. I guessed this was due to what happened to Dominic, which the other kids would have heard about and felt that the best way to protect themselves was to go and stand on a different corner. They would always come back though; knowing that they would lose regular custom, their pimps would have told them they had to. Another possible reason for their absence was that the police had steamed in with pictures of Dominic and scared them all off. In that case they would still return, but it might take longer. Fear of the police was stronger in boy junkies than fear of serial killers. I sat in the pub all of that day and for most of the evening.

During the morning of the second day, a couple of lads showed up. I was glad. I didn't want to go traipsing all over Dalston and out to Stoke Newington to find the place they'd decamped to. I waited in the pub. When the number had risen to four by midday I took a stroll past to see if any of them was the boy I had seen with Dominic. No luck. I thought about asking them anyway but decided against. The word might get round and the place would be dead again. I went back to the pub.

It was difficult to see but by late afternoon I thought the boy had arrived. I put my bag over my shoulder again and walked out on to the street. I walked past the twenty-

four-hour store and crossed over the road. I passed the
Thameslink station and walked up towards the derelict
kebab shop where the boys were waiting for pick-ups.
There were three of them, standing together in tight jeans
and bomber jackets. They looked just like any three teenagers, hanging out, trying to be cool, either chewing gum
or smoking. Other people walked by, most not noticing
them. A young girl checked one of them out. An old lady's
face drew up into a frown when one of the kids spat on
the pavement, not seeing her, forcing her to make a small
diversion in her path.

When I was twenty feet or so away from them, I could
tell that the boy was not there. None of them was him. I
was disappointed but this time I did decide to speak to the
others anyway as I was quite confident that I could do it
without spooking them. I approached the nearest one, but
spoke so that all of them could hear me.

'Listen, guys,' I said. 'I don't want to get you all
nervous. I'm not the Bill or anything. I was just wondering if any of you knew that kid Mikey. He used to work
from here.'

The three of them looked suspicious but not overly
worried or defensive. The one nearest said, 'No, mate.
Never knew him. Heard of him though. You sure you're
not Bill?'

'I'm positive.'

'What are you then?'

I never got a chance to answer. I was stood facing
towards the Cross, and I was about to speak when another
boy walked around the corner towards us. He was black,
about fourteen years old, and he was dressed in a bright
orange puffa jacket and a blue cap which he had on backwards. The boy's face was bruised some, the damage

hidden to a large degree by the natural colour of his skin, but evident nevertheless. He was walking with his hands in his pockets, his face a sullen mask of worry, and as he approached us one of the boys I was talking to looked up in a way which told me that he knew him. He nodded slightly and the black boy nodded back. I thought the black boy was going to say something, to make some sort of greeting but he didn't. He slowed down suddenly and came to a stop.

He came to a stop because of me.

Given warning, a second or two to get a hold of himself, the kid might just have bluffed it out and said hi to his mates and kept walking. But the surprise at seeing me was instant and as his gaze automatically locked into mine, his expression gave him away. He was afraid that I was there looking for *him*. Even then he could have shaken it off, if it were not for the fact that he could tell I had seen it. Seen his surprise. I stared into his eyes, trying to place him. I could feel recognition cogs wheeling into place and I knew that I'd have him in a matter of seconds.

Then I did have him.

The boy looked away from me and turned around immediately. He began to walk.

'Excuse me,' I said. He turned round very briefly but didn't stop. 'Excuse me,' I said again.

He was off.

How he wasn't killed by a cab accelerating away from the lights up towards the Angel I will never know. The shock and terror on the driver's face as he swerved straight into the goods van in the other lane was like a Munch sketch in motion. I ignored the havoc and the car horns and followed the kid over the road, keeping sight of his orange jacket as he ran and jostled through the crowd of pedestrians going to and from King's Cross. He ran towards the station and I just about kept up with him, fifteen or twenty yards behind him as he burned past the *Standard* vendors and the winos and the bus queues and the suits standing in line by the taxi rank. I ran after him, hampered by my hold-all which thudded against my hip with every second stride I took. I lost him as he turned right and ran up towards the Pancras Road.

Why the fuck was he running from me? I saw his face, nervous in the gym, just before he started sparring. Holding his coat. And earlier, just stood there, after I'd come out of the weights room. He'd come looking for me too, it must have been him Alberto saw in the café. Why was he . . . I thought of his bruises. Sal would never have let that happen to him in her gym. No way. Where did he get them? Why did I make him so terrified? No point worrying. He was running. He'd seen me and he was running.

I was on to him again as soon as I'd turned the way he had. He cut a right down a small road behind King's Cross station itself. I cut an earlier right and managed to beat him to the end, seeing him run out up ahead of me. He turned left and kept running and I followed, my side breaking as my ribs pulled apart where the cracks were beginning to knit. I pounded on, knowing that if he kept his pace up I was going to lose him. A boxing gym? He should have been at Crystal frigging Palace.

He took another right and I had an idea as to where he might be going. Again there was an earlier right, an old, cobbled mechanic's yard, and I took it, stopping myself before I flew out of the end of it. I held on to the wall and peered around the corner, just catching sight of a blur of orange as it came out ahead of me. I ducked back in and then heard the sound of his feet coming to a stop. Then there was the scuff sound of a quick sprint which stopped again, abruptly.

I pushed my ribs into my side and tried not to let my lungs pull in so much of the air it so desperately needed. Each breath was the ghost of the size tens I'd received at York Way. I left it a second and looked round the corner again, still breathing heavily. The kid was nowhere. I jogged up the street, up to the cast-iron fence-cum-wall at the top of it. I looked left and right but couldn't see the kid in either direction. I looked at the wall again and jumped up on to it, holding myself steady as I peered over the top.

The area I was looking into was land owned by British Rail. It was big, perhaps as big as two football pitches. I'd read somewhere that the land had been offered as part of a sweetener deal for companies interested in buying into the network when it was privatized. The land was central, perfect for high-rent office blocks and designer security homes. This hadn't happened yet though. The land was derelict, patched with the remains of abandoned fires lit by kids or the homeless, out for fun or heat. I could see rusting shopping trolleys and a punctured football, pieces of old carpet and a scorched three-piece suite.

And I could see a young boy in an orange puffa running directly away from where I was perched. He was running more slowly than he had been before, his head moving left and right as he looked around for me. As he moved his head and shoulders all the way round to take a look behind him, I dropped back out of sight.

After leaving a couple of seconds I pulled myself up again, this time getting a better hold so that I could duck down without coming off the wall completely. I looked over. I could see the boy jogging towards an old caravan, still looking all around him. The van was a hundred yards away. It was old and knackered, resting on six piles of bricks. I watched as the boy approached the van, reached up and knocked on the door. He pulled the door open. I ducked down again, knowing that he'd have one last look behind before stepping into the van. I came up to see the door closing. I took out my camera and zoomed in. I tried to see through the stained plastic windows but they were covered by brown curtains. I couldn't make out any movement behind them.

I focused on the door and was surprised when, after five minutes, it was thrown open. I caught a pair of hands, pushing the same boy out of the van on to the concrete. The door of the van shut and the boy got up. He held his knee where he'd fallen on it and then put his hand up to his face. Through the lens I could see that his nose was bleeding. The kid then hobbled off, one hand on his damaged knee, the other palm down, trying to staunch the flow of blood from his nose, wiping some on to the sleeve of his coat and then trying to wipe that off with his hand.

The boy walked off at a right angle to where I was sitting, towards a derelict building protected by wire meshing. He could probably get through there on to the street. It may even be where he slept. I looked up from the viewfinder and then put the camera back in my bag, still watching to make sure no one came out of the van.

I had it now. The gym. He wasn't scared of fighting. That wasn't why that doubt had come into his face when he saw me there. This kid looked like he got into fights quite often, and never came out of them too well. No. He was frightened of me. He was frightened of the picture that he'd seen me showing to Sal; it had been lying on the table in the weights room. He must have seen it. He was frightened because he knew the man in the picture and even more frightened of what might happen to him if he told me who the man was. I got the impression, thinking about it, that what frightened him most of all was that he really did want to tell me. He was terrified that that was exactly what he was going to do. That would have been fine if nothing could link me to him, but when he'd seen me on the corner with his colleagues he was sure he was in big trouble. If they knew he'd been looking for me, to tell me who the man in the picture was, they'd tell the man and he'd be as good as dead.

But now he had told me. I knew who was in there.

I jogged towards the van, trying to keep in line with the corner, away from the window. I thought about calling Ken Clay, but I wanted this guy for myself. I studied the curtains of the van but they didn't move. When I'd covered the distance from the wall I stood at the corner of the van and thought how to do it. From inside I could hear the sound of an efficient boom box tuned in to Radio One. Mark Radcliffe was assuring his listeners that he was very sorry indeed that his show was over for another day. I was glad of the noise; it would be a distraction. I waited until the next DJ had come on and assured his listeners of how glad he was to be with them for the next two hours. Still, I waited. Then the DJ announced that the next track would be a huge house-jungle crossover smash and was bound to break into the charts on Sunday. I wasn't ready to give an opinion on his prophetic statement but there was one thing I did know. The track was loud. I set my bag down on the ground beside me.

I walked round to the side of the caravan, where the door was, keeping my head below the level of the windows. I stood outside the door and reached for the handle. The kid had knocked but opened the door straight after he'd done so. It hadn't been locked. Was it now? I was about to find out. I pulled the handle.

I was inside the van. He was on the left, lying on a bed. He was propped up on some cushions and was just putting a beer down next to a half-empty litre bottle of cheap vodka on a small, built-in table to the right of the bed. At the foot of the bed, nearer to me than him, was a sawn-off shotgun, presumably the same one he had aimed at my head only a few days previously. In the split second before all hell let loose our eyes met.

He wasn't wearing a baseball hat now, and it was then that I realized what a perfect disguise his hat had been, why nobody had recognized him from the picture I'd been showing round; why he could know Rollo but Rollo didn't recognize him. The man was balding, with long, black greasy strands of hair hanging down from the sides of his head and down over his shoulders. On the top of his head, running down from the centre, and making a sharp turn to the left just above the brow, was a scar which dominated not only his head but his whole face. It was like a brand, the scar tissue old but still livid, something your eyes could not avoid, something which seemed to define him. I didn't know the cause of the scar, whether it was surgical, accidental or given to him on purpose, but I did know that with a hat on he was a different person. His hat was lying on the bed next to him.

He came forward towards the gun but I beat him to it. I was turning it on him when he took hold of the barrel with both of his hands and forced me back. For a split second the gun was pointing straight into his chest but I didn't pull the trigger. His momentum had taken him up into a standing position on the bed and it forced me backwards as he came off it and on to me. I backed into something, hard, and the gun went off, blowing a hole in the ceiling of the van and sending down a shower of debris. I pulled the trigger again, deliberately this time, blowing out one of the plastic windows. Knowing the gun was empty he released a hand from it and went for a straight right but I managed to get my head out of the way of his fist and it smacked into the plywood behind me. I got the butt of the gun into the side of his face. It straightened him up and before he could swing again I jabbed the end of the gun full into his face with as much of my weight behind it as I could get. It sent him the two feet towards the bed and he tripped backwards, thanks more to the contact with the bed than to what I'd done to him.

His face was pulsing blood. I wasn't sure how much he could see. He should have taken the count then but he didn't. He came up at me but before he could get to his feet I used the gun again. He went back further this time and his hand went for the nearest of the two bottles by the side of the bed which, to my relief, was the one that held the Becks. His fingers curled around the green glass and with one last effort he threw it with all his force, coming in after it, screaming like a stuck pig. I was showered with beer but the bottle missed me. I stepped to the side and the man missed me too; he crashed into the plywood which his fist had gone into. I used the gun again. He put his hands out to keep himself upright. I hit him again. Even then there was something left in him. It was like trying to fell a tree. I used the gun again and then one more time and then he didn't have anything left. I stood back from him and he slid down the wall of the van, settling on to the floor as gently as a lift in a four-star hotel.

The Spice Girls. I'll never forget that it was the Spice Girls which was all I could hear. I reached over and turned the sound off. I wanted it off because something else was trying to make me hear it. Or see it. I'd expected feelings of relief, even euphoria at finding the man who was now unconscious at my feet but all of a sudden it seemed trivial. There was something else, something bigger. My eyes went towards the unit at the top of the bed. My thoughts were racing ahead of me. The bottle. As he'd gone for the Becks bottle he'd knocked the litre bottle of vodka on to its side. It was still there. Even as he had done so it had started to come to me, though I didn't know what it was. Now I stared at the bottle. I got an uncomfortable feeling. I felt a racing in my stomach to match that in my head. There was a picture, a picture that I'd missed, something I'd seen but which hadn't registered. A bottle. A hand, the way it held . . . The vodka in the litre bottle swayed slightly, looking for equilibrium. It looked gentle, unconcerned. I stared at it.

I saw a man holding a bottle, holding it in a way which at the time had called out to me but I had failed to hear it. His hand on the bottle. Certain, calm, smiling. Holding it like . . . like he had some sort of affinity with it. I saw a bottle rammed into a young boy's throat. Other bottles. The pictures were becoming sharper. A boy, a truck driver. I felt the horror that comes from realization and the need to act, now, not wait another second, act before it all went out of focus. I didn't know how I knew what I did but I did know. I was certain. I *knew*. I could see it. It was the way he had held that bottle. I'd sat across from him as he smiled at me, and I'd been struck by it at the time but not struck hard enough. But now I knew what I knew and suddenly I knew how I could prove it. All of the inconsistencies, all of the elements which I couldn't fit into my scenario of what had happened to Edward, all suddenly made sense. Why I wasn't killed at York Way, why the killer didn't care about the video, why Teddy was preoccupied, how Dominic had become involved. The knowledge that had just come to me slid into the events easy as Cinderella's left foot. I snapped my eyes away from the vodka bottle and looked quickly round the caravan.

The man was lying on his side, curled up like he was asleep. Now I knew why he hadn't killed me; it was because he had never killed anyone. Not him. I searched for his mobile. I knew he'd have one, he was a pimp, wasn't he, at the very least? I tore the place apart until I finally found it in the pocket of a black leather jacket and used it to call Andy Gold. He wasn't there so I asked for Ken Clay. He came on the line and I told him that I was in a caravan on old BR land behind King's Cross.

'If you want the man in the hat,' I said, 'you better get here soon. He's unconscious but I don't know how long he'll be out.'

'Stay there,' Clay said. 'Don't fucking leave him.'

'I can't,' I said. 'Just get here.'

I was in a hurry. It wasn't a logical hurry, but it was speeding through me so fast I had to go with it.

'Just get here,' I said.

I could hear his protestations as I looked for the button to turn the thing off. I put the phone on the bed and took out my wallet. Andy Gold had given me a card which his bleeper company had issued and which had his number on it. I called it and told the woman the message I would like to leave. She wanted me to read it back to her.

'Just send the fucking thing!'

I dropped the phone and pushed open the door of the caravan. I grabbed my bag and ran to my car. There was a face in front of my eyes and as I ran I felt that I was running straight into it, my fists clenched, and I was about to smash a big hole in the confident smile that played on its broad lips.

I didn't feel the pain in my ribs any more.

When I got to Andy Gold's flat in Camden I double-parked and jumped out. He was already there, just getting out of his Astra. He locked it, and walked towards me, digging his flat keys out of his pocket. He looked puzzled.

'You've got the video?'

'Yes,' he said, 'it's inside. I never got round to taking it back. But I already gave you the picture.'

'Come on,' I said, 'quickly. I need to see it.'

We went inside. I asked Andy to find the place on the tape where he'd found Teddy, and the man in the hat. It didn't take him long.

'I already went through this about . . .'

I took the remote from him and hit the fast-forward button. I went back and forward over the next section of tape, going fast, and then slowing the tape right down. I couldn't see anything, but maybe it was because the door of the shop kept closing. I asked Andy to do the same thing with the other tape, the one from the concourse, which had shown Teddy and the man but had been useless due to the man's baseball cap. Again I hit the forward button, but this time the slow-mo. Andy sat beside me, not particularly engrossed in the screen, not knowing what to look for. The crowd of people inched past like a wave of zombies. Slowly. Slowly. My eyes flicked around them. I watched for five minutes, until I was almost ready to give up. Suddenly it didn't seem so obvious to me. Maybe I was wrong, maybe I had left the real villain lying unconscious in a caravan behind King's Cross. Andy started to fidget. Once again he told me that the tape was useless, you couldn't see enough of him. He wanted to know why I was looking at the time *after* Teddy and the man had gone by. He made a crack about wasting police time.

And then I saw him.

I hit pause on the remote and a hundred people stopped still. I looked at him, just catching the front of his face as he walked into the frame. No hat. Not a clear picture but a definite one. I stared at him. I'd stopped him, just like he'd stopped at least three people. The fuzzy V-hold on the screen made him shake like a fly caught in a web.

I put my finger on the screen. It took Andy a second to recognize him and another to realize why I was pointing him out. His breath stopped, as his mind processed the myriad objections to what my finger was telling him. He didn't say anything. He moved closer to the tiny shivering face in the top left corner of the screen. I could see him scouring his mind for a reason, a reason why it couldn't be him. Another second passed. Then Andy's eyes moved away from the screen and into space.

Suddenly, he made a grab for the telephone.

*

When I got to the airport it was busier than the last time I'd been there but it still wasn't crowded. I stood amongst the sparsely filled tables of the Pavilion Bar looking at a tall, slim figure who was chopping lemons at the bar. Alex Mitchell had his back to me but he must have felt my eyes on him because he stopped what he was doing and turned round to face me. He smiled but his smile disappeared immediately when he saw that I wasn't smiling. His face turned to chalk. Almost immediately he moved along the bar and turned to walk away but stopped when he saw Andy Gold blocking his exit. He backed up and hurried to the other end of the bar only to find an airport cop, complete with automatic rifle, standing square on to him, blocking his path that way too. It was then that he looked past me and saw the other six airport cops, all of whom Andy Gold had briefed, surrounding his bar.

Alex Mitchell should have given up then. But he didn't. He raised the knife he was still carrying high above his head and ran straight at the nearest cop. The bullet hit him almost exactly in the middle of his forehead.

PART FOUR

Chapter Twenty-Three

The smoking room of the Portman Club was no more crowded than it had been the last time I was there. This much was different though: the man sitting opposite me was no longer a Shadow Minister in Her Majesty's Opposition and would not even be an MP for that much longer. Sir Peter Morgan had recently announced his intention to stand down at the next election, a decision which was greeted by both the press and his colleagues with a great deal of respect and understanding. The press coverage which his announcement had received was shocking only in its restraint.

I hadn't wanted to meet Sir Peter at the Portman Club. I'd suggested we go to a café somewhere, or to my office, but Sir Peter had insisted and since he was paying me it was up to him. I'd turned down lunch though, not wanting to sit through another hour of small-talk before we got to the real meat. The crème brûlée was tempting but this time I let it pass. I arrived at the club just after two and was immediately shown upstairs and led through the polished mahogany door which swung open silently before me.

Sir Peter Morgan wanted me to tell him about it. He knew, as indeed the whole world knew, that the man who had murdered his brother had been shot dead by the police. He knew the name of that man but he didn't know a lot else. It was only a couple of days since Alex Mitchell had been confronted at Heathrow airport and the police had not yet revealed any more details about him or how he had committed his crimes. Not even to Sir Peter.

After I had joined the MP a different girl brought us coffee with the same good manners and diligence as her colleague had shown. We sat in the same seats we had used before and we were dressed about the same and there was the same hum of traffic from the street below as well as the same ticking of the grandfather clock which this time I noticed as soon as I entered the room.

Sir Peter looked older than he had done, almost frail. He seemed relaxed enough though but I still couldn't tell if the slight tension he demonstrated in his posture was due to the circumstances or was just the way he always sat. I'd never met him under what you would call normal conditions so I couldn't tell. Before he did anything else, Sir Peter reached into his breast pocket and pulled out a chequebook. He took out a fountain pen and scribbled on the cheque before snapping it off and setting it down on the table between us. It was face down so I couldn't see the amount Sir Peter had written it out for but I wasn't worried about that. I left the cheque there.

We both took sips from our coffee. A silence hung heavy between us which eventually the MP sought to break.

'Before you say anything,' Sir Peter began. 'I want to thank you.'

I put my cup down. 'There's no need.'

'I know. But . . .' He hesitated, his thoughts hovering. 'I want to thank you,' he reiterated. He took a deep breath and put his cup down on the table.

'So,' he said, clasping his hands together in his lap. 'So it was the barman who killed all those people.'

'Yes,' I said. 'It was. Alex Mitchell.'

'He was from Australia I understand.'

'Manly, I believe. A small district just across the bay from Sydney.'

Sir Peter thought for a second. 'I've never been there, to Australia. Too far away. Have you ever?'

'Yes,' I said, 'as a matter of fact I have. I went there with my brother, a few years ago.'

'Oh, I didn't know you had a brother too.'

'Yes,' I said, 'I do.'

'So this Mitchell man came over to work and started attacking innocent men.'

'Well no,' I said. 'No actually. He didn't start here.' I pulled a piece of paper out of my trouser pocket which I had collected from Andy Gold that morning. It was a fax from a detective with the Sydney PD, listing six names, two with question marks against them and the other four with ticks.

I looked at the fax and then handed it to Sir Peter.

'These men were all killed in Australia between four and seven years ago. Most were homosexuals and all but two had been murdered after having sex with someone it is believed they had never met before.'

'And he killed them? The same man killed all these men?'

Morgan was stunned. He held on to his glasses as he looked down at the sheet.

'I don't know,' I said. 'And neither do the police, but they're looking into it. Each of those men was killed with either a knife or a bottle and Alex Mitchell was resident in Australia at the time. All the killings took place within a hundred-mile radius of where he was working. I think he was probably responsible for some of them.'

'Christ!' The MP sat back in his chair. 'How on earth did they connect them?'

'I remembered the cases,' I said, 'from when I was there. I even remembered them when I was at the airport two weeks ago, interviewing Alex Mitchell. I told Andy Gold about them the day before yesterday. They were all over the Sydney papers as I recall and even when I'm on holiday I tend to notice things like that.'

'*Deformation professionelle.*'

'Sorry?'

'It's what the French say when you can't escape your job even when you're not doing it. I think you have a bad case of that.'

'I think you're right,' I nodded. 'I do.'

Sir Peter looked at me and pursed his lips softly.

'How did you know?' he asked. 'That it was Mitchell?'

'It just came to me,' I said. 'I just suddenly knew it was him. I just knew it.'

'And that was all?'

'No,' I said. 'Once I'd realized, when I'd connected the use of the bottles with his job as a barman and the way I'd seen him handle bottles, I went round to DI Gold's house. We went through the airport videos. The police had only bothered to scrutinize them for the moments before and during the time when Edward actually left the bar. It was natural, I suppose, given that they already had a pretty obvious suspect.'

'But you looked further on.'

'Yes.'

'And you were looking for Mitchell.'

'That's right. I remembered him saying that the night

barman had just come on. That meant that *his* shift was over. And there he was, following Edward. He was only a few minutes behind. He didn't need to keep too close because he knew where Edward was going.'

'To the car park?'

'Yes. They have a separate area for the airport staff. He may have heard Edward talk about his car or just guessed that he had one. Either way he knew where to go.'

'But what happened? I mean, had Edward arranged to meet him?'

'No,' I said. 'My guess is no. I think he followed him there and then begged a lift off him. He may have said that his car had broken down or something, and then pretended to suddenly recognize him from the bar where Edward had been sitting. Edward won't have been too concerned about taking him. Why should he be? The man was friendly enough behind the bar, he won't have asked Edward to drive out of his way. Edward was a kind man, he would have taken him.'

'And then . . .' Morgan's words tailed off. I left a second and studied Morgan's face. He wanted me to go through it all.

'Well, I think that Mitchell just assumed your brother was gay, having seen him chatting to a man and then leaving with him. Apparently, some gay flight staff did visit his bar. Maybe he thought he could kill both of them, and this new twist was too good to pass up. But the other man had gone, so he begged a lift and then instead of Edward dropping him off somewhere he took him home. To his house.'

'And . . .'

'And then they shared a bath, and had intercourse and . . .'

'No!' the MP said. 'Not Edward! I just can't see it. I just can't. He wasn't gay, he *wasn't*.'

'Mr Morgan,' I said. I leant forward in my chair and lowered my voice. 'He didn't have to be. You, for instance. You *are* gay, yet you're married.'

'Yes, but that's different. I didn't know, not for a long time . . .'

'But if you had known, would you not have ever thought of sleeping with a woman? Wouldn't you have been curious to know what it would have been like, to do that?'

The MP looked confused. 'I don't know. No. Yes. Yes, maybe I would. I see what you mean.'

'You don't have to be certain you're gay or even really think it to wonder. Edward wondered. And I suppose Mitchell came on to him in the car. And Edward's wife was away, and they hadn't been getting on too well. Edward just thought he'd try it. You yourself said he was very open about things like that, and there was no reason anyone would find out. So he did what he did and then he was unlucky. Very unlucky. Just like Mitchell's other victims.'

'God,' the MP said. 'It's all so . . . God.'

I let him take in what I had told him. There really wasn't any doubt about it. The police had found something in Alex Mitchell's flat which could only have come from Edward. I didn't tell Morgan about that yet though. I watched him as a look of incomprehension came over his face.

'How could a man do such horrible things?' the MP asked, as if I could tell him. 'I mean, how on earth? To Edward, and all these other people?'

'It's impossible to say,' I told him. 'No doubt there'll be

some lawyers who'll come up with reasons, and some faux psychiatrist-cum-hack writer who'll put a book out blaming it all on his childhood. But no one will ever really know. Not really. I doubt he knew himself. If he had he might not have felt the need to do it. My own theory is that it's all about power.'

'Power? In what sense?'

'The most basic sense of all. Something about him told him he had no power in his life. Maybe he came from a very straight background and hated the power his sexual feelings had over him. He tried to pretend he had power over them by murdering homosexuals, these men who he saw sometimes and couldn't help feeling attracted to. This also had the effect of making him feel empowered because, as soon as he had begun, he could feel the power that he had over the police, who couldn't catch him. It made him feel strong, like he mattered.'

Sir Peter nodded. 'And the boy in your flat. More of the same?'

'Probably,' I said. 'Mitchell had nothing on me. I think it irked him. I think, when I spoke to him at the airport, that I gave the impression of being in control, of not being fazed by what he was doing. What I was really feeling was that I was wasting my time, that I was just going through the motions investigating it for you. I was blasé because I thought I was on an easy way to pay the phone bill. I think he wanted to bring me into it, to involve me in his actions, to make me really feel them.'

'And he saw you talking to the boy?'

'Yes,' I said, 'he was following me. I'd given him my card which had my office address on and he hooked me there and then tailed me to my flat. He followed me to King's Cross and saw me talk to Dominic Lewes. I remember sensing that someone was watching me but I thought it was just kids out to rip off my stereo. But it wasn't. I'd actually tried to reach Mitchell at the airport a couple of times, but he wasn't there; he was keeping tabs on me. I'd even made the mistake of worrying about him, thinking of him only as a potential witness the killer may have wanted to eliminate.

'A couple of days later he killed Dominic and then sat outside my flat waiting for me to leave. He may have planned a ruse to get me out of there himself but if he had he didn't need it. He got lucky; someone else got me out of bed, and I ran off on a fool's errand to York Way, giving him time to leave the body on my bed and put me in the frame for it. My road is quiet, it's an alley really, no one would have seen him. Later, when he'd seen me come home, he called the police and said he'd seen something strange, a man with a knife, and they arrived to find me there.'

Sir Peter sat back in his chair. Behind him, across the room, the door opened and a man stepped in and stood by the side of it, waiting quietly with his hands clasped in front of him. Sir Peter let out a long breath.

'It was my fault,' he said. He was serious. His voice came up from a deep well of regret and impotence. 'It was me. I never should have spoken to Edward, never. About the way I felt. I put it into his head. If it wasn't for me he wouldn't have gone with that man. He told me that he'd never even considered it, not ever. It was my fault.'

'No,' I said. 'He didn't go with a man because you suggested it. That simply isn't what happened. It wasn't as if he'd never heard of gay sex. It wasn't that that killed him.' I was telling this to Morgan because it was true. I wasn't trying to make him feel better. He didn't argue.

'Whatever you say.' Sir Peter smiled. He was a long way off. 'It doesn't make a lot of difference now though, does it?'

'No,' I said.

'It's over. It's over now.'

Sir Peter shifted forward in his chair and went to pick up the cheque, no doubt to hand it to me. His hand stopped in mid-air, however, when I said, 'No, Sir Peter, it's not. It's not quite over yet I'm afraid.'

The waitress came over with the coffee jug. As she poured, Sir Peter Morgan didn't take his eyes off me. When she had gone I reached into the side pocket of my jacket and drew out a photograph. I reached over to hand it to Sir Peter and he took it from me. He didn't have to use his glasses to see what it showed. The blood fled from his cheeks like ants from a burning nest.

'The police found it,' I told him. 'In Alex Mitchell's flat. He took it from Edward. There are more but the police have those. This kind of sums up the general mood though.'

Morgan was completely still, unable to take his eyes off the picture.

'I made some mistakes,' I told him. 'I got all ravelled up in Graham Lloyd. You're right about him being a bastard by the way, though it was never likely that he was involved, not really. But it was only a short while after I'd quizzed him that I got beaten up by the man in the video still. I was sure that Lloyd was paying him but if he was, what for? He certainly wouldn't have employed him to be a serial killer but he may have paid him to kill Edward. He had a motive. Yet Lloyd surely couldn't have been stupid enough to get the man he'd hired before to have a go at me after he knew I was interested in him. He would more likely have shut up tight and covered his tracks.'

Morgan was sitting very still, his eyes on me now. He still had the photograph in his hand.

'I knew this, and I had actually discounted Lloyd, but when I found Dominic Lewes' body in my flat it really threw me. I knew then that the same person had killed all of the men, just as the police had known all along. But I tried to make myself believe otherwise, to tie Lloyd in, largely because I didn't like him but mainly because it was the only way I could figure it. You see, I couldn't square the man in the baseball hat with his presence in the airport video. He would only have been there if he was the killer, but the killer had been meticulous and controlled and to a large degree very careful. There were only a few occasions when Mitchell had taken any real risks, and killing Edward was one of them. Except it wasn't much of a risk in retrospect because he knew that if he killed Edward everyone would think it was the man in the hat, who he'd been seen drinking with. And he was right, we all did think that. You were probably the only one who knew it wasn't him. Which is why you hired me. The killer had been careful and here was this guy getting caught on camera, meeting me but not finishing me off, letting me hear his voice, telling me who he knew. I couldn't square it so I hung on to Lloyd and hoped he was the answer.'

Sir Peter didn't say anything. I didn't have to go on. He knew what I was going to tell him. But he had asked me to come here and tell it to him and that is exactly what I was going to do.

'I made another mistake,' I said. 'A small one but

important, something I didn't check. The officer who initially interviewed Edward's co-pilot reported that Edward had asked him to go for a drink when the flight landed but that wasn't true. They sometimes did go for a drink together but Chalkley begged off that night without even being asked. He remembered that when I phoned him this morning and said he hadn't meant to give any other impression.'

'Does it matter?'

'Not now,' I said. 'But it gave the impression that Edward wanted Chalkley along when he certainly did not. It would have made it a lot easier for me if Chalkley *had* wanted to go because he would then have remembered how Edward put him off.'

'What does this show?'

'I'm sorry, Sir Peter, it really doesn't show that much. Call it my *deformation professionelle*. All it shows is that Edward knew he was going to meet someone. He was going to meet the man in the hat. The man who got me out of bed and proceeded to kick the shit out of me. A pimp, a petty hood and blackmailer. The very man who took the photograph you're looking at.'

But Sir Peter Morgan wasn't looking at it any more. It dropped from his fingers and fell down on to the table right next to the cheque Morgan had written out for me. Morgan held his hands up to his face and began to sob quietly, streams of water coming through his fingers almost immediately, like water through the sluice-gates of a dam.

'You said it was your fault,' I said, though I couldn't be sure he heard me. 'And it was. Not for making him want to know what it was like to sleep with a man, no. But it was your fault that Edward went to sit at that bar.'

'I'm sorry. I'm so sorry.'

I didn't say anything. He wasn't speaking to me.

'I told Teddy I wanted to go. I told him. I never should have mentioned the man, never. If I'd gone to meet him instead it would have been me the barman met. I'd have taken him home. Home or somewhere. It would have been me, not Edward.'

Sir Peter couldn't get any more out. He was sobbing, his shoulders jerking with the effort like one of those small wooden toys whose joints are sprung with string.

I glanced down at the table where the photograph lay. It was face up. It was a colour photograph, taken from behind a curtain which explained the blurring round the edges. The rest of the shot was clear enough though. It showed the inside of a small room. It showed a boom box, the same one that I'd seen in the caravan two days ago. I imagined it was there to mask the sound of the camera shutter as it captured the events taking place. It also showed a young black boy bent over a table, naked except for his socks. He was the boy I had first seen at Sal's gym and who had later run away from me. I cannot describe the expression on his face except to say that it conveyed far more than the immediate pain he was feeling. Behind the boy was a tall, rather thin white man who was also naked. The man was quite clearly Peter Morgan and it was also quite clear what he was doing.

Morgan was hunched over in his hands. I looked past him to see that Andy Gold was getting impatient. I turned back to Morgan and went through the rest of it quickly.

'The boy's brave,' I said. 'He's going to testify, against both you and the man who was pimping him. He hated what you did to him. He recognized you on the news one day and pegged you for one of his regulars. He told his pimp, a guy called Smile, to please him. You see, this Smile was seeing the boy's mother. He beat all shit out of her and only promised to lay off the boy's kid sister if the boy went to work for him. He wanted to get in Smile's good books because though he hated him he thought it would help keep his sister safe. That didn't work too well though. Apparently Smile was keeping the sister for his own enjoyment.

'Smile was glad of what he heard though. About you being a prominent politician.' I picked up the photograph. 'He set this little show up and then started to hit you for cash. You panicked and told your brother, and he agreed to help you. Maybe he insisted, like you said, or maybe you begged him to go and meet the guy for you. I'll go with your version of that as it happens. Edward was a good guy; I think he would have insisted on helping.'

Morgan was nodding his head. His tears had dried up but his shoulders kept heaving up and down.

'He had the cash in the boot of his Rover, and after meeting up with Smile at the bar, and making sure who he was, he went off to the car park with him. Mitchell said they stuck around for thirty minutes before leaving but that was bullshit; he wanted to make it seem like Edward had never met the man in the hat before and was being picked up by him at the bar. That would make it seem more like Smile was the perpetrator, because the perpetrator had never previously known any of his victims beforehand. Telling the police that the two men sat at the bar for a while made a pick-up more plausible than if they had only been there two minutes.

'When they got to the car Edward gave the cash to Smile in exchange for the pictures and the negatives, which were found at Mitchell's place. Other copies were found in the caravan Smile used. He wasn't going to rest at one payoff; blackmailers never do. He'd have been back and you'd have had to do it all over again. Everything went OK this time though, it all went smoothly. Smile got the money and drove off. But that's when Alex Mitchell decided to show up. He went home with Edward and killed him, knowing that the guy he'd seen Edward with would be the prime suspect. And he was. Smile saw the video-still I was showing round, and he knew in what context he was wanted. He knew he'd likely go away for murder if I found him so he came after me to warn me off.'

Morgan was quite still now but his hands remained covering his face. I left a second and then said, 'You shouldn't feel guilty about what happened to your brother. Not about that really. But you should feel guilty.'

Andy Gold couldn't wait any longer. He walked across the room towards us, followed by two uniforms who had been standing out in the corridor. Without standing up I removed the wire I'd been wearing inside my jacket and handed it to him. Gold already had the pictures but wanted to catch Morgan talking about it in case the kid didn't come through. I knew it wasn't necessary, feeling pretty sure that Morgan would confess to it all on his own, but I couldn't see what harm it could do. Andy read Sir Peter Morgan his rights. One of the uniforms put some cuffs on him and stood him up. Morgan didn't look at me. His eyes were closed and he was mouthing something. I think it was the word 'sorry' repeated over and over again but the movement of his lips was so small I couldn't really be sure.

As the two officers walked the MP over to the door, Andy stopped and asked me if I was coming.

'No,' I said. 'Not yet.'

Andy shrugged and followed the two officers as they escorted Sir Peter Morgan from the room.

I sat back in the armchair and gazed at the elegant array of old leather furniture. Shafts of sunlight cut through the residual haze of homeless dust and old tobacco smoke. The clock ticked. I reached for my coffee before it went cold.

I'd wait there ten minutes and then slip out. I didn't have any desire to see Sir Peter Morgan being led out of his club by the police, past the grave portraits of his predecessors and the horrified eyes of his fellow members. I'd never wanted to meet him here anyway. I felt a curious heaviness, not the sort of feeling I associated with the other times I'd helped put away someone who preyed on people more helpless than themselves. I felt strangely rueful, and wondered why I should feel like that.

It was because he must have known. When he'd hired me he must have known what would happen to him if I was successful in pursuing my investigations. And plenty *would* happen to him, so much that I doubted whether he would be able to handle it. He had known who the man in the hat was and what I would find out if I found him. I guessed that was why he'd already announced his retirement, to cause as little embarrassment as he could. Putting his affairs in order like a Samurai before he falls on his sword. I remembered his fervour when he was urging me to go on with the case. It seemed strange to me now, that fervour, as though he did want to end it all but he needed me to help him; he couldn't plunge the blade in on his own. I had to admit that I felt a certain amount of pity for Sir Peter Morgan. I couldn't condone what he'd done with that boy and I didn't want to, but he knew that what he'd done was disgusting and it was his actions subsequently which led to his paying for it. No one would have known otherwise. He really didn't care what happened to himself, he didn't care at all. He just wanted to catch the bastard who killed his brother no matter what the consequences were. He loved his brother and wanted, in the end, to do right by him.

I could sympathize with that. I knew how that felt.

Chapter Twenty-Four

I left the Portman Club with Sir Peter Morgan's cheque in my pocket. I didn't have any qualms about taking it; I'd done what he'd asked me to do which, after I thought about it, was a more important service than I'd initially realized. I'd helped him to atone. I deserved the money. I banked it and did some sums and figured that I could afford to take a couple of weeks off.

During those two weeks I avoided buying a paper and I turned the radio off whenever the news came on. There was only one story, which I knew only too well, and even if the press had got all the facts, which I doubted, it would never be anything more than that; a story. No matter what words you use to describe a thing, words that are measured or those that are lurid and sensationalist, all you really have is words. Pictures don't help either; they're fictions too. I had entertained so many scenarios in my head about what had occurred with Edward Morgan and his brother that I didn't trust the final one, the one the world was busy putting together. I didn't read the papers just as I wouldn't go to a public execution. I now knew what the order of events had been without needing to be told again, and what did even they tell you about what really went on inside people? It was all just speculation, with varying degrees of malicious joy. I didn't need it.

The weather was cold and clear. I walked in the park and got over my cracked ribs and saw my face slowly reappearing in the mirror. I had a few drinks with Nicky but I never stayed late. I went to the gym, driving down there past the kids who were still on the corner like carp rising for the bait seconds after one of their number has been yanked away. At the gym I took it slowly, working out lightly and spending some time on the bike. Each time I went down there I saw the young boy, who never acknowledged my presence nor ever chatted to anyone else in the gym. He just concentrated on his business, whether it was curling a dumbbell or working with the rope. Sal told me that he was coming along well. He was focused, she said, and committed. Watching his set face and his narrowed eyes as he laid hell into the bag, I think I knew what he was focusing on.

I watched the dust grow on my answerphone and left the machine on. Sharon called me a couple of times but I didn't know what to say to her so I didn't pick up. Charlotte Morgan called to tell me that she was not going to go to the papers about her affair with Lloyd now that she knew he wasn't involved in her husband's murder. I'd guessed that she wouldn't and as much as I would have liked to see Lloyd's career take a serious knock I was relieved for her. Charlotte told me that she had, however, decided to invest in the vineyard Lloyd had mentioned though not in partnership with the MP, but with her accountant, who thought the investment very sound now that it wasn't tied to a failing concern. Lloyd was close, apparently, to putting a deal together himself, and was apoplectic to discover that he'd been gazumped by his former mistress. Revenge, it seems, is a dish best taken with a glass or two of English table wine.

I plucked up enough courage one morning to call Dominic Lewes' mother and arranged to meet her in Grimsby the next day. I drove up and we had coffee in a Little Chef on the outskirts of the city. She wouldn't hear of me apologizing for my part in her son's death, even though she now knew exactly what had happened.

'You didn't make him hate himself enough to go out and sell himself for drugs,' she told me. 'I know who did that.'

I told her about the times I'd seen her son and also the timetable I'd found in his room after he'd been killed. It didn't even begin to penetrate the cloak of sorrow she wore round herself.

'There is one thing though,' she said, as we were getting ready to leave. 'One thing which I like to think of. The police told me that this animal was due to strike again, that it was longer between murders than before. I like to think of the young man who he didn't kill because he got my Dominic. I like to think of a normal young boy with something to live for. I picture him sometimes, laughing with his mates or holding hands with someone special. He's a nice boy with a happy life. He doesn't live the sort of life Dominic did. When I imagine him sometimes I'm even glad it happened to my Dominic and not to him. He goes home and sees his parents at the weekend. He's happy. Dominic was never happy.'

I still didn't call Sharon. I just didn't know what to say to her. Every time I thought of her the images which played out in my mind were too much and I shut them down as soon as I realized I was thinking of her. After the first week the images were almost constant and I either walked them off or tried to dissolve them in Irish whiskey. One evening the phone rang and it was Trish, the woman I'd met at Nicky's when he'd conned me into going down to meet him. She asked me if I wanted dinner and I thought it might take my mind off things so I said yes, and we went to a new place on the Liverpool Road. Trish was a vivacious, attractive woman and we got on well together. She was also very interesting to talk to, something which I had completely failed to notice the first time I had seen her.

We chatted about this and that until the conversation eventually came round to families. I found myself telling Trish all about mine, about Luke and what had happened to him. I think I was a little drunk and I wound up telling her all about Sharon too and the night we had spent together. How bad I felt about it but how I couldn't stop a million different thoughts rushing round in my head. Trish nodded to herself as though something I was saying made sense.

'I could tell there was someone,' Trish said. 'When we were together. I could tell you weren't really into it.' I started to protest but she shook her head and laughed. 'It's OK,' she said. 'I don't mind. It was just that I could tell you weren't really up for it, but you couldn't think of a polite way to say no.'

Trish asked me what I was going to do about all of it. I told her that I didn't know. We had a long talk and at the end of it, after we'd left the restaurant and I'd walked her back to her car, she looked at me and smiled. She got in but before she drove off she wound her window down.

'I think you know what to do,' Trish said.

And suddenly, I did.

I stayed up that night and read all the poems that were in the file Sharon had given to me. I still hadn't looked at them. I couldn't stand the idea of knowing what my brother's thoughts were. Not after what had happened between me and his fiancée. Even before. Something in me had been aware for some time of feelings towards Sharon which were out of place, and it was horrified of them and scared of how my brother would feel if he knew. So I had avoided his thoughts and tried to view him as simply an inert piece of flesh, the subject of pity and remorse, to be visited and sanctified. I'd been far more cowardly than Sharon had. I'd talked about football matches and skiing as a way of avoiding the truth of what was going on. She had confronted her feelings and decided to be brave enough to go with them, to admit what we both knew: that we had become very close to each other. I couldn't face up to that because if I did I would also have to admit that Luke was irrevocably gone, that my brother was alive in name only. I could only ever love Sharon if I could first accept what she already had accepted and I had always turned away from knowing. That Luke was dead.

In the morning I drove out to the hospital. I sat next to Luke for ages, all day in fact, and I spoke for hours non-stop, telling him everything I felt about him and everything I felt about Sharon. I held his hand, pressing his grey knuckles hard against my forehead, occasionally soaking his palms and his wrists with my tears, the first time I had ever done so. I told Luke how sorry I was about what had happened to him. It was not the first time I had told him this, and I never did it from a knowledge of rational blame, but this time I felt more sorry than I ever had done before. I was now aware of what Luke's life had been like before he was attacked. I knew what he had given up. He had not only cast off his own life so that I could keep on living, he had also given that life to me. I held on to Luke's hand and begged for some sort of sign from him, a word to show that he understood what I was about to do. I waited for a long time before realizing that, though I had the chance in my life to know a happiness greater than I had felt possible since that night four years ago on the Westway, there was one thing I would have to do without for ever. I could ask for my brother's blessing until I was blue in the face, but he would never be able to answer, or to give it to me. Not now, not ever.

Eventually I kissed Luke's cold dry lips and said goodbye to him, and then to Hazel, who smiled at me fondly. I smiled back, feeling strangely elated. I drove back into London, all the way nursing a smile which seemed to be growing within myself, opening out inside my body like a huge orchid. A latent sense of guilt fought to stem it but the flower was too strong. I drove quickly, amazed and self-conscious about the way I was feeling, until the car was parked outside Sharon's building in Ladbroke Grove. It was dark by now and when I looked up I could see a light behind the curtains of Sharon's flat.

I hadn't told her I was coming. I sat in the car for five minutes, enjoying the expectation, the almost physical knowledge that I was about to see her. Her face was alive before my eyes but there was nothing I could do about that now, even if I wanted to. The orchid inside me had grown so huge it was trying to break through my ribcage. I wondered what Sharon was doing up there: reading a law report or *Marie Claire*. Or maybe she was with another man, the lover I had suspected. I didn't care. I was going up there, whatever the outcome was.

Simple as that.

As I reached for the door handle a poem came into my head; one of Luke's poems. The poem was about Sharon. It was about how Luke couldn't write about her, because she destroyed his centre, made him feel like a child, how his faculties had dissolved into a rush of sentiment he couldn't express without sounding ridiculous. But how, at the same time, he couldn't stop writing about her, even if he knew he was sounding stupid. It was one of my favourites in the collection because it was so fresh and honest. I remembered the ending:

> She's sweet as a wish
> and soft as a prayer
> and the sun hides out in her golden hair
>
> when the moon saw her face
> he decided to take early retirement
>
> and I love her more
> than a sailboat loves the water.

I couldn't argue with that.